D0810680

Never Say Never

Never
Say
Never

Dwayne S. Joseph

www.urbanbooks.net

Never Say Never

Urban Books
6 Vanderbilt Parkway
Dix Hills, NY 11746

ISBN 0-7394-5933-3

Printed in the United States of America

Dedicated to:
all of the Reesa's, Carmen's and Erica's out there.

Acknowledgments

Writing acknowledgments is always a big deal to me because each time I do so, I'm reminded that I've been blessed to have achieved my dream of being a writer since I was thirteen. That is truly fulfilling for me!

Ok, I've got my Maroon 5 CD playing...let's get going!

God: That I've achieved this dream is all due to you. The relationship I have with you is special to me because it's all mine. I cherish, honor, and respect it. Thank you for listening to me.

To my beautiful wife, Wendy and my precious little ladies Tatiana and Natalia: Even as a writer it's almost impossible to put into words what you mean to me. Believe me when I say that my life is complete with you in it. I love you Wendy(mi reina) I love you Tati. I love you Nati. To my parents: what more can I say? Thank you for being true role models. Dad, I love you. Mom, I love you. Daren: Howard U graduate!! Proud of you, kid. It's your time now. Take advantage of it. Stay true to yourself as you become the next Pharell! I love you, kid. Teens: You're a mommy now. It's weird to see my lil sis all grown up! I love you. To my nephew Evan: listen to your mother! To Granny and Grandmother: I cannot tell you how special it is to me to see you two with my little girls. Granny thank you for everything! With Evan in the mix now, I think we need to put a sign up in the house that reads "Granny Day Care" I love you. Grandmother: Thank you for being you! I—we—love you for that. Thank you also for that special gift. To Lourdes and Russell: I cannot tell you how lucky I am to have in-laws that I love and that love me back! Were you guys ever not in my life?? Ivan, Grace, Prianna, Leila: Love you guys for real! Ivan, you're holding things down and I love that. Grace, keep cracking that whip LOL. To my uncles and aunts and to my cousins, Kirt (in your corner forever, kid), Mike, Aleah, Greg, Tremaine, Dahlia, Mark, Brian, Ronald: Love you guys.

To my friends for life, Chris, Lisa, Jessie, Jasmine, Gregg, Kristie, Brian, Mia, Carlos, Mariana, Julian, Micah, Tiffany, Tho: I'm lucky to have friends like you guys!!

To my friends in the industry: Carl 'call him Da' Man' Weber: Congrats on everything. You keep giving me something to reach for. Martha: Thank you for everything! Maria and Arvita: it's a pleasure working with you! La Jill Hunt: Drama Queen for real. I love you, sis! Eric Pete: Life got even crazier when you joined the crew! Gregg, Chris, Brian and I are still waiting for you to join us Live on XBox! LOL. Roy Glenn: Will you please stop leaving me hanging like that! Thanks for everything man! Stephanie Johnson: It's great to have gotten to know you! I still have to school you on Mint Condition. You need to pick up their CD's! Angel Hunter: BIG congrats on your marriage and For The Soul bookstore in SC! Can't wait to come and visit!! Thomas Long: He's a hustler...a hustler! Jihad: I'm just trying to be like you, kid. Robilyn Heath: Still the mother hen. Richard Holland: Congrats on everything! Still looking to hire you as the hype man!! C. Kelly Robinson: It was a pleasure meeting you. Looking forward to the next book. AC Arthur: Definitely waiting for the next book. Peace to the fellas from SHAI. Glad to see you back on the scene.

Thank you Portia Cannon for being in my corner. Round two now. Thanks once again to the USF crew for the support: James Scott, Crystal Green, Leslie Ramirez, Kirsten McCree, Heather Seegel, Mahlon Adams, Elizabeth Smith, Shirley Merrills.. with a special thanks to Mario Merrills (looking forward to seeing you in the NFL), Kara Taylor, Steven Hong, Gifford Wright, Amy Santa, Sheanea Powell, Jenaye Dickerson, Nakyia Savoy, Amber Kerr, Tanyen Kerr, Lisa Purkey, Shantel Boykin, LaKeysha Glenn, Felicia Johnson. Thanks also to Charles Kumbersmart for the site and Candace for the BOMB cover!

To the Cushcity.com book club!!! BIG THANK YOU for all of the love!! I can't wait to meet with you all again!! Thanks also to Nalo Ervin and The Woman in Me 2002 book club! And much thanks to the entire Ujima Nia book club!!

Much appreciation to Peggy Hicks, and the Tri-Com staff for setting up all of the radio interviews. Tee C. Royal of Rawsistaz.com, Jacki Miller of Realreviewers.org (Much love for you), Yasmin from APOOO.org, author Cydney Rax of Book-remarks.com, author Cheryl Robinson of Avid-readers.com, Troy from AALBC.com.

Finally, to the readers that have taken the time to pick up anything I've written: From the bottom of my heart: Thank you, thank you, thank you for the support and all of the e-mails! They mean the world to me. Please keep them coming!! I keep all of them! Chris Licorice..I got you, kid. Tell your girl my wife hates the XBox too!! Will and Karl at House of Barbers.. much love to you guys!! Jocelyn Lawson: you've made this an even greater experience for me! Julie May, Joy Young, Shiekia Brown and Renee Green: BIG thank you!! And to everyone that posted reviews on amazon.com, barnesandnobles.com, and BlackExpressions. com: THANK YOU!! Watch out for my next book, If Your Girl Only Knew!

Lastly: For those who've been following me, you know I can't end this without a shout out to my New York Giants: Plaxico, Shockey, Tiki (meeting you was the biggest deal to me), Toomer, Manning, Strahan....weapons. I'm amp'd for the '05 season!! Till I die..I'm a NY Giants fan!

Peace,
Dwayne S. Joseph

www.DwayneSJoseph.com

Djoseph21044@yahoo.com

Reesa

"That's it. I'm through with his ass!"

I threw the covers off me, got out of bed, went to the living room, and turned on the TV. I was pissed, and sleep wasn't an option. I banged on my remote control as I switched channels, not really looking for anything to watch, but just hoping to release my anger and frustration. I meant it when I yelled it a couple of seconds ago. I was through with his ass. Simon. My man—or maybe I should say my headache—for the past two years. He's the reason I was losing sleep yet again.

I cursed out loud and threw the remote over to the couch across from me, leaving the channel on an infomercial for some butt and thigh machine that my fat ass would never use. Okay, it's not fat. Just healthy. Damn it, why couldn't Simon just come home like a good boyfriend was supposed to? It was damn near four in the morning! I know he was out doing his thing, but damn, did it have to be at this time of the night? I mean, shit, couldn't he wheel and deal during the daytime? Of course he couldn't. I don't even know why I was asking.

I sighed and squeezed my eyes shut tightly and tugged on my braids. The stress I was going through was all my fault because I knew what I was getting into when I first got together with Simon. He was one of those good-looking brothers with a body straight out of *Muscle and Fitness* magazine, and he hadn't earned an honest day's worth of pay in his life. You know the type of man I'm talking about, ladies. Simon schemed and hustled any and every way he could to put cash in his pocket. He'd been a car dealer, drug dealer, pimp, male escort, thug for hire, bouncer, chef, stick-up kid . . . the list goes on and on. Basically, if you name it, he'd done it. I could tell by the way he strolled the first night we'd met that he didn't live nine to five like the rest of us.

Usually, I wouldn't have given a brother like Simon the time of day. I mean, let's face it, he was a playboy, and I was a future financial planner. But ladies, I won't lie to you. I hadn't had an orgasm in four months, and when Simon stepped to me that night, it was damn hard to ignore his LL-like lips, his reach-out-and-squeeze-me pecs, and his abundance in the crotch area. Like I said, I knew the minute he approached me that he wasn't the type of man I'd marry, but I had drinks in my system. I was horny, and before I could even stop myself, Simon and I were leaving the club and heading back to my apartment to get our multiple-orgasmic freak on. It was only supposed to be a one-time sexual romp with Simon. I mean, come on, we were like oil and water. We just didn't mix.

Until we hit my bed.

I swear I have never had a man work me over the way Simon did. Brother had me singing opera beneath my sheets. He obviously must have been just as impressed with me because he called me up the next night looking for more. Of course I obliged. Night after night, Simon and I would hook up and work off our calories. Normally, after we were done freaking, he would go home. But one night after we did our do, he held me in his arms and didn't leave.

I wish I could say that my relationship with Simon had been nothing but roses, but obviously, since I was up at four A.M., pissed and ready for the umpteenth time to kick his ass out, it hadn't. Simon brought so much drama into my world it was ridiculous. If I wasn't dealing with his son's mother, Cecilia, who couldn't stand me, then I was dealing with the stack of bills that were all in my name. The phone, the credit cards, *his* cell phone, the car payment, and the rent—all under Reesa Sheree Nichols. And since I was the only one with a real job and credit, I was the one who had to worry about making sure the bills got paid. Oh, don't get me wrong, Simon helped when he could, but you probably already know that didn't happen too often.

"Damn it, I'm through with his ass," I said again.

How many times had I said that? Too many. But this time I meant it. I deserved better. I deserved more. I'm a woman. An attractive, caring, giving, successful, independent, intelligent black woman who should have a man of equal stature to lie next to at night. But damn it, why did I have to be thirty-three years old? You're probably wondering what's wrong with my being that age. Well, I can tell you the answer to that with one word: children. See, I'd always planned to have about three kids by now because I wanted to be like my mother: a young, fit, forty-something with grown-ass kids. But instead of having kids in my twenties like I wanted, I went from one unsatisfying relationship to the next. And then for about three years, I hit a drought and couldn't find a good man to save my life.

Now here I was at thirty-three, with no little rugrats to call my own and my cut-off age of thirty-five fast approaching. Yes, I said cut-off. I always said I wouldn't have kids past my mid-thirties, and I intended to stick to that. I wasn't like these new-age women who want to have kids in their forties and fifties. Oh nooo. Not me. Not my body. Thirty-five or it was none at all. And there lay my problem. Simon might have been far from being any kind of real man, but he was still a man with working sperm. And I won't lie . . . for all of his faults, I had to admit I did have feelings for him. But here's the problem: If I left him, what the hell was I going to do? Start over? Spend another couple of who knows how many days, months, or years searching for Mr. Right? And who's to say that I'd find Mr. Right anyway? Let's face it, the older men get, the more they want the video/model magazine female with perky breasts and bone-thin bodies. They don't want real women with mature curves. Mr. Right? How about Mr. Right Now? Simon wasn't perfect and had a long way to go to becoming a man, but I have to say, he'd accepted my hips and my C-cup breasts that had a little jiggle to them. He didn't shy away from the slight pouch I'd developed. I'm not saying he was Mr. Right, but at thirty-three, he just seemed to be the best chance I had to reaching my goal by thirty-five. Did I really want to take the chance of being alone and lonely? I don't think so.

I grabbed the remote control and shut off the television. Standing still in the darkness, I said to myself, "I'm through with his ass," then I went back to bed.

Erica

Where the hell are all the real brothers?

I mean, what more do they want? I'm a single, sexy, intelligent, and professional sister. I'm a real-ass woman: 36-28-34. Dark brown piercing eyes. Succulent, full lips. Dimples.

What the hell is their problem? Are they so caught up in their quest to be the "man" that they don't know a good thing when they see one? Are they really that blind? Or is it my fault? Am I being too picky? Is wanting a good, intelligent brother to love and be loved by too much to ask for? Should I not be looking for a faithful brother who understands that bling-blinging don't mean shit to me if he can't treat a woman right? I am so tired of falling for brothers who keep forgetting that being seventeen years old only happens once.

I'll be damned if I live my life like my mother did. During the twenty years she and my father were married, he fooled around on her more times than Hugh Hefner had Playboy bunnies. And the whole time it was happening, I'm sure my mother had to know about it, because the whole damn neighborhood did. Why my mother remained faithful to his trifling behind I'll never understand. About the only decent thing he did for her during all that time was leave her for a twenty-five-year-old bitch who he claimed to love.

My father spent his entire life being a teenager. I can only imagine what he was like before I came along. I have no respect for him or his trifling ways. That's why he and I don't speak. He's just another example of a sorry black man. No, check that. He's another example of a sorry-ass man. His immaturity goes beyond color.

I swear, sometimes I feel like I have LOOKING FOR MR. DO WRONG etched right into my forehead, because those are the only type of brothers that seem to pay me any mind. Men may complain about women being gold diggers, and I'm not going to say that they aren't out there, but let me tell you one thing: I've met just as many money-hungry brothers. It's pathetic the way these sorry men wine and dine and then stop once they discover what kind of salary I'm pulling in. But unlike some sisters out there—and I won't mention any names—I am not the one to allow a man to leech off me without reciprocating.

But it's not just the pain and suffering of finding a good black man that bothers me. The only thing more frustrating than that is *seeing* one with a Barbie attached to his hip. That shit I just don't understand. I swear, to see so many good brothers succeed and date Barbies, as if to say black women aren't good enough, is really disheartening. But unlike a lot of sisters, I don't fault the white women. Let's face it: Black men are some fine-ass men. And white women—shit, no woman—can deny that. It's not Barbie's fault that black men seem to flock toward them like wolves to raw meat. And I keep telling my girls that it has nothing to do with Barbie's submissive, freaky, easily-manipulated, spend-anything-for-a-brother ways either. Hey, I give white women their props. They snag the Mr. Do Rights and do whatever they need to do to keep them.

You go, girl.

Of course, I would do that too—if I could find a good one! But unfortunately for the brothers, I just don't have enough of the qualities they're looking for. Because I'll be damned if I let a brother manipulate me. And forget the whole spend-my-entire-paycheck-on-a-nigga-while-he-flaunts-me-like-a-prize bullshit. Remember Homey the Clown? Well, Erica Blige don't play that. A brother better come and come correct when he's stepping to me. Which brings me back to my question: Where are the real brothers?

Shit, but you know, forget the brothers. I'm tired of wasting my time waiting on them. Oh, and when I say that, I don't mean that I'm gonna do the lesbian thing or look for a man outside of my race. I just mean that I'm gonna do me and go out and do my thing, and if one of them wises up and steps up to the plate, then cool. But if not, oh well. I'm not gonna lose sleep pining over them. I don't need a man to define me or bring me happiness. I can do bad all by myself. Having said that, let me pull out my little black book.

Surprised?

Don't be.

Trust me, men aren't the only ones with a name and a star for when they want a little tune-up. Let's see . . . yeah, Jared. He'll work. Brother's not the brightest, but he knows his shit in the bedroom. Plus, he's good for a night of free drinks. Where are the real brothers? I don't know. But I'll tell you what . . . I'm done asking.

Carmen

"Carmen, you should dye your hair blonde."

Huh? I looked at my boyfriend of three years out of the corner of my eye. "Why, Anthony? What, you want me to look like Shakira?"

Anthony kept his eyes glued on the television screen, or maybe I should say on Shakira as she gyrated in her video, and shrugged. "Nah. You can't look that good," he said, nibbling on his bottom lip. "Shakira is hellafine. I'm just saying it would look good, that's all."

I cut my eyes at his remark. "What the hell do you mean I can't look that good?"

I couldn't believe he'd just said that. Well, yes I could.

"Baby, Shakira is the shit. There are only a few women that fine. Beyonce, J. Lo, maybe Ashanti."

"So what are you saying? That I'm not fine?" I folded my arms across my chest and pressed my lips together tightly.

Anthony shook his head and exhaled. "Will you calm the hell down, Carmen, and let me enjoy my damn video?"

"No, I will not calm down," I said, standing. I stood directly in front of the television, blocking his view. "Answer my question, Anthony. Am I not fine?"

Trying his best to see past me, Anthony said, "Carmen, I never said that you weren't fine. I just said that you weren't as fine as Shakira."

"That's real ugly, Anthony," I said, cutting my eyes at him. "How are you gonna say some shit like that to me?"

"So you'd rather I lie?"

"Go to hell," I yelled out. "Why do you always have to be so insensitive? Why do you always have to say some shit to hurt me?"

"What the hell did I say that was so wrong, Carmen? So I told the truth and said you weren't as fine as Shakira . . . so what? Not many women are."

"How would you like it if I said that I'd dump you for Maxwell in a heartbeat?"

"I'd say go for it. And stop tripping, because I didn't say all that about Shakira."

"You may as well have!" Anthony groaned and flopped back on the couch. I stared at him with hard eyes. He was always saying something insensitive to me like that. Most men are smart enough or care enough about their women to lie and never say some shit like that. But not Anthony. I don't know if it was that he didn't realize what he said hurt me or that he just didn't care, but I was tired of his comments. "So you wouldn't mind if I left you for Maxwell? That doesn't bother you at all?"

Anthony looked at me and smirked. "Why the hell should that bother me, Carmen?"

"I'm saying that I'd leave you for another man."

"Yeah. A man that you're never going to meet!"

"But what if I did?"

"Jesus!" Anthony said, sitting up. "This conversation is ridiculous." He grabbed his car keys from the coffee table and stood.

"Where are you going?"

"I'm going out for a drink. You're getting on my fucking nerves."

"I thought you wanted to see your video."

"The video's over."

"Oh, I'm so sorry I ruined your moment."

"Whatever, Carmen. I'm outta here. And if I see Maxwell, I'll tell him you're looking for him."

"Whatever, Anthony. I'm just sorry I'm not as fine as Shakira!" Anthony walked past me, shaking his head, and slammed the front door behind him as he left. "Jerk!" I yelled out loud.

Maldita Sea! Why did that always have to happen? Why did Anthony and I always have to argue like that? I cursed him and his insensitivity in Spanish again and turned off the television. "No more videos," I said. No more half-naked, damn-near perfect female bodies prancing around on my screen to piss me off. I moved to the stereo, hit the power button, and pressed play on my CD player. As salsa sang out from my speakers, my phone rang. I would have let it go to the answering machine, but when I looked at the caller ID and saw that it was my girl Shay, I lowered the volume on the stereo and hit the talk button. "Hey, Shay," I said.

"Hey. What's up, Carmen! What are you up to?"

"Nothing much," I said, plopping down on my leather sofa.

"Uh-oh. What happened this time?"

"What do you mean?"

"Don't 'what do you mean' me," Shay said. "I can hear the frustration in your voice. You and Anthony had it out again. So what did he do this time?"

I sighed. "Would you believe he had the nerve to say I should dye my hair blonde?"

"Huh?"

I sucked my teeth. "He was sitting down watching videos on TV, and when I came in the living room to ask him what he wanted for dinner, he told me I should dye my hair blonde."

"What made him say that?"

"Because he was watching a damn Shakira video, who, by the way, I am not as fine as."

"What?"

"He had the nerve to tell me that I wasn't as fine as Shakira."

"Huh? What made him say that?"

"When I asked him if I should dye my hair so that I could look like Shakira, he was like 'Nah, you can't look that good.' Stupid *pendejo. El se puede ir al carajo con esa mierda!*"

"Whoa, whoa, slow down, *chica.* You know I don't understand what you're saying."

I blew out a frustrated exhale. "Sorry. Didn't mean to vent like that. I'm just frustrated."

"Girl, you're always frustrated."

"I know, I know."

"You were frustrated the day we met, remember?"

"Yeah, I remember." I sighed and thought back to that day. I'd gone to the gym to get rid of some frustration from an argument that Anthony and I had the night before after I'd come home close to midnight from a business dinner. Anthony didn't appreciate the fact that I'd gone to dinner with another man without letting him know first. And it didn't matter that I'd tried to call him on his cell phone, which he hadn't answered, and left several messages. I was his woman, and no woman of his should be going out with another man. Business or no business.

Anthony's over-possessiveness hadn't been anything new, but what had been new had been the hurtful way he'd spoken to me. Showing me a complete lack of respect, he compared me to a whore and implied that my business dinner had been an effort to try to sleep my way to the top. I went to bed in tears that night.

The next day, I went to the gym and met Shay. We were both on the StairMaster, sweating our pounds away. I'd seen Shay before, but never spoken to her. I had no intention of speaking to her that day either until she looked over at me and asked me what was wrong. When I asked her why she asked me that, she said, "I recognize the look of frustration, girl. And I know that's not exercise that's got your forehead all knotted up and your face all screwy."

I've been venting to her ever since.

"Carmen, I don't know why you just won't take my advice and leave Anthony's ass."

"You know why, Shay."

"Yeah, yeah. Because you love him," Shay said disapprovingly.

"Yes, I do."

Shay sucked her teeth. "Carmen, are you a glutton for punishment? I mean, for real, how long are you gonna keep dealing with Anthony and his shit? I keep telling you that any man that's causing you as much stress as Anthony has been causing you is not the man you need. You're supposed to be living stress-free, Carmen. I know you love Anthony's sorry ass, but honestly, he ain't doing nothing for you but dragging you down emotionally. And believe me, you don't want that. You know about all the shit I put Ahmad through when his ass wasn't acting right. Believe me, I loved him, too, but I wasn't going to allow him to disrespect me. And that's what you're doing, Carmen. You're letting Anthony disrespect the hell out of you."

"He's not always bad," I said, defending my man, even though I knew Shay was right. "He doesn't always disrespect me."

"Oh please. That's BS, and you know it. But you know what, let's just switch to a new topic. I really don't feel like listening to you lie to yourself or me anymore. If you want to stay with Anthony, then by all means, you go right ahead. So are we all still on for going out for drinks and dinner on Friday night?"

"I think so. I just need to call Reesa and Erica to make sure."

"Okay. Is Reesa still hanging tough with Simon?"

"Yeah."

Shay sucked her teeth. "Another sad case," she said.

"We're not all lucky like you, Shay. Ahmad is an exception to the rule."

"Carmen, he wasn't an exception until I set him straight."

"Yeah well, Anthony's not trained like Ahmad."

"Trained? Please. Girl, Ahmad loves and respects me. I'm just talking shit when I say I set him straight. I mean, I did put him through some hell, but ultimately, his changing came down to his feelings for me and his desire to be with me. As many times as you've argued with Anthony over the things he says and does, has he made any effort to change?" Shay paused to give me a chance to answer, but I didn't say anything. She was just hitting the nail on the head too damned hard for me. She mmm-hmmed. "That's what I thought."

"It's not as easy as you think, Shay. Both Reesa and I have a lot of time invested in our relationships."

"Yeah, wasted time. And I never said it was easy. Anyway, I need to get off this phone and take care of some things. I'll call you later this week to see if you've come to your senses at all."

"Whatever."

"Yeah, whatever. You know I'm right."

"Good-bye, Shay," I said, shaking my head.

"Truth hurts, don't it?"

"Byeeee!"

Shay laughed. "I'll talk to you, girl. Bye."

"Bye." I hung up the phone and as soon as I did, my smile disappeared. Shay had given me the speech before, but for some reason it really got to me this time. I think it was her comment about Ahmad willingly changing for her that did it. Just hearing that made me think about Anthony's feelings for me and wonder just how strong they were. Like Shay said, no matter how many times I'd argued with him, he just didn't seem to care enough about my feelings to stop putting me down and disrespecting me. I knew he wasn't the same type of man that Ahmad was, but couldn't he try to care just a little? Shay said he was dragging me down emotionally. I wanted to say she was wrong about that, but when I thought about how many nights I'd gone to bed crying or pissed off, it was hard to do anything but think that she was right.

I can't look as fine as Shakira?

Bullshit.

I may not have her body, but I did more than enough work in the gym to know that I could come pretty damn close: 36-22-38. Shit, I'm not Shakira, but I have a body on me too. And personally, I think I'm prettier with my hazel eyes, full lips, and long, curly brown hair. Not as fine as Shakira? Anthony might not have thought so, but I knew plenty of other guys who thought differently. Maybe it was time for me to really give Shay's advice some heavy consideration.

Erica

"Girls' night out! This was long overdue, wasn't it, ladies?" I clapped in time with the rhythm of Beyonce's song, "Baby Boy," as I led the way into the Silver Shadow night club. I moved my head and worked my hips; I was feeling the music. I'd been so busy with work lately that it had been a while since I'd stepped out. I scanned the packed venue, going from one brother to the next. That one had no style. That one too much style—who told him he could rock lavender? That one had no money. Oh, and that one, no job. I shook my head with disappointment. "I think it's gonna be slim-pickins in here tonight. I haven't seen anything that's caught my eye yet."

"That's okay," Reesa said, standing beside me. "I didn't come looking for a man anyway."

I rolled my eyes. Why did she always have to say some shit like that? "Reesa, why don't you loosen the hell up? So you have a man. So what? That don't mean that you can't come in and enjoy the sights. Damn. Carmen, will you please talk to your girl? I came here to relax, have fun, and have some drinks on some brothers that ain't gonna get shit but a smile. Am I right, Shay?"

I looked over at Shay as she smiled. "Damn right. I love Ahmad and wouldn't cheat on him for anybody, but I won't turn down a free drink."

"Thank you!" I high-fived Shay and looked at Carmen. "You did come to have some fun, right?"

Carmen smiled. "Please. I came to have too much fun."

"Uh-oh," I said, raising my eyebrows. "I'm scared of you."

14

Carmen laughed. "Don't be scared. There's plenty of men to go around."

My eyebrows went up even higher after that comment. I watched her as she moved her hips to the music. She always dressed stylishly when we went out, but this night, she was exceptionally styled out in a black tube top, a long white skirt with a slit rising up to the top of her thigh on one leg, and a pair of black high-heeled pumps. Since I met everyone here, I hadn't really had a chance to check Carmen out before. "What's up with your outfit, *chica?* I know Anthony didn't approve that."

Carmen sucked her teeth. "Anthony is my man, not my mother, and I don't need his approval."

"Since when?" Shay and I asked at the same time.

Carmen rolled her eyes and showed us her palm. "Whatever. I'm going to touch up my makeup. I'll be back." Carmen walked off, leaving us shocked. I looked at Reesa.

"Don't ask me," she said.

We both looked at Shay. She shrugged. "Hey, I've told her enough times how worthless Anthony is. Maybe she's finally listening to me."

"Hopefully," I said.

Reesa shook her head. "Why do you two always have to be getting in someone's business? Carmen's in love. Can't you just be happy for her?"

"I'll be happy for her when she gets rid of her dead weight and finds a better man," Shay answered.

"I hear that," I said. "Anthony ain't shit."

"I'm just glad I don't have to deal with a man like him," Shay said.

"I know what you mean," Reesa said. I rolled my eyes and sucked my teeth. Reesa looked at me out of the corner of her eye, and I think for a moment thought about saying something to me. But instead, she focused on Shay again. "Hey, did I tell you about the interview Simon had today?"

"No, you didn't," Shay said.

"It was with Johns Hopkins doing medical billing, I think."

"Really?" Shay asked. "I didn't know he had experience in that field."

"Don't you mean any experience . . . period?" I said.

15

Reesa looked at me. "Excuse me? You have something you want to say?"

I looked away to the dance floor with a scowl and said, "You don't want me to say anything."

"What was that?"

"Oh Lord," Shay said as I turned back to the table and stared at Reesa. "Ladies, chill please," she said, knowing where we were about to go.

"Don't you ever get tired of putting on a show?" I asked Reesa, ignoring Shay's request.

"A show? What does that mean?"

"An interview, huh? I bet Simon's lazy ass didn't even go to it."

"For your information, he did so, and they're supposed to call him with their decision next week."

I clapped and said sarcastically, "Whoopee. Maybe your man is finally deciding to be a man."

"Why do you always have to talk about my man like that, Erica?"

"Why? Oh please, Reesa. You can talk him up all you want, but you know that just like Anthony, Simon ain't shit either."

"You're just jealous because I got a man and your lonely ass don't."

I laughed. "Jealous? Of who? Please. I'd rather be a lonely ass than be with a little boy. A man? Whatever. Tell me . . . are you still paying all his bills?"

"Ladies," Shay said, trying to keep the peace again. But we were too far gone for that.

"You know, Erica," Reesa said, taking a step toward me. "I'm tired of you always putting my man down. You don't know shit about him."

"I know that he don't have a real job and hasn't had one since I've known you. I also know that you know he ain't worth anything. You just don't want to admit it."

"Whatever, Erica," Reesa said, turning away, only proving my point.

"Yeah, whatever. Simon ain't nothing but a pretty boy with a body. And truthfully, his body ain't all that."

Reesa turned back toward me and stared at me with evil eyes. I returned her venomous glare with my own. If it weren't for Carmen, Reesa and I would never have been friends. And even with Carmen as our common denominator, *friends* was still a term that was used loosely. I just didn't like Reesa's ass. She was opinionated, judgmental, and thought her shit didn't stink. Especially when it came to Simon. She was always talking him up like he was God's gift to women, when everybody knew he was nothing but a free-loading, broke-ass brother. The exact kind I stayed away from.

I don't know why she was always trying to put on an act about Simon and her relationship with him. She should have just kept it real and admitted that she knew her man wasn't shit but he knew how to fuck. But no. She'd rather put on a show and look down on others. Talking about me because I didn't have a man? Please. I'd take no man and no dick over Simon—or any man like him—any day. I continued to hold my glare with Reesa's. This always happened when we went out.

"Ladies, ladies!" Shay said, stepping between us. "Y'all know I don't do this too often, so can you please chill out? We came to get our drink and dance on, not argue."

Neither Reesa nor I said anything. We just continued to beat each other down with our eyes.

"Am I talking to myself, here?" Shay asked.

I cut my eyes at Reesa then looked at Shay. "I hear you."

Shay nodded. "Thank you." Then she looked at my opponent. "Reesa?" she asked.

Reesa gave me another hard stare then said, "I'm going to get a drink." She walked off without saying anything else.

"Erica, why'd you have to go and start up with Reesa?" Shay asked as we moved to an empty table close to the dance floor. "You don't always have to do that shit."

I sucked my teeth. "She gets on my nerves with her shit. Talking about why we have to be in other people's business, knowing she only said that because it was hitting too close to home for her, because just like Anthony, her man is a joke. Jealous of her ass?" I paused as a lanky brother with an eighties flat-top came over to our table and asked me to dance. I gave him a look that said *nigga please* then went back to talking to Shay. "What the hell is she smoking to even say something like that? Hell, I'd rather have no man than to settle with someone like Simon. I ain't that desperate."

As I said that, Carmen arrived and sat down. "Where's Reesa?"

I curled my lips and said, "Gone, hopefully."

Carmen looked at me then at Shay. "They got into it again, didn't they?" Shay didn't even have to answer her. "Erica, do you and Reesa always have to argue when we go out?"

I twisted my lips. "Why do you even invite her ass?"

"Because she is my sistah-girl, just like you are," Carmen said. "That's why."

I sucked my teeth. "She gets on my nerves."

"Yeah well, I'm sure she shares the same sentiment."

"Whatever. I'm not the one trying to push my man off as gold when he's not."

"Erica, first of all, I don't think that's what she's doing. And honestly, if she is, it's her damn prerogative to talk about her man anyhow she wants. That's her man, her relationship. You don't have to like him or it. But you have to respect her. And me. You can't keep going head to head with her just because she says something about Simon that you may not like."

"Simon is worthless," I said.

"He's not your man," Shay said.

"I swear, Erica, the way you're acting, I can't help but wonder if maybe you want a little piece of Simon," Carmen said.

I looked at Carmen through slitted eyes while Shay chuckled. "You can kiss my mahogany-colored ass with that comment. You too, Shay, for laughing. Y'all know damn well I have no interest in a man like Simon."

"Then why trip on Reesa about it and give her such a hard time?"

"Because I don't like her," I said.

Carmen shook her head. "Come on, Erica. I know you. There are a lot of people you don't like, yet you don't give them a hard time like you do Reesa. What's up? What is it about her that brings out the ugly in you?"

"You mean besides her nose-up-in-the-air attitude?"

"Yes, besides that. And just for the record, your nose is up a lot higher than hers."

"Speak the gospel," Shay said, laughing.

I chuckled. "You both know where you can go. Anyway, the main reason I give her such a hard time is because I have no respect for her. I mean, she's a successful, intelligent, attractive black woman. There's absolutely no reason for her to be dealing with a tired-ass brother like Simon. None."

"I hear what you're saying," Shay said, "but that's her prerogative."

"Yeah well, it irks me. We are women. Independent, strong, driven women. Men should be stepping up to our pedestal. We shouldn't be stepping down to theirs. As far as I'm concerned, Reesa hasn't just stepped down from her pedestal by being with Simon, she's jumped off. That's a lack of self-worth to me. And her lack of it bothers me. That's why I can't stand when she brings his name up. He's a waste. We all know it. Why try to put on an act for us? And Carmen, I would get on your case, too, but judging by what I've seen tonight, it looks like you may have finally woken up."

Carmen opened her mouth to respond to my comment, but before she could, Reesa appeared. She and I locked eyes for a moment. I silently dared her to say something. She opened her mouth then looked from me to Carmen. "I have to get going," she said.

"What?" Carmen asked, looking at me. "You just got here."

Reesa sighed. "I know, but Simon just called me. He needs to borrow the car to take care of something."

"Now? Didn't he know you were going out?" Shay asked.

"Yeah, but it just came up."

"Can't he find another ride?" Carmen asked.

"He tried."

I was about to make a comment after that, but bit down on my tongue and instead stood. "I'm going to get a drink." I walked past Reesa without saying a word. As I walked to the bar I shook my head with disgust. It was ten-thirty at night and Simon needed her car to take care of something. How pathetic. That only fueled my feeling of disrespect for Reesa.

Educated.

19

Attractive.

Independent.

Financially successful.

Stupid.

I sucked my teeth and ordered a Cosmopolitan. Not me, I thought. No way. No how. A vibrator'll be my man before idiots like Simon or Anthony.

As the bartender handed me my drink, a deep, velvety voice said, "Drinking alone?"

I looked over to my right and stared up at a tall, dark-chocolate, put-Denzel-to-shame brother who was staring at me with a pair of intense bedroom eyes. I licked my lips. "The question is, are you?"

The too-fine brother flashed a damn near perfect smile. "I am," he said, nodding. He licked his lips LL style. "Now, what about you?"

I hadn't even had a sip of my drink, and I was feeling warm. I looked over toward the table where Carmen and Shay were still talking to Reesa. Then I looked back up at Dark Gable. "I am too," I said.

Dark Gable held out his hand. "Dominic."

I slipped my hand in his. "Erica."

"So, Erica, pardon the use of this line, but what is a fine woman like yourself doing drinking alone? Or are you only alone until your man arrives?"

I smiled. I'd heard the line too many times, but it sounded damn smooth coming from his lips. "No man, and my girls are over there, but they're getting on my nerves, so I'm drinking alone."

"Well, good for me, and sorry to hear that."

"Good for you, huh?"

Dominic smiled. "Very."

"And what about me?" I asked, enjoying the flirtation. "Is it good for me too?"

Dominic licked his lips again and upped the bass in his voice a notch. "It could be."

"Could or would?"

"Would. Definitely."

I nodded and finally took a sip of my drink. It had been a long time since I'd had a one-night stand, but I had a feeling that I was about to have one. I shamelessly looked Dominic up and down and allowed him to do the same as the raw sexual lust between us sky-rocketed off the charts. "Your wife at home?"

"I'm not married."

"Wife, girlfriend . . . same difference."

"Don't have one of those either."

"Boyfriend?"

"Don't swing that way. I thought that was obvious."

"Nothing's obvious these days."

Dominic sipped his beer while I finished my Cosmo.

"Would you like another?"

I shook my head. "I think I'm ready to leave," I said, my eyes on him.

"You sure?"

"Yeah. I'm sure."

"What about your girls? Won't they be disappointed that you're leaving?"

I looked toward the table again. Reesa was gone. Carmen and Shay were looking in my direction. "They'll be alright," I said, putting my empty glass down. "They're big girls." I moved away from the bar, gave Dominic another look then walked out of the club. I was leaning against my BMW 325, enjoying the fifty-degree chill in the October air when Dominic approached. I looked at him. He looked at me. Neither one of us spoke for a few seconds. Just stood, enjoying the breeze and the sight of each other. Finally, sound broke the silence.

"You sure?" Dominic asked.

I pulled my car keys from my purse. "Follow me."

Minutes later I was leading the way down Little Patuxent Parkway, with Dominic's Nissan Z350 trailing me. We were headed toward the Columbia Hilton. I picked the Hilton because I wasn't willing to go to his home, and there was no way I was taking him to mine. Figured the Hilton was a safe bet. He was paying, of course.

When we got upstairs, words were no longer needed. From the moment the door closed, our lips did all the talking, and our fingers did all the walking. Dominic wasn't the best kisser, but I was willing to ignore that. Especially after removing his shirt and running my hands up and down his sculpted chest. Dominic knew how to work his finger. Fondled me so good, I dripped when my thong slid down my legs. I removed his boxers and caught my breath at the size of him. Hadn't had a man his size in a long while. I put my hand around him and felt him throb. Completely naked, we made our way to the bed where I lay back and ordered Dominic to go diving. His kissing had been subpar, but his fondling and his girth were well above average, so I figured that his swimming would be just right. I was wrong. Dead wrong. Dominic had no skill with his tongue whatsoever. He was so bad that I told him to stop and just slip on a condom.

"What's wrong? You don't like it?" he asked.

I looked at him. "No," I said bluntly.

"Maybe you need to loosen up a bit."

"Hard to be loose with you slopping it up down there."

"Whatever," he said, obviously bothered by my callous remarks.

I didn't care. "Whatever," I said. "Just slip on the condom."

Dominic nodded and grabbed his condom and put it on. I smiled. Thought to myself: size like that, the episode could only get better.

Goddamn was I wrong.

Again.

Never in my life had I been with a man so unskilled underneath the sheets. Not even my first sexual partner, Charlie Wilson, who was a virgin, had been as bad as Dominic and his non-satisfying ass. From the moment he slid inside of me, I knew the experience was going to be terrible, because he damn near came seconds later! *Pissed* wouldn't be the appropriate word to describe what I was feeling as he asked me to lay still while his bloodflow slowed. *Homicidal.* That's the word. I don't know why, but I tried one more time to give him the benefit of the doubt. Figured my lovebox just felt that damn good. I should have kicked his ass out the bed though, because the frustration never went away. We had to stop and start three more times before he was able to finally work up the most off-beat rhythmic fucking. I swear, a man with no arms and no legs could have moved smoother than Dominic's ass.

"Get the fuck off me," I yelled.

Dominic, who was sweating for no reason at all, looked at me. "Huh?"

"I said get the fuck off me. Now!"

"What? Why?"

"Why? Nigga, have you ever fucked anything other than your hand?"

"Aww come on, Erica. I was in a long-term relationship before this. I'm just a little rusty."

"A little rusty? Please, your shit is broken. Now get the fuck off me." I hit him and kneed him until he did what I asked. "I can't believe you have absolutely no skills. What a fucking waste!"

"Why you gotta act like that?" Dominic asked, his ego obviously bruised. "I told you I was in a long-term relationship. I fell into a rut. I just need a couple more minutes to work out the kinks."

"Whatever," I said, getting dressed. "You can work your pathetic-ass kinks out by your damn self. I'm leaving. I can't believe you can be so fine and so sorry. What a fucking waste!" I yelled again. I slipped into my black leather pants, threw on my beige blouse, slipped on my shoes, and grabbed my purse.

"You need to chill with that noise, bitch," Dominic said, getting up from the bed. "I'm a fucking man. You can't be talking to me like that."

I gave Dominic a you-must-be-crazy look. "Nigga, I'll talk to your sorry ass however I feel like it. A man? Please." I walked to the door. "Here's a tip for you, lame-o. Why don't you go and get some lessons with that thing? Then you can try calling yourself a man. Until then, spare yourself any more embarrassment. Oh, and if you ever see me again, don't even think about speaking to me. Because I swear if you do, I will make sure that *every* female knows that you need to hang a damn out-of-order sign on your worthless dick." Leaving him speechless and embarrassed, I stormed out of the room and slammed the door. A waste! I couldn't believe he was that bad.

When I got in my car, I grabbed my Kelis CD from my case, slid it in, and pumped her song, "Out There," as I peeled away from the Hilton.

Reesa

"Where the hell have you been?" I tapped my foot furiously on the ground and folded my arms across my chest as Simon walked through the door as though he hadn't been gone all night with my car and made me miss work for the day. "I thought you said it was only going to take you an hour to get your shit done."

Simon closed the door behind him. "I got caught up," he said, slipping out of the leather jacket I'd bought him for Christmas a year ago.

"Caught up?"

"Yeah." He walked past me without a kiss or an apology. "Shit got kind of hectic."

"And you couldn't call me?"

"I told you things were hectic."

"Damn it, Simon," I said, following him into the bedroom. "I had to call off work today because you weren't back with my car."

Simon sat on the bed and took off his Lugz boots then looked up at me. "No you didn't," he said, standing and sliding out of his jeans. "You could have gotten a ride with Joy, and you know it."

I didn't say anything right away because he was right. Joy worked on the floor beneath me and lived just twenty minutes away. Whenever Simon pulled shit like this, I'd usually call her for a ride. I could have called this morning when I knew Simon wasn't going to show up, but I wanted to be home when he arrived. "I'm really tired of your inconsiderate shit, Simon. You

25

may not care, but I have a damn job that I depend on. I needed my car, and you should have been here."

Simon sat back down on the bed in his boxers. "Look, Reesa, I'm tired, okay? I told you shit got hectic. What more do you want?"

"How about a damn apology?"

"Apology for what? You didn't have to call off today."

"How do you know I didn't need my car?"

"If you needed it, you would have called me."

"I was too pissed to call you."

"Yeah, whatever. Come on and stop tripping, Reesa." Simon rose from the bed, came over to me, took my hand in his, and placed it on his hardening crotch, which I had been trying my hardest to avoid staring at. "You know the real reason you stayed home," he said, opening my fingers and closing them around him. He leaned into me and lightly kissed my neck, sending shivers up my back.

"Yeah, because I wanted my car," I said, pulling my hand away.

He took it back and this time, guided it underneath his Joe Boxers. My body heat rose as he let go of my hand to do its thing while he kissed and licked at the base of my neck again. "Is that what you really wanted?" he asked, blowing his hot breath across my skin.

I shook my head in an attempt to fight the rising desire for Simon and the sex he gave so well, while my hands disobeyed my every command and worked Simon's manhood into a pulsating state of attention.

"You only wanted your car? Nothing . . . else?"

I tried to keep my lips sealed but his licking, his pecking, his hot breath, his erection forced my lips to part, allowing a soft moan to escape. Simon took my free hand and walked me over to the bed and laid me down. I didn't fight him, just lay back and let him remove my black dress pants, light-blue blouse, bra, and panties.

"Are you still mad, Reesa?" he asked, sliding his finger inside of me.

I didn't answer right away. His touch had me momentarily paralyzed and mute. Finally, I said, "Yes."

With three of his fingers inside of me, Simon fiddled with my clit and made the inside of my walls tingle. At the same time, his tongue did laps around my nipple then trailed its way down, pausing momentarily at my belly button before continuing until his fingers and tongue changed shifts.

"Still pissed?" Simon asked, licking, nibbling, burrowing.

I squirmed from the pleasure, lifted my waist for better dining, and put my hands on the back of his head. "Yes . . . Oh shit! Yes!" I answered, meaning every breathy word.

Simon asked me over and over until my walls opened and released a flood of ecstasy. Still pissed off, I rolled Simon onto his back, removed his boxers, and straddled him. I moaned as I slid down on him and rode him until we both exploded.

When we were finished, Simon lay on his back snoring, while I lay on my stomach crying. I shouldn't have fucked him. Damn it, why did I always have to be so weak? I thought back to the night before and my war of words with Erica at Silver Shadow. I defended my man like Condoleezza Rice defends President Bush: knew he was dead wrong, but wouldn't admit it. Erica had been right about everything she'd said.

Simon wasn't a man.

I looked over at him and watched his chest rise and fall as he snored. I'd put a hurting on him. Sexed him so good, I wore his ass out. To him it was good sex. It was angry sex to me. Tears cascaded down my cheeks.

He wasn't a man.

But he was all the man I had.

And like I said, I was pushing thirty-five.

I just wished that my fear of being alone and not having kids were the only reasons I wouldn't kick Simon's ass to the curb. As much as I hated to admit it, I loved his ass too. And even though I'd probably do better by letting him make another female's life stressful, I still didn't want him to be with anyone else.

Ain't that a trip?

I turned my head to the side and stared at my alarm clock until my eyes closed. Seemed like seconds later they were snapping back open when the doorbell rang. I looked at the clock; I'd been asleep for almost an hour. I shook Simon, but he didn't budge. Just snored. I sighed; slipped into my flannel pants, tank-top, and satin robe; and went to the door. I should have checked the peephole first. Had I done that, I would have never opened it.

"What are you doing here?"

I snapped my head back and looked at Simon's son's mother, Cecilia, like she had lost her fucking mind. "Excuse me?" I said, squinting. "Bitch, I live here. The real question is what is your ass doing here?"

Cecilia glared back at me like she wanted to do something devious. Cecilia was a five-eight Amazon with shoulder-length hair dyed platinum blonde, and hoop earrings in her eyebrows and bottom lip. Cecilia and Simon hated each other. They just fucked one night and ended up having a beautiful baby boy they named Jabari. Simon rarely used Cecilia's name. Bitch was his preference. That was mine too. Had been since the day we met.

I was at the movies with Simon when that happened. She was there with a date, too, but the minute she saw me and Simon, she forgot her date existed and caused a scene, yelling about how Simon wasn't shit. He could take some yellow bitch to the movies, but he couldn't send her some money for their fucking son. Simon spat back that he wasn't sending her shit because Jabari wasn't his. She called him a piece of shit. Said his ass was gonna start paying child support then told both of us to go to hell.

I never said a word. I'd been too stunned to speak. I'd been dating Simon for five months, and that was the first time I found out he was a baby daddy. I confronted him about it after we left the theater without seeing a movie. He insisted that Jabari wasn't his and that's why he never mentioned anything to me. I believed him until I saw Cecilia out with her son one day. I made Simon come correct after that, because Jabari is his spitting image.

I'm not sure what Cecilia's real problem with me was, but we couldn't be in the same room alone.

"Where's Simon?"

"I just asked you a fucking question, Cecilia. What are you doing coming to my house when I'm not here?"

Cecilia cut her eyes at me then pulled her son in front of her. I hadn't even seen him standing with her. I bent down, ashamed of the language I'd used. "Hey, Jabari! How are you?"

Jabari smiled and opened his mouth to respond, but before he could, Cecilia said again, "Where the hell is Simon?"

I frowned and stood. "Look, Cecilia, I'm not answering a fu—a single question until you tell me what your a . . . what you're doing here. You know you're not welcomed."

"Whatever, bitch," Cecilia said, not giving a damn about Jabari's presence. "Simon's taking us shopping."

"Shopping?"

"That's right. Jabari needs a new pair of sneakers, and I have a couple of outfits that I want."

"Excuse me? Outfits? Who the—"

"Bitch, what are you doing here?"

I turned around. Simon was standing behind me.

"Daddy!" Jabari raced past me and wrapped his arms around Simon.

"Hey, little man," Simon said, lifting Jabari into the air. "Do me a favor, a'ight." He put Jabari down. "Go in my bedroom and turn on the TV to Cartoon Network."

"But I want to stay here with you," Jabari said.

"I'll come back and join you soon."

"Okay."

Simon smiled as Jabari walked off. When he disappeared into our room, Simon turned back to Cecilia. "What the fuck are you doing here?"

"Don't even try to give me attitude because she's here, motherfucker. You know why I'm here."

"I said I was gonna come and pick you up," Simon snapped back.

I looked at Simon. "Pick them up? You mean she's telling the truth?"

"Damn right I am," Cecilia said, answering for Simon.

I turned and gave her the evil eye then looked back to Simon. "Is she telling the truth? You're taking her shopping?"

Simon looked from me to Cecilia then back to me. "Yeah."

I chuckled, although I didn't find anything funny. "Okay, I'm obviously missing something here, so why don't you clear things up for me? First, Jabari I can understand, but why is she talking about you taking her shopping at the mall? Second, you said you were going to pick her up. Just how the hell did you plan on doing that? Because as far as I know, I'm the only one in this room with a car."

"Look, Reesa, let's talk about this later, a'ight?"

I shook my head. "No, we will not talk about this later. I want my questions answered now!"

"Hmph," Cecilia said. "You let her talk to you like that?"

I looked at her. "Cecilia, why don't you keep your mouth shut?"

Cecilia raised her eyebrows. "Bitch, you better watch how you talk to me."

"I don't have to watch shit," I said, no longer able to keep the profanity away. "This is my damn apartment!"

Cecilia curled her lips. "You know what, bitch? You wouldn't have this damn apartment if it weren't for me."

"What's that supposed to mean?"

"It means that half of the damn rent for the past two months came from my pocket."

I closed my eyes a fraction and looked at her. "What?"

Cecilia smiled. "Ask your man how he managed to come up with half of the rent money."

I turned to Simon and stared at him. "What's she talking about?"

Simon stared daggers at Cecilia then looked down at me. "Look, let's talk about this later," he said again.

"I already told you that's not an option. Now, what the hell did she mean? Did you borrow money from her?"

Simon looked at Cecilia again, then back to me, but didn't say anything. But he didn't need to because his eyes said it all. "Why the hell did you borrow money from her?"

"Look, Reesa, shit was tight for a couple of months. Business wasn't running the way I would have liked."

"So you borrowed money from her ass?" I yelled, pointing in Cecilia's direction. "If you didn't have the money, why didn't you just say so? I would have taken care of the damn rent just like I always do."

Simon nodded. "That's the reason right there."

"Huh?"

"I don't like her ass, but I'd rather borrow money from her than have to listen to you talk shit about how you're always taking care of shit around here."

"That's because I do!"

"So what are you saying? That I'm a burden?"

"A burden? Please. You're a lead weight clasped around my ankle. You don't pay bills, but you sure as hell know how to make them."

"Why you disrespecting me as a man, Reesa?"

"A man? When the hell have you ever been that, Simon?"

"So what, because I don't have some fucking nine-to-five gig I ain't a man?"

"No, Simon. A job doesn't make you a man. What makes you a man is your ability to take care of your responsibilities. And that is what you don't know how to do. You're a hustler, Simon. Fine, I can deal with that. Some men are just that way. But damn, did it ever occur to you to be the best damn hustler you could be? Jesus! Doesn't it bother you that you don't own shit? That you never have money? That you can't pay a bill to save your life?"

"You don't know what the game is like, Reesa. Shit ain't easy."

"So if it's that damn hard then go out, be a regular fucking man and get a nine-to-five job! That would have to be a lot better than having to borrow money from a bitch you can't stand."

"Call me a bitch one more time and there's gonna be problems up in here," Cecilia said.

I looked at her and thought about saying something, but changed my mind. She just wasn't worth it. And quite frankly, neither was Simon. I shook my head, sucked my teeth, and threw my hands in the air. "I can't take this shit anymore." I looked at Simon. "I can't take your shit anymore. I've had it."

"What's that supposed to mean?" Simon asked.

"It means that you need to pack your shit up and move. We're through. I'm tired of the late nights stressing because you can't bring your ass home. I'm tired of paying your bills. I'm tired of your baby momma drama. I'm tired, Simon. Sick and tired of wasting my fucking time on you."

I turned and looked at Cecilia. "I know you two hate each other, but if there's any part of you that wants him back, you can have him." I turned back to Simon. "I'm going to change then I'm leaving. Don't be here when I come back. If you are, I swear I will call the police and have them come and escort your ass out of here."

I walked off to my bedroom without saying another word. When I walked in, Jabari was sitting on my bed watching BET. I looked at him and smiled. He smiled back. "Your mom is ready to go," I said, shutting off the television.

Jabari frowned. He and I always had fun together, and I know he wasn't looking forward to going back to Cecilia. Before he left the room, I gave him a hug and told him to be good. When he left, I closed the door, sat on the bed, and sighed. I couldn't believe I'd just done that. Ended everything. Now I was going to have to do what I feared: start over. Swim in the dating pool again and look for the king fish swimming with the sharks. God, I hated the dating scene.

I lay back on the bed and smelled the sex Simon and I had engaged in just a few hours earlier. I was going to be alone again. There'd be no one to make any random noise, no one to leave a mess after I'd cleaned up. No one to complain about, no one to lie next to, to keep me warm at night. No one to stoke my fires when they needed to be stoked.

Alone.

I hated being alone.

I wasn't needy, but I liked to have a warm body at my side. And Simon's warm body was going to be near impossible to replace.

I took a deep breath, held it for a few seconds, then released it slowly and got up from the bed. I dressed—put on a pair of jeans and a red V-neck sweater—and slipped on my all-white Nike sneakers. As I did, the bedroom door opened. I looked at Simon. He looked at me.

"Cecilia still waiting for her ride?"

"Why are you tripping, Reesa?"

"Simon," I said, grabbing my purse and car keys, "I've already tripped. What I did out there was pick myself back up."

"So just like that, we're done?"

"Just like that." I walked past him and tensed up just in case he decided to play stupid and grab me. He'd never put his hands on me before, but you never know. I walked into the living room; Cecilia and Jabari were nowhere around. Simon walked out behind me. I turned around and shook my head. "I can't believe you borrowed money from her."

"Like I said, I didn't feel like hearing your mouth."

"Was getting a regular job that hard for you?"

"Working regular jobs has never been for me. You know that."

I nodded. "Yeah, I did know that. So I guess the only person I should be pissed off at is myself, huh?"

Simon shrugged. "I never fronted on who I was," he said, which was basically his way of answering yes to my question.

I nodded again. "Don't be here when I get back, Simon. I meant what I said." I grabbed my coat from the closet, slipped it on, and walked out the front door. When it closed behind me, I heard Simon mutter, "Bitch."

I laughed to myself. I was a bitch. And it was about damn time, because although I was pushing thirty-five and had a real fear of being alone, I'd been a sucker for far too long.

Carmen

"Is it my birthday?" I'd just opened my eyes and was greeted by the sight of Anthony holding a tray stacked with a plate of pancakes, sliced apples, a small glass of OJ, and a cup of hot tea. Anthony watched me with a big smile plastered on his face.

"No," he said with a laugh.

I wiped crud from the corners of my eyes. "Did I miss an anniversary?"

"Nope."

"Am I going to die, and this is your way of breaking the news to me?"

Anthony broke out laughing and nearly spilled the tray. "No. Now, will you sit up so that I can serve you?"

I looked at him strangely. In our three years together, I could only recall two other times that Anthony had stepped foot in the kitchen to cook for me. The first time had been after I had fractured my wrist at the gym. I'd slipped during my aerobics class, and I landed funny on my hand. The other time Anthony cooked was when I'd caught the flu so bad that I could barely get out of the bed. Other than those two occasions, Anthony was a non-cooking fool.

"What's the occasion, Anthony?"

"Can't I just make breakfast for my girl?"

"No. Especially since I can't look as good as Shakira," I said, reminding him that I was still upset about his comment the night before.

"Whatever," Anthony said. "Just sit up, would you? This food's gonna get cold."

I gave Anthony another scrutinizing look then sat up. "I need to brush my teeth first."

"Brush them after you eat."

He waited for me to prop pillows behind me then set the tray over my knees. I took a whiff of the pancakes. "Mmm, you made my favorite!"

Anthony smiled. "Yup."

I cut a piece and slid the blueberry pancake into my mouth and opened my eyes wide. "These are good!"

Anthony cheesed again. "Of course they are."

I slid another piece into my mouth and took a bite of the sliced apple. After I washed it down with a swallow of orange juice, I looked up at Anthony. "Okay . . . so what's this for? 'Fess up. I know you didn't do this just to do it."

Anthony sat down on the bed beside me. "You're right," he said. "I'm guilty. There is something behind the breakfast in bed."

"I thought so. So what's the reason?"

"This was my way of apologizing for yesterday."

I watched him with a skeptical eye. "Oh, really?"

"Yeah, really. Look, what I said yesterday came out sounding all wrong."

"Is that right? So how was it supposed to sound?"

"You're fine, Carmen. You know that."

"Just not as fine as Shakira, right?"

"Can we please move past Shakira?"

"Move past her? Isn't she the reason I'm sitting here eating my favorite pancakes?"

Anthony groaned. "Look, Carmen, you're fine. Sexy as hell. Can't we just leave it at that?"

"Like *you* said, Anthony, I'm just not as fine and sexy as Shakira." I took another bite of my pancakes and apple slices and smirked. After the night out I'd had hanging with Shay and dancing my ass off with one fine-looking brother after the next, the last thing I had on my mind was Anthony's ignorant-ass comment to me. I'd forgotten all about that after the third Long Island Iced Tea. The only reason I was going on and on was because I was enjoying the frustration on Anthony's face. He'd dug the hole with his insensitive words, but even though I didn't care anymore, I wasn't about to let him climb out of it easily. "So am I at least second to Shakira? Or is there another female I can't look as good as?"

Anthony clenched his jaws and cracked his knuckles. "Look, I have to get going. I have to go to work for a bit. I just wanted to give you breakfast in bed, say I was sorry, and give you this." He placed a small envelope on the tray.

"What's this?" I picked it up.

"It's a gift."

"To where?"

"Open it and see."

I took a sip of hot tea then tore open the envelope and removed a small card. "What the hell is this?" I asked after reading it. "Is this for real?" I held it up and looked at him.

"What's up with the attitude?" Anthony asked.

"This is an appointment card to get my hair done."

"Yeah."

"I just had my hair done last week."

"I know, but this isn't just to get your hair done. It's to get your hair dyed too. I made an appointment with the best hairstylist there. I got the recommendation from my sister. I spoke to him and arranged everything. All you have to do is show up and sit in the chair."

I looked at Anthony with my mouth hanging open. *No way,* I thought. He had to have lost his mind. I shook my head. "So you arranged everything, huh?"

"Yeah."

"Even the color *I* said I want my hair dyed, huh?"

"Yeah."

I took a deep breath, held it in for a few seconds, then let it out slowly, all in an effort not to lose my cool. "Anthony," I said, moving the tray from over my legs, "you . . . are . . . a . . . piece of . . . work. This is some real bullshit. I guess this is your way of trying to make me fine like Shakira, huh?"

"Carmen—"

"Shut up, Anthony! Just shut up. I can't believe you had the nerve to do this. Jesus! And I didn't think it could get worse than your comment!"

"Carmen, will you just chill out and listen to me?"

36

"Hell no, I won't chill out! How would you like it if I pulled some shit like this? How would you like it if I said, 'Anthony, I think your dick is too small. Here's an appointment card to go and get it enlarged so you can be just as big as my ex!'"

"What the fuck kind of comment is that?" Anthony yelled.

"I'm making a point, asshole!"

"What the hell kind of point is that? And for the record, my shit is not small!"

I shook my head. Jesus. "Anthony, you're such an ass! How could you do some shit like this?"

"What the hell did I do that was so bad, Carmen? So I made an appointment for you to have your hair done. So what?"

"So what? What you did is ignorant and hurtful."

"Hurtful?"

"Yes! It's almost like you're saying I don't look good enough the way I am."

"Come on, Carmen. That's not what I'm saying."

"Oh really? Do you really expect me to believe that shit? Especially after you came out your mouth yesterday talking about how I should dye my hair blonde and how I couldn't look as good as Shakira's blonde ass."

"Will you give Shakira a fucking rest?"

"No, damn it! She's the one that's causing all of this."

"You're tripping, Carmen."

"No, you're tripping. Especially if you think I'm going to dye my hair for your ass. *Ay, no puedo entender como yo estoy contigo!*" I shook my head and continued to go off in Spanish, asking myself about my choice in men.

"Hey! I understood that," Anthony said. "I'm a damn good man. That's why you're with me."

"No, you're an ass!"

"Why, Carmen? Just because I want you to dye your hair?"

"Yes!"

"You're such a hypocrite."

"Excuse me?" I looked at Anthony with my hands planted firmly on my hips. "What did you just call me?"

"I said you're a hypocrite, Carmen. I mean, how the hell are you gonna get on my case about some shit like this when you've done something like this yourself?"

"What? I have never done something like this."

"Yes, you have."

"No, I haven't!"

"Remember the closet episode?"

"Huh?"

"Don't 'huh' me. I know you remember."

I closed my eyes a bit and tried to figure out what he was talking about. The closet episode? And then it hit me. "Oh my God! You are not really going to compare that to this."

"Hell yeah I am because it's the same thing."

"No, it's not!"

"I never said I wanted a new wardrobe, Carmen. But sure enough, when I came home from work, a new wardrobe is what was hanging in the damn closet. And all of my clothing, which I had no problem with, had been donated to Goodwill."

"I did you a favor, Anthony, and you know it. You had no style."

"I didn't care about style, Carmen. I was just fine with what I had."

"What you had was for kids. I gave you a man's wardrobe."

"And I never asked for it!"

I rolled my eyes. "Whatever, Anthony. I sure as hell don't hear you complaining now, and I really don't see how you can compare my wanting you to dress like a man to your fucking gift."

"Carmen, I didn't give you that gift to say that you aren't fine. I gave you the gift because just like you thought a wardrobe change would be good for me, I think a change in hairstyle and color might be kind of cool. I've seen you in the stores browsing at the hair coloring section before, so I know you've thought about it."

"There's a difference between thinking and doing," I said.

"I know that. But you've thought about it, and that's what matters."

I folded my arms across my chest and pouted.

"Look, Carmen, can't you just give it a try? You might like the new look."

"You mean *you* might like it."

"Just like *you* liked my new wardrobe."

38

I gave Anthony a hard, cutting, didn't-appreciate-his-last-comment stare, but didn't say anything. Instead, I thought back to the day Anthony came home and found a brand-new wardrobe waiting for him in his closet. To say that he wasn't happy would be an understatement, because he damn near had an aneurysm. He was so pissed that I gave his clothing away and replaced it with a style that he'd "never wear!" He felt that my actions were just my way of not accepting him for who he was.

Of course that hadn't been the case. I just wanted to see him wear something other than casual clothing with brand names etched on them. Anthony's an attractive, high-yellow Kenny Lattimore look-alike, but the style he used to wear took away from his appearance. And I wanted him to stand out the way he should. It took some repetitive explanation on my part—and some ass—but eventually, Anthony came around and decided to give the new wardrobe a try. Now you wouldn't catch him in anything that didn't come from Banana Republic or Nordstrom.

Anthony looked at his watch and sighed. "Look, Carmen, just forget about the damn gift, okay? I was just trying to do something nice for you. Just like *you* did for me. If it's too hard for you to give the new style a try, then fine." Anthony picked up the appointment card I'd thrown to the ground and shook his head. "I gotta go. I'm late for work." He turned and started out of the room. I watched him walk, his shoulders slumped and his head hanging just a little lower than before.

"Wait," I said, frowning, rolling my eyes and sighing at the same time. "Give me the card."

Anthony turned around. "Huh?"

"Give me the card," I said, putting out my hand.

"So what are you saying?"

I rolled my eyes one more time. "I'll go to the appointment. I'll try the new look."

"You serious?"

I hesitated then said, "Yeah."

Anthony smiled and came toward me. "For real?" he asked, the pitch in his voice higher than before.

"Look, I already said yes. Do you want me to change my mind?"

"No, don't do that!" Anthony came forward, grabbed me in his arms, and planted a kiss on my lips. "Thanks, baby. You won't regret this. And I know the new color's gonna look good on you." He slid the card in my hand, kissed me again then stepped back. "Damn," he said, still holding the Kool-Aid smile. "If I didn't have to be at work today, I'd scoop you up, lay you on the bed, and keep you there all day."

Anthony licked his lips, rubbed his palms together, and gnawed on his bottom lip. He was obviously giving his last comment some thought. But I wasn't having it. "Look, you already missed a couple of days last week because you were sick. You need to go in to work."

Anthony frowned. "Yeah, I guess you're right." He glanced down at his watch. "All right, let me jet before anymore time goes by. Can I get a raincheck on keeping you in the bed for later tonight?"

"Sure," I said with little emotion.

Anthony hurried out of the room. I waited until I heard his car start then pull off before I sat down on the bed and grabbed the remote control for the television. This was supposed to have been a relaxing day off for me. I checked the appointment card I was still holding and shook my head. I couldn't believe I'd given in and said yes. I sighed and hit the power on the remote. Seconds later I yelled, shut off the television, threw the remote to the ground, crumpled the appointment card then got up to get dressed to go to the gym. The television had been on MTV, and of course Shakira's video just had to be the one that was playing. I had to get out of the house.

Erica

"Carmen, I'm telling you, I was *this* close to going to jail, brother was so bad. All I needed was a gun!"

"Come on, you're exaggerating," Carmen said, laughing.

"Exaggerating my ass!" I said, sucking my teeth. "I wish I were exaggerating. At least then I wouldn't be sitting here contemplating going back to Silver Shadow just to find his pathetic ass so I could serve him with papers."

Carmen broke out laughing again and some of her drink spilled from her mouth. I took a sip of my lemonade and shook my head. I was still pissed off about how disastrous my episode after leaving the club had been. I was so mad I didn't even go home right away. I just headed down 295 toward DC, pumping my Kelis CD. When I was done screaming along with Kelis, I switched CDs and played Ashanti's song, "Rain On Me," to calm myself down.

I drove around DC for a while, thinking about going in one of the clubs—maybe Choices or Dream—for a drink, but changed my mind and eventually headed home and did what that jackass couldn't do—satisfy my urge. When I was done, I filled the bathtub with as-hot-as-I-could-stand-it water, added some Bath and Body Works bubbles to take me away, lit a few cinnamon candles, played my Will Downing CD, and took a bath.

"I tried and I tried. I tried and I tried."

I sang right along with Will as the bubbles floated over me.

"I tried and I tried."

Damn it, what the hell did I have to do to have a little company in the tub with me? I know I said I was done asking, but where the hell were the real brothers?

Damn it.

As I lay in the tub, letting the water go from hot to cool, I thought about Reesa's comment about me being jealous of her because she had a man and I didn't. At the time, I scoffed in her face, saying that my being jealous was an impossibility, but as I lay in the bathtub I couldn't help but admit that she had been right. I was jealous. Not because I wanted Simon's good-for-nothing ass, but because alone in the bathtub, with a dildo waiting in the bed was the last thing Reesa was. Simon may be a waste of a man, but he was still a man with working parts; a man whose body you could feel beside you at night, keeping you company, shielding you from the brutality of loneliness. Although I wouldn't admit it to anyone, I was missing that so bad.

My last relationship, which I thought was going to be the end-all-be-all , ended on the worst note possible. My ex, whose name I won't even mention, got another woman pregnant. His ex if you must know. A ghettofied bitch with an easy-access coochie. I thought my ex and I had something. We complemented each other well. He was a lawyer, me a web designer. We were both driven, both paid, and we looked damn good together. At the time, I had a short, sexy hairstyle, kind of like Nia Long in *The Best Man*. My body was still curvaceous and thick in all the right areas. My ex was a former football player in high school and college and had kept his fit physique. Like I said, we made heads turn.

I can't lie, I was in love with him. He was every woman's fantasy. Paid, fine, and had serious skills in the bed. He had me wrapped around his finger. Could have told me the world ended and we were the only two people left on the face of the earth, and I would have believed him. I know, I was that bad.

I wouldn't have believed he'd been messing around on me if his ex hadn't made an unexpected visit to his place to deliver the news to him. I had answered his door that night. I didn't normally do that, but he was in the shower washing off the funk we'd created in the bedroom. I stared at his ex for a couple

42

of minutes but didn't say anything. I'd never met her, but I knew of her from old pictures in his photo album. She knew about me too. Said I was uglier in person. She was hating of course, because truth be told, she was the one who resembled a pit bull.

Our conversation didn't last long. I asked what she was doing there. She handed me an envelope, told me to read its contents then spread the word. Then she walked away. I closed the door, tore open the envelope, and read the results of the pregnancy test that had been inside. Then I re-read it. And re-read it again. Did that until my ex came out of the shower. I confronted him about it, and of course he denied it. Said that there was no way his ex was pregnant by him because he wasn't fucking her. Like a fool, I believed him—until a few months after she had her baby. The bitch showed up at my job. She didn't say anything, just let me see her son who was the spitting image of my ex. I went home that day and packed up all of my shit. I've been going on two years without a man now.

"I'm for real, girl. I want to sue his ass for fraud. Brotha has no right being that fine and that pitiful with his dick."

Carmen chuckled again and said, "Well, at least he wasn't gay."

I twisted my mouth into a sneer. "I think a gay brotha would have satisfied me better than his ass."

Carmen laughed again, and this time I laughed with her. It wasn't funny, but what else could I do? Carmen took a bite of the salad she'd ordered. We were sitting in Olive Garden waiting for our lunches. "You're crazy," she said between bites.

I nodded. "It's these brothas that have got me crazy."

"I hear that."

We high-fived each other.

"So, what's up with the new hair color? What made you do it?"

"I was wondering when you were gonna say something."

"I had to vent first. So what's up with it?"

Carmen shrugged. "I don't know. I just wanted to try something different. You don't like it?"

I gave her now platinum-colored 'do a once-over. "I like it. I think the color and style look good with your hazel eyes. What did Anthony say about it?"

Carmen let out a frustrated sigh. "He loves it."

I took a sip of my lemonade and peered over the rim of my glass at my sistah-girl, who I'd known for five years. It was obvious by her expression that there was something behind what she'd said. "Okay," I said, putting my glass down. "Spill it. What's up with Anthony loving your hair?"

"Nothing," Carmen said, doing a terrible job of being convincing.

"Come on, *chica*. What's up?"

Carmen looked at me. "The hair coloring was his idea," she said.

"Huh?"

Carmen passed her hand through her hair. "He wanted me to dye my hair."

"Okay, and?"

"And he gave me an appointment card to get it done."

I looked at her with one eyebrow raised. She'd done it again. "Carmen, I know you're a Latina and it's in your culture to take care of and satisfy your man, but why do you keep doing things to satisfy Anthony when he doesn't deserve it?"

"He wanted me to try a new look," Carmen said.

"Is that right? Since when?"

"Since Shakira was on TV."

"Huh? What's she got to do with you getting your hair dyed?"

Carmen groaned then went on to tell me all about Anthony's comments about Shakira and then about her waking up to breakfast in bed, then getting her "gift." When she was done recounting everything and explaining why she'd given in, I pressed my lips together tightly and gave my girl a disapproving stare.

"Carmen, Carmen, Carmen," I said, shaking my head. I paused and let out a long, exaggerated sigh. "You know you were wrong for giving in to him, right?"

"He gave in to me with his clothes, though."

I sucked my teeth. "So?"

44

Carmen shrugged. "So shouldn't I bend if he's willing to?"

"Hell no! First of all, his style was terrible with a capital T. He needed for you to be his fashion police. Second of all, you're a woman, and as a woman, you don't have to bend for shit. Damn, girl, you do enough for Anthony's lazy ass with all of the cooking, cleaning, and sexing that you do."

"I just like to take care of my man."

"Taking care of him is one thing, Carmen. Waiting on him hand and foot is another. And now you're changing your hair color because he wants you to? When are you going to draw the line, girl? When are you going to start demanding that he take care of you?" I paused as the waitress brought our food—chicken penne for me, spaghetti for Carmen. When the waitress walked away, I looked at my girl with apologetic eyes. I didn't mean to jump down her throat the way I had, but I was really disappointed and bothered that she would dye her hair just because Anthony wanted her to. God, she needed some backbone. She was always doing something for Anthony's benefit. Always compromising herself in some way, shape, or form, granting whatever wish he had. I'd lost count of the number of times I'd told her she shouldn't do everything for Anthony.

"Look, girl, I don't mean to be all on your case about this. I'm just trying to get you to open your eyes and see Anthony for what you know he really is—a selfish, spoiled, insensitive jerk." Carmen gave me a cutting look; obviously she didn't like my last comment. But I wasn't about to retract my statement because it was true. "I'm just being honest with you, Carmen. Anthony is spoiled as hell. When's the last time he made a payment on his car?" I didn't even wait for her to answer. "Never," I said, shaking my head. "Girl, his mother makes his car payment."

"He doesn't have the best job, Erica."

"So? Let him get another one. He's twenty-nine years old. I mean, come on, if it's not his car payment, then it's his credit card bills. If it's not those, then it's his half of the rent. He's supposed to be a grown-ass man. Not a little boy who's still reaching into his mother's pocket. There's absolutely no reason why he can't pay his own damn bills, Carmen, and you know it." I stopped talking to allow time for what I'd said to sink in.

Carmen opened her mouth to respond, but then closed it and instead reached for her drink and took a long sip. I checked out her hair. Until she'd told me all about Anthony and his "gift," I thought it looked great. Just knowing now that getting her new 'do had more to do with pleasing Anthony than pleasing herself changed my opinion.

Self.

Always first.

Always the most important.

Carmen needed to realize that.

"Look, let's switch topics, okay?" I'd lectured her enough, and it was time to lighten the mood. "How's work going?"

We BS'd about work for the next twenty minutes until Carmen received a call on her cell from her sister. Ten minutes after that, she had to rush out. Her sister was in a bind and needed some help. I would have gone with her, but I'd ordered a piece of Tiramisu before she got the call, so I decided to stay behind. Besides, I didn't feel like dealing with the crazy drama that her sister usually got into.

Luckily I had stopped at the bookstore before I got to the restaurant and bought La Jill Hunt's latest book, so I had something to keep me company. With nowhere special to be, I wasn't in the mood to rush out of there. I grabbed my fork, opened the book to page one, and started eating and reading at the same time. Tiramisu gone, I was all into the drama La Jill created when a deep, baritone voice I never expected to hear again interrupted me.

"Erica? Is that you?"

I looked up from my book with an immediate scowl. "What are you doing here?" I said, my voice raw and biting.

"Damn! Hello to you too," my ex, Kenny, said.

I twisted my lips even more. "What do you want, Kenny? Why are you bugging me?"

Kenny, still looking as fine as ever, nodded and stroked the faded goatee he was now sporting. "I see you're still carrying around issues from the past."

46

"Yeah well, some issues are harder to get rid of than others."

"You still look good, Erica. I like the new hairstyle. You've got the whole Kelis thing going."

I gave Kenny a sour look then exhaled angrily. "Do you need something, Kenny? Because if you don't, I'd appreciate it if you'd get out of my face."

Kenny shook his head and flashed the subtle smile I used to love. "Erica, are you gonna hate me for the rest of your life over a mistake I made?"

"A mistake?" I said loudly, not giving a damn about others around us.

Kenny looked from side to side. "Yes, a mistake," he said, lowering his voice, and I'm sure hoping I'd lower mine.

Of course that's the last thing I was about to do. Especially after what he'd just said. "A mistake would have been a one-night fuck, Kenny, not a fuck that lasted for four damn months that climaxed with another bitch's pregnancy." I closed my book, shoved it in my bag, and stood. I was almost face-to-face with Kenny now; he's about five inches taller than me. I looked up at him. "I know us being in the same place is coincidental, but if it happens again, do yourself and me a favor, don't approach me. As a matter of fact, don't even look in my direction." I grabbed my half-empty glass of lemonade from the table and threw the drink in his face. "Asshole!" I said then walked away. On my way out, I passed my waitress and told her Kenny was paying for the check.

I left the restaurant and hurried to my car. When I got in and slammed the door shut, I let the angry tears I'd been holding back, fall. I was so pissed. Of all the people to bump into, it had to be him. Damn it. I slammed my hand down on the steering wheel then buried my face in my hands and cried even harder. After a few minutes the tears ceased, and I wiped my face and blew my nose. *It had to be him,* I thought again.

I started the car.

It had to be him.

I slipped in my Kelis CD, blasted my anthem, and pulled off.

"I hate you so much right now!" I screamed.

47

Two years, and I still hated him.
Damn.

Reesa

Let it go to voice mail. That's what I was going to do as my office phone rang. Let it go to voice mail. I didn't feel like talking to anybody. I was miserable.

Unhappy.

Lonely.

Depressed.

Horny.

I was a wreck. Two weeks had passed since I walked into my apartment and Simon wasn't there. Two weeks had passed since I'd kicked him out. Two weeks had passed, and I hadn't heard a peep from him. Not a phone call, an e-mail; not that he'd do that, since he didn't really know how to use the computer, but still . . . No late-night knocking at my door; no surprise visits to my job. Nothing. I ended our relationship, told him to get to stepping. I was through, had had enough of the games. Like Mary J., I didn't want no more drama. Two weeks. Where the hell was he?

I looked at my phone and watched the red light come on, letting me know that the caller had left a message. Could this be the one? I picked up the receiver and dialed my log-on and password to access my voice mail. So far I'd been zero for five. Maybe this message would be from Simon. Unfortunately, it wasn't. Just another work-related voice mail that I wasn't going to respond to. I deleted it, put down the receiver and sighed. Where was he and why hadn't he called? I wondered again. I shook my head. Although Simon hadn't given me any indication that he was going to, I really expected to hear from him by now.

"Why, Reesa? You did kick him out," I said to myself.

I kicked him out. I'd had enough.

Damn it, I was missing him.

I tried to go out with some women from work a couple of times. Figured since I didn't have much time before thirty-five came, I'd better jump back into the dating pool and start swimming quickly. But even though I met some attractive, educated, doing-something-with-their-lives brothers, I couldn't stop thinking about Simon, and for the life of me, I couldn't figure out why. Simon wasn't exactly the best catch. I acknowledged that. But still, he was my man. And now I didn't have one.

"God bless America!"

I rolled my eyes. Bernice was going off again. She was a coworker in the office next to mine, who had no right being in an office setting because she absolutely couldn't handle pressure of any kind. If her phone rang, she wigged out. If she received an e-mail, she wigged out. If someone came by to ask her a question, she wigged out. If mail of any kind or amount came, she wigged out. Basically, she wigged out all day, every day.

"Give me a break, God!" she said as her phone, which was too damned loud, rang.

Normally, I'd get up and close my door whenever she got on the phone because she had an annoying habit of speaking for everyone to hear her business, but today I just sat and listened to her.

"Hey, honey . . . Oh, I'm having so much fun I can hardly stand it. As usual I can't get any work done because my phone won't stop ringing. I don't know . . . everyone just seems to be calling me . . . Yeah, I know. I'll probably have to skip lunch like I do every damn day . . . How? If I take lunch, I'll just get backed up with more voice mails that I can't get to and e-mails that I won't have time to respond to . . . I know what the doctor said, but he doesn't work here. Look, I have my Gas-X with me, so I'll be fine. And I'll see if I can step away from my desk for five minutes and get something from the vending machine, although I don't see how that's going to be possible since the receptionist seems to be forwarding all calls over to me . . .

Yeah. Anyway, will the bathroom be fixed today? I haven't been able to take a decent shower in days."

Okay, enough.

I got up and closed my door. Enough about the imaginary endless phone calls, the imaginary amount of work that's keeping her from lunch; enough about the Gas-X and the decent shower that she hasn't taken.

Enough.

The only reason Bernice was still there was because our supervisor's wife was her husband's secretary. If not for that, she would have been gone a long time ago.

I stared at my phone as it rang again. When the message light didn't come on, I let out a frustrated breath.

Two weeks.

I took a sip of my peppermint tea, which was now only lukewarm, and picked up the phone and called Carmen. I'd called her after I came home to an empty house and told her what went down.

"US Foodsupply, Carmen speaking."

"Hey. What's up, girl?"

"Hey, sistah-girl. What's shaking? I thought you were taking the day off."

I sighed. "I changed my mind and decided to come in, although I don't know why because I'm not doing a damn thing."

"Still bummed out, huh?"

I looked at a picture on the corner of my desk of Simon and me, and frowned. "I shouldn't be missing him the way I am, Carmen. He's lazy, has no goals or desires to do anything but hustle, and I really don't need the baby momma drama he's got with Cecilia."

"This is true."

"I deserve a real man."

"Speak."

"A better man."

"Go on, girl."

"A man who is deserving enough to be with a woman like me."

"Preach!"

51

"A man who can handle all I have to offer!"

"Hallelujah!"

"I deserve . . ." I paused and stared at the picture again. I looked at Simon's smile, his eyes. I looked at me standing beside him with his arm around my waist, my head leaning on his chest. I sighed.

"Reesa?" Carmen said, breaking me out of my trance. "You still there?"

I cleared my throat. "Yeah . . . I'm here."

"You didn't cancel his cell phone, did you?" she asked, knowing the answer.

"No," I said.

"You're going to call him, aren't you?"

I didn't reply right away and instead looked at the photograph again. It was taken at a club we went to in DC. We were standing in front of a painted background with a picture of an Escalade, with the words *I ain't scurred* going across the top. Not a Sears portrait, but I liked it. "Yeah," I finally said softly.

"And what about the church session we were just having?"

I shrugged. "I can do better, I know, but I miss him. I know you may not understand or agree, but I have to call him."

"Believe me, girl. I understand more than you know."

I smiled half-heartedly. "Yeah," I said, thinking back to the countless times she'd called me to vent about Anthony. "I guess you do."

"Are you going to let him move back in?"

"I don't know," I said, raising my eyebrows. "I'm not even sure what I'm going to say when I call him."

"I'm sure the right words will come out."

"Yeah, I guess."

I didn't say anything for a few seconds, and neither did Carmen. There was something depressing about our silence. "Hey, Carmen?"

"Yeah?"

"Why are the bad men so hard to let go of?"

Carmen breathed out heavily into the phone. "I wonder the same thing sometimes."

"Everything I want in a man I had with James. He had a good job, his own car, his own apartment. He was considerate

52

and cared about my feelings, my needs. He loved the hell out of me. Why wasn't he enough? Why did I turn down his proposal?"

"That's easy to answer," Carmen said. "It's the same reason I didn't move to Florida with Javier. They weren't perfect, but they were damn close."

I sighed. "And we wouldn't have had anyone to train."

"Nope."

"Women . . . we are something, aren't we?"

"The best."

I exhaled. "Well, girl, let me make this call."

"All right. Be strong, Reesa. I'm here if you need an ear."

"Thanks, *chica*. I'll call you later on."

"Okay. Bye."

"Bye." I hit the button to end the call and took a deep breath as the dial tone hummed in my ear. "We're the best," I said with a smirk. I looked at the picture of Simon and me again and shook my head. Just before we'd taken that picture we'd been fighting. I had taken a short break away from the dance floor to go to the bathroom and clean my face and reapply my makeup. I figured Simon would have taken the time to get us some new drinks, but when I came out of the bathroom I saw that was hardly the case. Instead of standing by the bar waiting for my return, Simon was out on the floor, smiling while a light-skinned sister wearing a tiny piece of cloth for a skirt grinded her ass into his crotch. I watched in wide-eyed shock as Simon's hands moved up and down her bare shoulders, and he whispered in her ear, making the hoochie smile and blush. Eventually I snapped out of my trance and stormed onto the floor and confronted Simon. He and I went at it for a few minutes until I stormed out of the club, pissed that he would think dancing with another female like that was no big deal.

Simon came outside after me seconds later, and after listening to me go off for several more minutes, he apologized and took me in his arms. I wasn't going to accept, but as he did that, a photographer who'd been outside, and I'm sure had listened to us go back and forth, offered to take a picture of the "happy couple." I was going to decline, but before I could, Simon said yes and we were posing for our Polaroid.

I looked at my smile in the photograph and marveled at how perfectly fake and practiced it was. Fake because I was not happy, and practiced because I'd put that smile on so many other times. How many more times would I do that? "No more," I said, pressing the number pad. "No more."

My heart beat heavily as Simon's cell phone rang. After the sixth ring I let my shoulders, which I'd been squaring back defiantly, drop. Where the hell was he? I wondered again. I took a slow, deep breath, listened to the phone ring one more time then started to pull the receiver away from my ear.

"Hello?"

I heard that just before the receiver moved away from my lobe. I pressed it against my ear again. "Simon?"

"Reesa?"

"Yeah."

"What's up? I'm surprised you're calling me."

Playing with a pen on my desk, I said, "I was thinking about you. Wondering how you've been."

"Why? Because you kicked me out with no place to live?"

I sucked on my bottom lip and scribbled angry lines across a sheet of paper. "I was tired, Simon."

"Of what?"

"Of your shit," I said, drawing furious circles.

"So then you're calling me because?"

"I-I . . . Why didn't you call me?"

"Huh?"

"It's been two weeks. Why didn't you call me?"

"You kicked me out, Reesa."

"So you were just going to leave it at that?"

"You said you'd had enough. What did you want me to do? Call and beg you to move back in?"

"Nothing wrong with showing a woman how much you care," I said.

"Reesa, I care. But I don't beg. You know that."

"Yeah well, it would've been nice." Simon didn't say anything, and I continued to defile my sheet of paper. After a few seconds of silence I said, "Where have you been staying?"

"What?"

"Since I kicked you out . . . where have you been staying?"

54

"With a friend."

"This *friend* a female?"

Simon chuckled. "Would it matter?"

"Are you serious?"

"Why? You ended our relationship and kicked me out."

"So, just because I did that, you went and shacked up with another female?"

"Who said anything about shacking up with another female?"

"You did."

"I never said that."

"You never said you didn't."

Simon breathed. "Look, Reesa, did you call me just to argue? Because I don't have the time if you did. I got things to take care of."

I put the pen down and looked at our picture again. Stared at the way the shirt he wore fit around his arms, his chest. I didn't want to, but it made me think of the last time I was with him. Made me think about how good it felt to feel him inside of me.

Damn it. "I miss you."

"Oh, really?" Simon said. By the way his words came out, I could tell he was smiling. "I thought you were through with me."

"I am . . . I was . . . " I paused and let out a long sigh of defeat. "Look, I just want some things to change, Simon. They have to change."

"I still have the spare key. I'll be there before you get home."

"Did you hear what I said, Simon?"

"Yeah, I heard you."

"You willing to do that? Change things."

"Sure, baby. Look, we'll talk later. I gotta take care of some things. I'll see you when you get home."

Before I could say another word, he hung up. I put the phone down and closed my eyes. I shouldn't have been, but I was smiling. Simon was going to be there when I got home. There was absolutely no reason for me to be excited about seeing him. No reason for me to think about leaving work early so that I could run to the liquor store to buy a bottle of wine; no reason for me to wonder if we still had enough Bath and Body Works solution for the tub. No reason at all, because I knew in my heart that although I'd been lonely, I'd been going forward since Simon had been gone. I knew that was going to change now, because I knew that by letting him move in I'd taken a step back. So I shouldn't have been putting my phone on send calls, e-mailing my supervisor to let him know that I wasn't feeling well and that I'd take my laptop home and work from there, and I shouldn't have been slipping into my coat while taking a loving glance at the photograph with Simon and me. I knew all of this. I also knew that Simon never said whether his *friend* was a female. I knew. But my feet never stopped moving.

Carmen

"Hey, Carmen."

I looked up. "Hey, Jordan," I said, smiling broadly.

"I like the new hair color."

I blushed. "Thanks."

"When'd you get it done?"

"Two weeks ago. You didn't notice it before?"

"I just got back from vacation. You didn't know I was gone?"

I shook my head. "No. I had no idea."

Jordan Combs nodded and said, "Oh."

"It's been hectic around here lately." I looked at my coworker and felt my heart race. I lied when I said I didn't know he had been on vacation. I did know. And I'd been anxiously awaiting his return.

I'd been working with Jordan for a little over two years. He was the PGM for beverages, while I was the product group manager for non-foods. Jordan had always been attracted to me in a big way. More than a few times, he'd invited me out to lunch or out for happy-hour drinks, and more than a few times I'd turned him down. It wasn't because I wanted to, because believe me, I didn't. Jordan looked like an older, more sophisticated version of Eric Benet with a low-cut, wavy fade, and a salt-and-pepper goatee framing the sexiest pair of lips that I'd ever seen on a man. Point blank, Jordan was fine with a capital F. Not only did he have come-and-kiss-me-now lips, he also had a set of deep, dark brown, you-are-under-my-command-and-the-first-thing-I-want-you-to-do-is-strip-naked-now eyes as well. And to go with those looks was a fit, not overly worked out body, and a too-sweet personality.

Like I said, brother had it going on, and the last thing I wanted to do was turn down his offers. But I had to. You see, Jordan had actually laid all of his cards out on the table before and told me exactly how he felt about me. It was after hours one night. We were both working late on separate projects. He came into my office and closed the door behind him. I didn't think anything of it because we were always having closed-door business discussions. I smiled at him, he at me. Then he sat down in a chair on the opposite side of my desk and cleared his throat. His eyes, always intense, always serious, were fixed on me and refused to let me look away.

"What's going on, Jordan? You look like you have something serious to discuss."

Jordan continued to stare at me. His gaze was so intense that I actually felt a little uncomfortable. I squirmed in my chair a bit and tried, but couldn't turn away.

"I do have something heavy to talk about," Jordan said, his voice flat.

"Heavy?"

"Yes."

"Uh-oh. Who got fired now?" The company had recently lost its CEO, CFO, VP, and a slew of other members of upper management due to shady number reporting. We'd lost a few of our coworkers on our floor, and I expected Jordan to hit me with news of another surprise firing. But what floored me was not what I had been expecting at all.

"No one did."

"Oh, okay. So what was the heavy topic you wanted to talk about?"

Jordan cleared his throat. "Us."

I looked at him as he watched me. "Huh?" I hadn't even realized that I'd said that out loud until Jordan said again, "Us."

"Us?"

"Yes."

Jordan watched me while I watched him with my heart beating heavily. "Uh . . . Jordan . . . when you say us . . . you

58

mean us as in work-related, you and I have a project to do, right?"

Jordan raised his eyebrows and sucked in his lips. "No, Carmen," he said, shaking his head. "That's not what I meant at all."

"So . . . what did you mean?"

Jordan cleared his throat then stood up and walked over to my wall and looked at a motivational picture entitled *Perseverance.* I watched him read the bold-lettered slogan silently. I was waiting for him to finish the move he'd started. After a few seconds, he turned around.

"Carmen . . . I'm not going to waste your time or mine beating around the bush. There's an attraction going on between you and me . . ."

I opened my mouth to interrupt. I didn't want him to go where he was going. But he was determined. He put up his hand.

"Let me finish, Carmen. This is uncomfortable for me as it is. It took me a while to come and say what I have to say. I'm not one to do these things when a woman is involved with another man, but . . . " He paused and cracked a knuckle. "But I couldn't fight it anymore. I want to have a relationship with you outside of work."

"Jordan—" I tried to no avail.

"Carmen, not since Terry has there been a woman who's excited me the way you do. Honestly, I didn't think there ever would be a woman to do that again. When Terry died, a part of me died too. I shut down emotionally and shut myself away from people and the hopes of ever having true happiness again. I was pretty much intent on living out my life as a single, widowed man. But then I came here and met you, and—"

I shook my head. "Jordan," I tried, cutting him off again.

He wasn't having it, though. "—and everything changed." He paused and stared at me. I don't know why, but I didn't say anything. "Listen, Carmen, I know that I've pulled the rug from underneath you with all of this."

I opened my eyes wide. "Yeah," I said.

"Believe me, I've wanted to say these things to you for a while, but because we've only had a working relationship, I held my tongue. But I'm tired of doing that. I have feelings for you, Carmen. Strong feelings. And I think you have—"

"Jordan, stop," I said, cutting him off. And this time I wasn't going to give him a chance to shut me up. "I'm flattered. Shocked, but really flattered about the way you feel, about the things you've said. Maybe if things were different for me . . . Maybe if I weren't seeing Anthony—"

"Anthony doesn't deserve you, Carmen. Forgive me for overstepping my boundaries, but I've seen you come to work stressed out over him. I've heard you on the phone arguing with him. You work late nights sometimes, and I know you're not doing it because you *have* to get things done. I've only met Anthony once, but when I did, I couldn't help but ask myself what you were doing with him. A woman like you deserves to be happy all of the time, Carmen. I know I'm older, but Anthony can't bring you the happiness I know I could bring you."

"Jordan, I don't know what to say."

"Don't say anything."

"How do you expect me to not say anything?"

"I just want you to think about the things I've said."

"We have a great working relationship, Jordan."

"I know. And I think that we could have a great out-of-work one too."

"But—"

"Just think," Jordan said, moving to the door and resting his hand on the knob. "That's all I want you to do. Go home, look at Anthony, and think about what I've said. I won't put any pressure on you." Saying all he needed to say, Jordan opened the door and walked out of my office. I sat still for a long time after he left. I was stunned. Jordan came with his hands out, his palms open, his sleeves rolled up, and did what most men didn't have the balls to do. I'd found him sexy before, but after that . . . dayum, brother could have it! But as I thought that, I looked at the picture of Anthony sitting on my desk, and guilt immediately came over me. I sighed. I hadn't done anything wrong, but I'd let my mind wander.

Anthony doesn't deserve you, Carmen. . . . A woman like you deserves to be happy all of the time. . . . Anthony can't bring you the happiness I know I could bring you.

I tapped my tongue against the roof of my mouth as Jordan's words whispered over and over in my head. Anthony didn't deserve me.

I gave Jordan another smile. A month had passed since our conversation, and true to his word, he hadn't pressured me for an answer at all. I know I owed him some type of response. After all, he had approached me like a man. But giving a yes-or-no answer was far from being the easiest thing to do. I wished that wasn't the case, though. I wished Anthony was bringing so much joy into my life that the thought of being with another man was inconceivable. But inconceivable the thoughts weren't. They were pleasant, romantic, sensual, heated, and frequent. Every time I'd lay my eyes on Jordan and see his smile or hear his voice, every time Anthony would do something to piss me off, I'd entertain the thought of being Jordan's woman just a little bit more.

"So, how was your vacation?" I asked.

Jordan shrugged. "It was uneventful. I didn't really do much. Just some fixing up around the house. Other than that, I just took the time off to relax."

"Relaxing is always a good thing to do," I said with a smile.

Jordan returned one of his own then an awkward do-you-have-an-answer-for-me-yet-no-I-don't silence took over. It lasted until Jordan cleared his throat and said, "Well, let me head over to my office and begin the painful process of catching up."

"Okay," I said, disappointed he was leaving.

Jordan turned to leave, but before walking off, he turned and looked at me. "Hey, Carmen."

"Yes?"

"Maybe we could hook up for lunch sometime. That would be up to you, of course. I just figured I could tell you more about my vacation."

I smiled. "Sure. I'd like that."

Jordan nodded. "Maybe . . . tomorrow?"

"Tomorrow's good."

"Twelve-thirty?"

"Twelve-thirty works," I said.

"All right, it's a date then. Well, I mean a lunch date."

I looked at Jordan as he watched me. For two long seconds our eyes were locked on each other. Finally, I said, "It's a date."

We exchanged another silent but telling stare before Jordan smiled and walked off. *Anthony doesn't deserve me.* I looked at Anthony's picture and thought about the breakfast in bed and the appointment card he'd given me. I passed my hand through my blonde hair and frowned. "He doesn't deserve me," I said out loud before realizing my lips had parted. I looked at the picture one more time then rolled my eyes and turned it around so I wouldn't have to see it.

Erica

My ass hadn't even had a chance to relax and enjoy the feel of my chair before my life got really complicated.

"Don't get too comfortable, Erica." That was my boss, Rodderick. He'd just stepped into my office with an unusually jovial smile spread wide across his face.

"What's up, Rod? What's with the smile? It's been a while since I've seen you smiling like that."

"Excitement and opportunity," Rod said, rubbing his palms together.

I looked at him with curious eyes. "Excitement and opportunity, huh? Okay, fill me in."

"I'll fill you in on the way to the breakroom. I need a refill."

"Deal." I got up and hustled alongside Rod as he went to get his morning cup of coffee. His excitement was contagious. I didn't even know the reason for it, but I was excited as hell too.

"Have you ever heard of the author Kenneth Heart?" Rod asked, avoiding our mail carrier.

I shook my head.

"He wrote a nonfiction book called *A Man and Happiness: Why He Can't Have It*. It's been the number one *New York Times* bestseller for five weeks in a row now."

I thought for a moment then shrugged. I had no clue who he was talking about.

"Come on, Erica," Rod said, stepping into the empty breakroom and practically lunging for the coffeemaker. "It's the book all you women are reading right now."

"Not this woman," I said. "I don't really do nonfiction books."

Emptying what seemed to be his tenth packet of sugar into his cup of coffee, Rod said, "Well, it's a huge book. Similar to Michael Baisden's, *Never Satisfied: How And Why Men Cheat.* It's all about why men can't have happiness with a woman because we can't keep our zippers from falling down. It's the kind of book we men hate and you women love."

"Mmm-hmm. I see. Sounds like something I need to read then. Anyway, why'd you mention his name to me?"

Rodderick's smile broadened, and his caramel skin darkened by one shade as we headed back to my office. "He's on his way here."

"And that's a good thing because . . . ?"

"He wants us to design a website for him."

"Doesn't he have one already?"

"Nope," Rod said.

I sat down in my chair. "That's weird. Most authors, especially bestselling ones, do. It's like singers and videos—you have to have one to have huge record sales. A website for an author is a validation of sorts."

"Yeah well, Kenneth Heart is validated."

"So why does he want one now? And why is his wanting a website such a big deal?"

"Answer to question number one: don't know, don't care. Answer to question number two: It's a big deal because no one has ever seen the guy!"

"What do you mean no one's seen him?"

"I mean no one has ever seen his face. He's sold a crazy amount of books. Women all over love this guy, men hate him, but not a single person has any idea what he looks like."

I shook my head. "That doesn't make sense. He must have done signings or interviews by now. Someone must have seen him somewhere."

"Nope. No interviews, except for phone ones. No signings. No sightings of any kind. Not even people in the industry know what he looks like."

"So how did he sell so many books?"

"Great marketing for a great product. Like I said, women everywhere are reading or have read that damn book—except you of course."

"Hey, I told you I don't do nonfiction books."

Rod reached across my desk and grabbed my phone. "Rhonda, bring your copy of Mr. Heart's book to Erica's office right away please. Thank you." He hung up the phone.

"Why are you having her bring me the book?"

"Mr. Heart will be here in about an hour. Start leafing through it because I'm giving you the project."

"Me? But I'm working on the site for the Lawson law office."

"Push that aside. This site is high priority. Besides, he actually requested that you be the one to design it."

"Me?"

"Yup. He said he heard you were the best developer here. And I told him that he heard correctly."

"Aww thanks, Rod.

"Yeah, yeah," Rod said, rolling his eyes playfully. "Anyway, I want all of your focus and energy on his site. Make him and it look good, because this is going to be huge. Everybody—readers and the media—is going to be visiting this website because his seclusion's actually made national headlines."

"I assume the preferential treatment is also due to the fact that he's probably paying top dollar for our services."

Rodderick nodded. "Top dollar." As he said that, his secretary, Rhonda, appeared. "Here's the book. I had to run out to my car to get it." She handed it to me.

"You've read it too?" I asked.

"Hasn't everybody?" Rhonda asked before walking out of the office.

Rod raised his eyebrows at me and said, "Make sure you can quote some passages for him. Make him think you read it too." Then he left, leaving me alone with the book. I exhaled, took a sip of my green tea, which was still hot thanks to my Starbucks mug, and looked at the book's cover. A huge heart was laid out in the middle, while a jagged line, splitting it in half ran down its center. I hmphed and out of habit, opened the book to the acknowledgment/dedication page because I like to see who the author is thanking or dedicating his work to. Kenneth Heart didn't have any acknowledgments. Just a dedication.

Dedicated to the happiness I threw away.

Interesting.

I opened to page one of chapter one. It was titled: "Why Do Fools Fall in Love?"

Men are fools.

That was the first sentence. I took a sip of my tea and hmphed again. I couldn't agree more. I read on, my interest piqued.

I'm a fool.

Oh, really?

I had a one-of-a-kind love, and I threw everything I had with her away for periodic nights of meaningless, unfulfilling fucking with another woman. My ex, actually. I use the word fucking because that's all we ever did. We fucked. I came. She came. I left to go back to the woman I loved and wanted to grow old with. If that wasn't bad enough, my ex ended up getting pregnant. The love of my life hung in there with me until my ex gave birth to my beautiful son, who is my spitting image.

I stopped reading and shook my head. There must have been a lot of assholes telling the same story. I took another sip of tea and kept reading. I was all into the book when my phone rang. It was Rodderick.

"Hey, Rod."

"Erica, Mr. Heart's here."

"Really?" I looked at my watch. Damn, I'd been reading for more than an hour. I looked at the book; I'd reached page 150!

"Rhonda's bringing him to your office now. I would have come, but I have a conference call in thirty seconds. Have you been leafing through the book?"

"A little," I said, bending the page to mark where I left off.

"Good. Do what you do best—give him an off-the-hook site."

"Will do. And Rod, don't try to use slang. It doesn't work for you."

Rod laughed. "Whatever. I'm keeping it real."

"Yeah, really stupid."

Rod broke out laughing again. "Anyway, stop by my office when your meeting's over."

"Okay."

I hung up the phone and made sure my desk was presentable. I didn't worry about myself because I always looked good. Seconds later, there was a knock on my door. Rhonda was staring at me through the thin pane of glass to the left of the door. I couldn't see the guest of honor. I motioned for her to come in.

"Mr. Heart is here," she said, opening the door.

"Okay. Thanks, Rhonda."

She smiled at the author, who remained just out of my sight, then walked off. I expected him to walk in, but instead he remained hidden. *Okay, he's taking this incognito bit a little too far,* I thought.

"Mr. Heart," I said, "you're welcomed to come in." I rolled my eyes as he remained silent and didn't move. This was ridiculous. I stood to approach him, and as I did, he stepped into the doorway.

"What the . . . ?" I paused as my ex, Kenny Owens, stared back at me. "What the hell are you doing here?" I snapped loudly.

Kenny looked behind him and smiled at Rhonda who just happened to be walking by and had undoubtedly heard my outburst. He stepped into my office and closed the door behind him.

"What the hell are you doing here?" I demanded again, remaining rigid behind my desk.

Kenny smiled. "I'm here about my website."

"Your website? You're Kenneth Heart?"

He nodded.

"No the hell you're not!"

"Yes, I am."

I folded my arms across my chest and stared jagged daggers at him. I couldn't believe it. "Get out," I said.

He didn't move.

"Get the hell out of my office, Kenny," I said again, my tone more venomous than before. "Now!"

Kenny looked from me to my desk and rested his gaze on Rhonda's copy of his book. "Did you read it?" he asked.

I didn't respond.

"It's dedicated to you. You know that, right?"

"Kenny," I said, tapping my foot furiously. "I said all I had to say to you at the restaurant, so I swear if you don't get the fuck out of my office, I will call security and have them remove your lame ass."

Kenny raised an eyebrow. "I don't think your boss would like that."

"I don't give a shit," I countered. "I want your ass out of my face."

"Sorry, Erica, but I'm a paying client—a well-paying client. I'm not going anywhere."

"Fine. You want to do this the hard way then we'll do it the hard way." I picked up my phone to dial the number for our security staff, which wasn't really a staff at all. Just Edmund, our sixty-five-year-old part-time retiree. I was bluffing, but so what? I just wanted him to leave. But that didn't happen.

Kenny stepped forward and snatched the receiver out of my hand. I gave him one hell of a cross look. "Give me back the damn phone, Kenny."

"No. Not until you listen to me."

"I'm not listening to a single word you have to say."

"Did you read any of the book?"

"Did you just hear what I said?"

"Did you read any of the book?" he asked again.

"Fuck you and your book," I snapped.

That didn't faze him. "I wrote it because I couldn't get over losing you."

"I told you, fuck you and your book! Now give me the damn phone!"

"Erica, I know it's been two years, but I'm still in love with you."

I slit me eyes. "Go to hell, Kenny."

"You were the best thing that's ever happened to me," he said, his voice softening. I pouted but didn't say anything. "It started out as a letter to you, but as I wrote it, words and feelings just came out of nowhere and spilled out onto the page. Suddenly my beg-you-to-take-me-back letter turned into what's lying on your desk. I only decided to publish it because my sister convinced me to. After she finished reading it, she insisted that I try to get it published. You know how my sister is, so you know I kind of had no choice."

"How is Rhea?" I asked, allowing myself a moment to calm down. His sister and I had always gotten along. When I ended the relationship with Kenny, I ended it with his entire family. Letting our friendship go had always been something I regretted doing.

"She's good. She said to tell you hello."

I nodded. So she knew he was coming. "Why are you here, Kenny?"

"I need a website."

"Cut the bullshit."

"It's the truth," he said, shrugging.

"Go somewhere else," I said.

"There's nowhere else to go."

"Look in the phone book."

"Erica—"

"Or try the Internet."

"Erica—"

"Hell, ask the homeless man at the end of the block."

"Erica—"

"Leave."

"I can't."

"Why?" I asked, a lump in my throat rising.

"Because I'm still in love with you, and I want you back."

A lone tear that I'd been trying to hold back fell from the corner of my eye. "I hate your ass," I said, my voice cracking.

"No, you don't," Kenny replied.

"How the fuck do you know?"

"Because I'm still here."

"So leave."

"I miss you, Erica."

"Ass."

"I have this enormously popular book. I never have to work another day in my life. I have a beautiful eight-bedroom home, I drive a Mercedes, and I am unhappy as hell."

"Good," I said, tears falling freely now.

"What will it take to get you back, Erica?"

"For hell to freeze over."

"I'll do anything."

"It wouldn't work."

"I don't care how long it takes."

"Forever sound good to you?"

"And a day," he responded, watching me intently.

"Get the hell out, Kenny. Please." I hated the fact that I was crying in front of him, but I couldn't stop; the tears fell without regard for my feelings.

Kenny watched me for a few seconds then sighed. "Okay, I'm going, but I'll be back in two weeks."

"I won't be here."

"Your boss know that?"

"Don't do this, Kenny," I said.

"I'm just trying to fix what I broke."

"When it was broken, I threw it away."

"It can still be recycled."

"Kenny—"

"Here's your phone back." He held out the receiver for me to take. I looked at him but didn't move. *Two years*, I thought. I'd gone through so much emotionally just to get over him. Why was he back now? And when I told him to leave, why had my words been so empty? I opened my mouth to say something, but before it could escape, Kenny put the receiver back on the base and said, "Two weeks." Without waiting for a reply from me, he turned, walked to the door, opened it, and left.

I stood motionless for a few seconds then sat down and buried my face in my hands. There was a knock on my door a few minutes later. I looked up.

"Are you okay?"

"Yeah, Rhonda. I'm good. Thanks."

Rhonda looked at me skeptically.

"I know it's hard to believe just by looking at me, but I'm fine, really."

"Okay. Um . . . Did Mr. Heart leave?"

"Yeah, he did," I said.

Rhonda nodded then turned to leave. I knew she was headed straight for Rodderick's office. I sighed and shut down my PC. I wasn't in the mood to deal with any more questions. "Rhonda," I called out before she could leave.

She turned around. "Yeah?"

I shut off my lamp, stood, and grabbed my purse and coat. "I'm not feeling well. I'm going to head home. Let Rod know, please." I moved from behind my desk then stopped. I looked at the desk, staring at Kenny's book. I grabbed it. "Here," I said, handing it to Rhonda. "I'm done with this." I walked out of the office before she could say anything. I was halfway toward the elevator before I stopped and turned around to watch Rhonda walking toward Rodderick's office. She was three doors away.

"Rhonda!" I cursed at myself as I called her name. "Rhonda," I said again, my feet carrying me toward her.

Rhonda stopped walking and turned around. "Yeah?"

"I changed my mind," I said, stepping in front of her. "I'm not done with it."

Rhonda nodded and handed it to me. I turned and walked away, cursing myself for letting Kenny get to me.

Reesa

I paced angrily in the living room and looked at my watch for the fifth damn time. "I can't believe he's doing this shit to me again!" I said out loud. "Damn it!" I sat down on the couch, crossed my legs, folded my arms and stewed while I thought back to Halloween when he'd done the same thing.

We were supposed to go out together to a Halloween party that my company was throwing. I'm usually not for doing the company thing, but I'd been feeling pretty good lately. Things had been different since Simon had moved back in. He'd gotten the job he'd interviewed for and had been working steadily, which was a very welcomed change when it came time to pay the bills. Along with the for-once reliable paycheck, Simon also put to rest Cecilia and her nonsense by paying back all the money he owed her. With that paid, he had no more obligations to her ass other than to take care of his son, which was a treat for him.

For the first time since we'd started dating, I was proud of my man. He was bringing home the bacon—not much, mind you, but it was something—and he was taking care of me in and out of the bedroom. With Simon doing his thing legally, I didn't hesitate to let people know we were going to be in attendance at the function. Shit, it wasn't often someone could ask me or my man what he did and there'd be an answer.

For the event, I did it up. I dressed up as the Bride of Frankenstein with the flat head, peg coming out of the neck, a thunderbolt scar running down my forehead, and green skin. Had the white tattered gown too. Like I said, I went all out. I didn't know what Simon was dressing as because he wouldn't tell me. He said he wanted to surprise me. And he did. Only it was far from being a good surprise. The company party, which went from eight to twelve, had been over for two hours when Simon came strolling into the apartment, drunk as hell and reeking with the smell of weed.

"Where the fuck have you been?" I yelled. I was still wearing my costume, and I'm sure I really looked the part then, as pissed off as I was. "You asshole!" I spat as Simon fell into the couch. I knew he got high from time to time, but this was ridiculous. "Get off the couch, Simon," I yelled, going to the window and opening it.

"What the fuck is your problem, Reesa?" Simon said, his words slow.

I turned and bore into him with my eyes. "What's my problem? Ass, we had a damn Halloween party to go to. I've been waiting for your ass to get home."

Simon put a closed fist over his mouth. "Oh shit! My bad. I forgot all about that."

"You forgot? We just spoke about it this afternoon."

"Yeah, yeah. My bad, my bad."

"To hell with your bad. You never had any intention of going, did you?" I asked. He didn't even have to answer that because I knew that was the case. "You're such an ass, Simon. I can't believe you rolled in here drunk and high like this. Get off the damn couch!" I went to the kitchen, grabbed some air freshener, and sprayed it all over the room, even on his ass.

He jumped off the couch. "Watch where you're spraying that!"

"I'm not watching shit! I can't believe you did this. I can't believe you had me sitting here all night waiting for you. I should have never given you my damn car."

"Look, Reesa," Simon said, walking back to the room. "I said my bad, all right? I forgot your stupid-ass party."

"Whatever, Simon. So where were you?"

"I was chilling," he said.

"Chilling where? With your boys, huh?" I said, standing close to the door. "You sure about that?" I'd had suspicions that he was messing around on me but I'd never actually confirmed anything. Of course I knew that I wasn't going to have anything confirmed then either. But I still asked. "Simon?" I said when he didn't answer me. I called his name again, but instead of an answer, I received a groan then the shower was turned on. I hit the door with the palm of my hand. "Asshole!" That night I made him sleep on the couch, and that's what was going to happen tonight too.

I waited for Simon for another half hour before I picked up the phone and dialed Shay's number. I was spending Thanksgiving at her house with her and Ahmad this year. Normally I'd go to my parents' for the holiday, but they'd recently moved to California, and they wanted to give thanks in their new home. Since I couldn't afford two trips, I decided to save my trip for Christmas.

"Hey, girl, weren't you supposed to have been here by now?" Shay asked, answering the phone. I was supposed to have been there more than an hour ago to help with the food.

I sighed. "I'm sorry, Shay. Simon's ass isn't here, and he has my damn car."

"Didn't he do something like this for Halloween?"

I groaned.

"You need a ride?"

I let out a long, extremely frustrated breath. "Would you mind?"

"Not at all. I'll have Ahmad come and get you. Did you make the stuffing and the rice?"

"It's sitting on the stove."

"Good."

"I'm sorry about this, Shay," I said apologetically. "I hate to have Ahmad drive out here."

"It's no biggie, Reesa. It's only a twenty-minute drive to your place. Besides, it's probably better that it's just you who comes over. You know Ahmad's not Simon's biggest fan."

"Yeah, I know."

"Okay. Well, let me go and baste this turkey. Ahmad'll be there soon."

"Thanks again, Shay."

"Anytime. See you soon."

"Okay." I hung up the phone and looked at my watch once again. *Asshole,* I thought. I called Simon out of his name out loud then went to pack an overnight bag. I know I didn't ask her, but I was sure Shay wouldn't mind me staying at their place. I wasn't in the mood to deal with Simon's shit. Damn it, I was through with his ass.

Carmen

"I just wanted to call and wish you a happy Thanksgiving."

I smiled. "That was thoughtful, Jordan."

"I'm not going to get you in trouble by calling, am I?"

"No. Anthony's in the bathroom. You don't have to worry about that anyway. You're a friend, and friends can call me anytime."

"Believe me, Carmen, I wish I could call you anytime."

I smiled again. I resisted the urge to say I wished he could too. Things between Jordan and me had slowly been heating up since our lunch date weeks ago. That day we went to a deli and sat and talked about general "safe" topics. I know Jordan wanted to talk about us, but I wanted to stay away from that subject. I was treading on very thin ice by being there with him, I knew that, and the more enjoyable and free-flowing our conversation, the thinner the ice became. Since none of our coworkers were around, we were able to really get to know each other. In a little more than an hour and a half, we discovered that we had a lot in common.

Unlike Anthony, Jordan was into a lot of the same things I was. For example, he loved salsa as much as I did, if not more. He also had a love for books, and during the course of our meal, we got into a passionate discussion about a book we'd both read, called *A Man and Happiness: Why He Can't Have It.* I was surprised that Jordan had actually read the book, considering the fact that most men hated it. We went back and forth about whether men could actually have happiness.

The book's premise was basically that it was impossible for a man to be satisfied with one woman. At least that's the way I took it. Jordan disagreed and insisted that the author, who'd lost the love of his life due to his own idiotic behavior, was not saying that men couldn't be satisfied, but rather that a man had to do a lot of soul searching before embarking on a monogamous relationship.

We argued playfully about the topic until we realized that we'd gone well over an hour for lunch. Before that day was over, we made plans for another lunch date the next day. After a week of planning, lunch between Jordan and me became the norm. Every now and then I'd invite other people to go along with us. I usually did that when I felt that the safe topics we usually talked about weren't going to be so safe anymore. I know Jordan knew what I was doing when I sent out invites, but again, true to his word, he never said anything.

But when he asked me for my phone number, I knew his patience was dwindling. To play it safe, I gave him my home phone number instead of my cell. Figured if he called me at home, our conversation could never be too long or could never venture into dangerous territory. He'd never called me—until now.

I took a look back toward the bathroom; Anthony was still in the shower. I cleared my throat and decided not to comment on Jordan's last remark.

"So you're headed over to your in-laws?" His parents were away on a cruise in the Caribbean.

"Yeah. My mother-in-law is anxiously waiting for me to get there and eat up her peach cobbler."

I laughed. "Sounds like she has a fan."

"Not just a fan. A would-be investor too. I keep trying to convince her to sell it."

"Uh-oh, sounds like I need to get me some of that cobbler."

"Hey, you're welcomed to come," Jordan said.

As he did, the shower was shut off. Damn. I cleared my throat again. "Why don't you steal a piece for me and bring it to work?"

"No problem. I'll steal two pieces for you."

I smiled then looked to the bathroom again where Anthony had just opened the medicine cabinet. He would be out soon.

"Hey, Jordan," I said, hating to have to get off, "I need to get going."

There was a short silence before Jordan responded. "Okay."

"Enjoy your Thanksgiving."

"Will do. You do the same."

"Thanks. Bye." I hung up the phone as the bathroom door opened. But as Anthony walked out, the phone rang again. I looked at the caller ID and felt my heart take a slight pause. It was Jordan again. I grabbed the phone as quickly as I could and prayed that Anthony, who had reached our bedroom, wouldn't answer the phone too. "Hello?"

"Sorry I called again, but there's something I needed to say."

I looked toward the room while my heart thudded in my chest. "Yes?"

"I know I said I wasn't going to put pressure on you, but it's been a while. I want to make you happy, Carmen."

"Jordan," I said, keeping my voice low and my eyes on the bedroom. Just as he did before, he wouldn't let me get a word in.

"I've told my parents about you. I've told them about how I feel about you. I've told them about Anthony."

"Jordan," I whispered, shocked at what he was telling me.

"I told them all of these things to get their advice. You want to know what they said?"

I sighed. There was no use in trying to stop him. "What?"

"They said I should keep pursuing you. That if I've met a woman that could bring me out of the darkness I've been living in, a woman that I feel I could spend the rest of my life with, then I should stop at nothing to make her mine. My parents are pretty intelligent people, and they've been married for over forty years. I've never hesitated to take their advice before, and I don't see any reason why I should now. Happy Thanksgiving, and I'll see you on Monday."

Before I could respond, Jordan hung up the phone, and as he did, Anthony walked out of the room with a bottle of lotion in his hand. "Who was that?" he asked.

I put the phone down. "Nobody," I said. "Just a telemarketer."

Anthony nodded. "Okay. Can you put some lotion on my back?"

I looked down at the phone then said, "Sure."

When I was finished making his back look brown again, Anthony clapped. "Thanks, baby. Now, let's hurry up and get to my parents'. You know my mom makes the bomb turkey."

I nodded and went to the bathroom to finish applying my makeup, with Jordan's words resonating in my mind. He was going to stop at nothing. Damn. I closed the door as 50 Cent blasted from the speakers in the living room, and stared at myself in the mirror. "What are you going to do, *mujer?*" I asked my reflection.

My reflection looked back at me and shrugged. "Be happy," it said. "Be happy."

I sighed and grabbed my eyeliner. As 50 Cent rapped about being a "motherfuckin' P.I.M.P.," I sucked my teeth. "Bomb turkey, my ass."

Erica

It was Thanksgiving, and I was eating a TV turkey dinner by myself in front of the television, watching a *Soul Food* rerun on Showtime. I'd canceled going over to my parents' for the holiday because I wasn't in the mood to fake happiness when emotionally I was a wreck. Seeing Kenny again really fucked me up, and I just didn't want to be around anyone. I didn't even call my girls to wish them well for the holiday. Damn it. Why the hell did Kenny have to come around? I was doing so well. I'd finally moved on. Other than not being able to find a good man, I was happy with my life. Good job. Great condo. No kids to slow me down. All that was missing was a man, and because I'd given up on trying to find one, I was cool. I had my black book when I wanted some company for the night, and that's all I needed.

Damn Kenny and his book. I looked at it sitting beside me and scowled. That book seemed to upset everything in my life. My reliable and expensive BMW caught not one, but two flat tires. The heat in my condo went out during the night, and I woke up with a cold. The heel on my Manolo shoe broke when a stray dog darted in front of me, causing me to stumble. And worst of all, my job situation was in some serious jeopardy because I was refusing to work with Kenny. In the three years that Rodderick was there, he and I never had a tense moment between us, but the day after Kenny's unwanted visit, tense only scratched the surface of how things were between him and me.

"What the hell happened yesterday?" Rodderick hadn't even closed the door behind him as he walked into my office.

I groaned, stood, went to the door, and closed it. Just before I did, I caught a glimpse of Rhonda looking our way. I sucked my teeth and went back to my desk, where I remained standing and stared at Rodderick. There was no other way for me to say what I had to say, so straight and to the point was it. "I can't work with him."

Rod looked at me as though I'd just said something foreign. "Come again."

I sighed. "I can't work with him, Rod," I said again. "I just can't."

"And when did you move up in management to where you had a say over what projects you did and didn't take on?"

I looked at Rod, shocked at the tone and choice of words he'd used. He stared back at me with an expression I'd never seen before, like I-am-the-boss-and-you-do-whatever-the-hell-I-tell-you-to-do. The lines were clearly drawn. "Rod, look, without going into details, there's some history between Mr. Heart and me, and it wouldn't be good for us to work together."

"Erica, I personally don't care what kind of history you and Mr. Heart have. He requested that you design his website, and that's what you're going to do."

"Rod—"

"Erica, this isn't open for a damn discussion. I pay you to design websites. I don't pay you to tell me what you can and can't do. Kenneth Heart wants you to do his website, and you're going to do it."

I slammed my hand down on my desk. "This is bullshit, Rod, and you know it. I told you we have history between us. Ugly history. How the hell do you expect me to do good work for a man that I can't fucking stand? Damn it, give it to someone else. Give the project to James. He's just as good."

"Don't even try it. James is nowhere near as good as you are, and you know it. Now I'm sorry about the drama you have with Mr. Heart, but I hired you to be a professional, and as a professional, there are times when you have to suck it up and take on projects, or work with people that you don't like."

My bottom lip trembled as I fought back tears of frustration and anger. "I can't . . . can't work with him," I tried again.

"Sorry, Erica, but it's either you do the job or you clean out your desk and find another company to work for. There's no compromise here. Now, Mr. Heart just called me and canceled his appointment coming in two weeks and rescheduled it for the beginning of December. I want your decision by the end of November. That gives you ample time to get your priorities in order. I hope you make the right decision." Rod stared at me for a second then walked out of my office. I hadn't taken a day off for the entire year, and before the day ended, I decided to use up my vacation, personal, and sick days in one shot.

I ran my hands through my hair in frustration then slammed my palms down on my leather cushions. *That book.* I looked down at it and scowled again.

It's dedicated to you. You know that, right?

"Did I ask for that?"

I wrote it because I couldn't get over losing you.

"Oh well, you'd better get over it."

. . . I'm still in love with you.

"And I hate you."

You were the best thing that's ever happened to me . . .

"Should have thought of that before you slept with that bitch."

I groaned out loud as I played the answer-and-rebuttal game in my mind. I was the best thing that's ever happened to him? Asshole. I grabbed the book and opened it to a random page somewhere in the middle. I looked at the first sentence on that page.

What would I do to get back the woman I love? Anything. That's what.

I slammed the book shut and thought it again: *ass.*

I threw the book to the floor, rose from the couch, and went to my bedroom. I couldn't believe I was about to do what I was about to do. I sighed then bent down beside my bed, stuck my hand underneath the mattress, and removed a photograph I had buried there. I sat on the bed and looked at the lone picture of Kenny and me, which I had never been able to bring myself to throw away. It was taken three summers ago before all of the shit happened. We were in Virginia Beach, standing on the boardwalk, leaning against the rail, entangled in each other's arms. It was hot as hell that day, and the last place I felt like being was out in the sand, sitting under an umbrella, bathing in the humidity, but Kenny, who'd grown up in Virginia, wanted to catch waves. Whatever. I went. Took the latest book I was reading, my radio, a couple of jazz CDs, my sun-block, my hat, and my DKNY shades and went to be with my man. We were on our way to the sand when Kenny stopped a couple passing by and asked the man to snap our picture.

I looked at the smile on my face and tried to remember the last time I'd felt like that. I was so in love with Kenny's ass. So in love and blind to the wool he'd been pulling over my eyes. Four damn months. He'd been splitting his dick for four months. Got her pregnant, which meant that he didn't really give a shit about me because he didn't bother to use a fucking condom. Four damn months. I was his fool, while he was my knight in shining armor. Four damn months, and I was supposed to be professional and work with his tired ass so that he could talk bullshit about wanting me back.

I studied the picture and the image of my former self. I had my hair in that *Best Man,* Nia Long style because I loved the way she looked in that movie: classic, in control and at the top of her game. After I cut Kenny out of my life, I was at home one day, depressed, bitter, angry, and heartbroken all at the same time. I was rifling through my music collection, looking for something that epitomized my mood when Kelis's CD fell from the rack. Since Kenny's betrayal, I'd been questioning God's existence. I mean, if there was a God, how could He let me go through something like that? But when that CD fell and the case popped open, all but saying *Play me,* I knew that God was there with me, because that song was the epitome of how I felt. I popped it in, turned the volume on my stereo up full blast and played that song for the rest of the year. Well, at least it seemed that way. I played the hell out of it. At home. In my car. In my PC at work. In my portable player when I went jogging.

"Out there." That was my anthem.

Screaming 'til I could scream no more. Didn't matter that I couldn't sing to save my life. "Out there." My anthem. My song.

I decided to do the Kelis thing with my hair a couple of weeks after that. I woke up one day and said to myself that it was time for a new look, a new attitude. My heart had been shattered, yes, but I had to stop letting Kenny be my world. Besides, my mother, who'd raised four kids on her own without help from a man, raised me to be a survivor. So that's what I did. Survived. Changed my hair, switched up my wardrobe, bought a new car, said to hell with Kenny, and lived.

I won't lie; It wasn't easy. Shit, honestly, it was damn hard in the beginning. I had more than a couple of relapses where I found myself picking up the phone and dialing Kenny's number only to hang up whenever he answered. He returned my call every time, but I never answered the phone. Just turned my ringer and answering machine off so that he couldn't leave any more messages like the pathetic ones he'd finally stopped leaving. Along with my phone relapses, I found myself driving by his job every now and then. Why, I don't know. I never planned on going inside to see him. Hell, I barely even slowed the car down. But I still went. Drove by, took a quick glance and kept going. When I wasn't letting my fingers do the walking or being a stalker in my car, I'd sit at home, soaking my shirt with my tears, going through old pictures of Kenny and me while I listened to depressing love songs. Like I said, I was hooked, and the withdrawal was a bitch. Eventually I kicked the habit, though, and said to hell with the love songs, stopped shedding tears, stopped calling, stopped stalking, and ripped up all of the photos in the album.

All but one.

I held the picture tightly between my index finger and thumb and stared at it. Stared at the way Kenny held on to me, the way I held on to him. We were the perfect couple in that picture. Me the perfect fool, he the perfect liar. And now we were reunited. I let out a long breath then ripped the picture to pieces.

Asshole.

I dropped the shredded pieces in the trash then walked out of the room.

Kenny or my job. That's the decision I was faced with when I went back to work. Damn. I already knew what my decision was going to be, and that really pissed me off.

Reesa

"Girl, who is that fine brother walking through the door?"

Shay sucked her teeth. "Peel your eyes away from him," she said with disgust as she gave a disapproving glance toward the entrance. "He ain't shit."

"Damn," I said. "What's the story on him? I don't think I've ever seen you get like that."

She sucked her teeth again. "His name is Mike. He's one of Ahmad's boys. And he's a playa with a capital P."

"I see. So why are you giving him the death stare?"

"He's partly to blame for all of the shit Ahmad and I went through a couple years back."

"Really?"

Shay nodded. "Yeah," she said, looking toward the door, where Mike and Ahmad were laughing. Then she shook her head and looked at me. "Anyway, talking about him is bringing up memories I don't want to remember. New topic."

"Sorry," I said.

"No need to apologize. Anyway, girl, your rice and stuffing was all that. I love the raisins you put in the stuffing. I've never had it like that before."

"Thanks! Believe it or not, I learned that from Simon."

"Really?"

"Yeah. He's actually worked as a chef before."

Shay didn't say anything.

"He's still trying to find himself," I said, answering the question I knew she had in her mind.

Shay raised her eyebrows and without saying a word, said *Whatever*. I sighed. "Look, I know Simon's not the best catch out there."

"So why do you put up with him and his shit?" Shay asked. Her candidness surprised me.

"It's—it's not that simple," I said.

Shay frowned and pulled me past a few of her guests into the kitchen. "Reesa, I'm sorry to sound like Erica," she said, "but you're really wasting your time with Simon."

"Shay—"

"Just hear me out for a sec, girl. I'm not saying this to be on your case, but I hate to see you wasting your time with Simon. Erica's absolutely right. You can do so much better than him, and you know it! You deserve a better man. Not one who's going to do the shit Simon does. I mean, for real, girl, the brother isn't worth the pennies I have in my pocket. He doesn't have a steady job, he doesn't have his own car, he's inconsiderate as hell. I mean, damn, it was bad enough he left you hanging for Halloween, but today too? His ass should be here with you right now. Don't get me wrong, I'm glad he ain't here, but still."

"I know, Shay," I said, leaning against the counter.

"So why don't you drop his ass then?"

"You wouldn't understand," I said, shrugging and looking down at the ground.

"Try me."

I looked up at Shay. "Simon's my last chance," I said softly.

Shay looked at me with bewildered eyes. "Huh? What do you mean he's your last chance?"

I took a deep breath and let it out easily. "I'm thirty-three, Shay. I don't have much time left."

"Time for what?"

"To have kids."

Resting her hands on her hips, Shay said, "You lost me, Reesa."

"I'm thirty-three," I said again.

"Okay, and?"

"And I need to have kids now, because once thirty-five hits, that's it. My time will be up."

"Huh? Okay, you really lost me now."

I sighed and moved away from the counter. "Girl, I'm not trying to have a baby after thirty-five. I don't want to be some old woman chasing after some damn kids. So the way I see it, Simon's my best chance at making sure I have a bun in my oven before my deadline."

Shay shook her head. "Reesa, are you serious? Please tell me you're not serious."

"I am."

"So you mean to tell me that you'd rather settle with a boy like Simon so that he can father your children instead of dump him and find a man that's worthy enough to be at your side?"

"I don't call it settling," I said. "I'm just doing what's necessary."

"And it's necessary for you to have Simon be your baby's father?"

"Like I said, I only have 'til I'm thirty-five."

"First of all, Reesa, doesn't Simon already have a son? How do you know he wants another child?"

"I don't. But he has Jabari with Cecilia, who he can't stand. I would think he'd want to have a child with a woman he can stand."

"Don't be so sure about that. Most men like him don't want any additional responsibility." Shay looked at me with a raised eyebrow and waited for me to reply, but I didn't say anything. She sucked her teeth. "Anyway, moving along, this thirty-five-year-old cut-off that you have is insane. Plenty of women are having kids at an older age and are doing just fine chasing after them."

"Yeah well, I don't want to be one of them."

Shay rolled her eyes. "Whatever. Even if you insist on sticking to your cut-off, what's wrong with finding a different man? It's not like you can't."

I sucked my teeth. "Come on, Shay. Let's be real here. Finding a man is not that easy. Especially a good man. I know Simon's not the best, but honestly, I'd rather be with him than without him. I don't want to have to go through that whole dating process again, trying to find a man among dogs."

"It's not that bad."

"Oh yes, it is, and you know it. Just think about how things were before Ahmad came along. You can't tell me that life was all roses and daisies for you then."

"No, it wasn't all that," Shay admitted, "but it wasn't so bad that I would settle for someone that wasn't worth my time."

"Yeah well, you had time on your side. You were younger."

"Oh please, Reesa. You're acting like you'll be some kind of senior citizen when you hit your mid-thirties."

"Not a senior citizen, but too old to be having kids."

"Reesa, I love you, you're my girl, but you are insane. As far as I'm concerned, you have absolutely no legitimate reason for staying with Simon."

"I told you, you wouldn't understand," I said, shrugging.

"No, I don't, Reesa. You are a beautiful, intelligent, successful, independent, *young* black woman. Finding a man for you ain't that damn hard."

"I beg to differ."

"Beg to differ? How the hell can you beg to differ when you aren't even out there to see what you're missing?"

Shay paused and shook her head while I went to the kitchen sink and stared at my reflection in the window above it. I knew there was a lot of truth to what she was saying but still—it was easier for her to say that when she was standing on the opposite side of the fence from where I was. Yeah, my Prince Charming was possibly out there somewhere, but honestly, I was just too damned scared to take the plunge and start over.

"I'm thirty-three, pushing thirty-four in a couple of months, Shay."

"So? You're not an old hag."

"I'm not exactly a spring chicken either. And from what I was seeing these days, men are going for younger women with perky breasts."

"Not all men, Reesa. You're keeping yourself from being happy, girl. Why would you do that?"

I looked at the frown that covered my face and sighed then turned around and faced Shay. She had the most disapproving look on her round face. I shrugged again. "Sometimes you have to make sacrifices to get the things you want," I said. "My clock is ticking, girl. I want a baby."

"I hear what you're saying, Reesa, but still, you're talking about sacrificing your happiness to have a baby with a man who doesn't know the meaning of the word *responsible*. And when you have a child, that word is the personification of what having a baby is all about. Do you really want to go there with Simon and his track record?"

I blew out a sigh and was about to answer when Ahmad stepped into the kitchen.

"Hey, sorry to interrupt, ladies, but Reesa, Simon's at the door."

"Simon? Here?"

Ahmad nodded and didn't look too happy. "Yeah. And just so you know, he's standing outside. I don't let people who are high come into my home."

I looked at Ahmad then frowned. I let out a slow breath. "Thanks, Ahmad."

"You gonna be okay, girl?" Shay asked as I moved to walk out of the kitchen.

I shrugged. "Yeah. I'll be fine. I apologize to the both of you for this."

"Don't sweat it," Ahmad said.

"Yeah, just handle your business," Shay added. "Handle it for good. You don't need this shit."

I sighed and walked out of the kitchen. I grabbed my coat from the closet behind the door and took a deep breath before opening it. Simon was high. He actually came to my friend's house high. That son of a bitch. I opened the door and saw Simon leaning against my car, with his head lying back on the hood. *He is high,* I thought again.

Enough.

Goddamnit, enough.

I stormed over to him. "Give me my fucking car and apartment keys and get the fuck out of my life!"

Simon pushed himself off the car and looked at me through red eyes. "Hold up and let me explain what happened tonight."

"I don't want any fucking explanations, Simon. I want all of my keys, and I want your tired ass gone."

Simon looked at me with a smirk but didn't say anything and didn't move.

"Give me my keys, ass. Now!"

"Not until you let me explain where I was and why I was late."

"I told you I don't want any damn explanation."

"Then you're not getting your keys."

I stared at him and tightened my lips. "Son of a bitch," I said. I folded my arms across my chest. "What's your damn explanation?"

"I was at Cecilia's."

"What? What were you doing there?"

"I was on my way home to pick you up when she called my cell to tell me that Jabari was really down about not seeing me for the Thanksgiving holiday."

"Okay, but you're going to see him for Christmas."

"Yeah, I know, but he's still missing out on the holiday. So anyway, to make him happy, I swung over to her place to see him. I wasn't planning on being there long, but she had all of this food cooked . . . "

"Wait a minute," I said. "You mean you ate Thanksgiving dinner with that bitch and not me?"

"Look, I didn't want to disappoint my boy."

"So you'd rather disappoint me?"

"You're a grown-ass woman who should be able to understand where I'm coming from."

"Oh, I do, Simon. And believe me, I applaud you for wanting to make Jabari happy, but just like I understand where you're coming from, Jabari's got to understand that his parents aren't together and because they're not, there are going to be some holidays when he won't see you."

"Yeah well, I was out, and there was no reason for him not to see me today," Simon said defiantly.

"You were out, huh?" I said. "You know what? You seem to forget that there's only one owner to that car, and your name is nowhere on that title."

"Whatever, Reesa," Simon said.

"So when did your ass get high? Before or after you left her place?"

"You know I don't do that shit around my son."

"Oh, how admirable of you."

"Why don't you give it a fucking rest, Reesa? I had one or two blunts. So the fuck what? That don't do nothing to me, and you know it."

"I don't give a fuck what it does to your ass, Simon. Damn it, it's bad enough you left me stranded, but to disrespect my friend's home like this? Do you have any idea how embarrassing this shit is?" I shook my head and stuck out my hand. "Give me my damn keys. I'm tired of your ass. I can't believe I took you back," I said more to myself than to him. "I can't believe I put up with your shit over and over." I chuckled. "To think I was actually willing to sacrifice my happiness just to—" I stopped talking, put my hand on the back of my neck, and blew out a sigh of relief. I'd finally come to my senses. I was through. For good this time. I stuck out my hand again. "Keys. Now."

Simon gave me a condescending stare. "I ain't giving you shit," he said easily.

I jerked my head back. "Excuse me?"

"You heard me. I ain't giving you shit."

"Simon, you better give me my damn keys."

"Or what?" he asked. I took a cautious step backward but kept my eyes focused on him. "What are you gonna do, Reesa?" he asked, matching my step back with a forward step of his own.

My heart was beating quickly as my lips became dry with nervousness. "Don't be an ass, Simon. I want my keys."

"I already told you I'm not giving you your keys."

I turned and looked to the front door, hoping it would open and someone would walk out. Simon had never been physical with me before, but he was high, and there was something about the tone of his voice and the look in his eyes that I didn't like. When the door never opened, I took a slow deep breath and looked back at Simon. "Why are you being like this, Simon?"

"Because you're a fucking bitch."

I slit my eyes. I hated to be called out my name like that. "So then if I'm a bitch, do us both a favor and give me my damn keys and leave! I'll call you to let you know when you can come and pick up your shit, so you may want to answer your phone."

"Shut the fuck up!" Simon hissed. "Just shut the fuck up. You ain't the only one that's tired. Shit, for real, if you wanna know the truth, I'm tired of your ass. That's why I don't come home, that's why I leave your needy ass stranded. Living with you is like living with some fucking old-ass woman. Shit, other than you paying my bills, the only thing you really been good for is fucking. And you ain't even the bomb at that. That's why I get straightened out every now and then by Cecilia. She's a bitch, but she knows how to put it on a brotha."

My mouth dropped open slightly as I stared at Simon while he bore down on me with evil in his eyes. I'd had suspicions that he was messing around on me, and although the last person that came to my mind was Cecelia, it actually made perfect sense. "Asshole," I said. And then before I even knew I was doing it, I spat a slimy glob of spit in his face. "You broke-ass, pathetic-ass waste of a fucking man!" I yelled.

Simon wiped the spit from his cheek and glared at me. "Stupid bitch," he said, raising his arm. I tensed in anticipation of a slap that I could feel coming. But before it could, the door opened.

"Don't even try it, nigga."

As Simon looked past me, I turned my head and glanced at the door. Stepping outside was Ahmad's friend, Mike.

"Who the fuck are you?" Simon asked. As his attention shifted from me to Mike, I stepped out of Simon's reach.

Mike walked toward us. "I'm a nigga that ain't gonna allow you to put your hands on a woman."

"Fuck you, and keep out of my business before your ass gets hurt," Simon said.

Mike continued walking toward us. "Trust me, motherfucker, the only one getting hurt is gonna be you. And then after I beat your ass down, I'll take you to jail for assaulting an officer." Mike removed a wallet from his pocket and flashed a badge.

Simon didn't say anything for a few seconds. Just stared at Mike and his outstretched badge. "That shit ain't real," he said finally.

Mike, who was standing less than two feet away now, chuckled. "Make your move and find out."

I looked at Simon. I could tell by his stance that he was wary of Mike and his badge.

"What's it gonna be, man?" Mike asked. His badge was back in his pocket now, hands down at his sides, fist balled. "You man enough to find out if I'm bluffing?"

Simon looked from Mike to me, then back to Mike. Finally, he nodded and said, "Whatever, man. I don't have time for this shit."

"Yeah. That's what I thought," Mike said. He looked at me. "Everything cool now?"

I shook my head. "Not yet. He has my keys."

Mike looked back to Simon. "Hand 'em over, man."

Simon glared at me with his jaws clenched. I didn't try to suppress it. I smiled and held out my hand. "Car and apartment," I said. Simon clenched his jaws again, dug in his pants pocket, removed my keys, and dropped them in my hand. "I'll call you and let you know when to come and get your things," I said with another wide smile.

"And I'll be there to help you pack," Mike said. I looked at him. He gave me a wink.

Simon gave us one last stare-down, said "bitch," then walked off.

I let out a sigh of relief and faced Mike. "Thank you."

Mike flashed a sexy-as-sin smile. "No problem. I wish he would've been stupid enough to test me. I really wanted to beat his ass."

I laughed. "Simon's stupid, but he's not that stupid."

"Maybe not, but he's still a fool to disrespect an attractive woman such as yourself."

I blushed. "Thanks."

"My pleasure. My name's Mike, by the way." He extended his hand.

I took it. "Reesa."

"Nice to meet you, Reesa. What say we get out of this cold and head back inside?"

"Sounds like a good idea."

"Cool. Oh, and I meant what I said about being there to help your boy pack. I'm not gonna let you be alone with him."

I looked at Mike as he flashed another smile at me. I thought back to Shay and the contempt she'd had in her eyes when Mike first arrived. She'd called him a playa with a capital P. Looking at him and talking with him, it wasn't hard to see that she was right. But damn, he was fine. I smiled back. "I guess we'll have to exchange numbers," I said.

"I guess so."

Erica

I shut off the engine but I didn't open the door. Just sat unmoving, my hands wringing the hell out of the steering wheel. Breathing in and out slowly, forcing myself not to turn the key in the ignition, hit the gas, and go back home. I didn't open the door. Just sat and listened to Najee, which was playing in my CD player. I switched from the Kelis I usually listened to because I wanted my mind and soul to be as clear and calm as they could possibly be. I sat still, parked in the last row of the company lot, and stared up at my office building that was too damned close.

I clenched my fingers around the steering wheel and sighed as my gaze moved from my building to the clock on my dashboard. Thirty minutes. That's how long I had. I called Rod the day after Thanksgiving and told him I'd be in on the first of December. That's when he told me that Kenny would be coming. "He's scheduled to be here at ten o'clock," he'd said. I opened and closed my fingers around the steering wheel and sighed again. I had twenty-nine minutes until Kenny arrived.

I looked at the key in the ignition. It was begging me to turn it. Begging me to let it start the car. God, I wanted to.

Turn me, it seemed to say. *Turn me, turn me, turn me.*

I took a deep breath and held it.

Turn me.

I released the air from my lungs.

Turn me, damn it!

Then I looked at the clock. Twenty-eight minutes now.

I grasped the key and turned it completely off, shutting down Najee and his sax. I took another slow breath then removed the silver key from the ignition and dropped it into my purse. I didn't want to, but I finally opened the door and stepped out of my car, allowing the crisp, cold morning air to slap me for not listening to the key's demands.

"Professional, girl," I said to myself as I moved one foot in front of the other. "You are a professional. You can handle this." I stopped walking. Turned my head and looked at my car. It was there, waiting for me to come back to it. Almost looked like it was waiting with a smile. "I'm a professional, damn it," I whispered. I turned back around and continued to the building.

I didn't take the elevator like I usually did. Instead I labored up the staircase. Did that because no one ever took the steps, and I wanted to be alone for a few more minutes. I needed to be alone. Just my luck, every damn body was hiking it. When I got upstairs to my floor—the third—I found out the elevators were out of service. Figures.

Rhonda smiled at me and gave me her usual "Good morning," but it wasn't the same. Neither was the way she looked at me. She was wondering if I was going to be able to go through the meeting with Kenny. Wondering if her ears would be privy to another blow-up in my office. I gave her a fake-ass smile and headed into my office and closed the door. I should have listened to that damn key, I thought as I turned on my PC and my lamp, and grabbed my Starbucks mug. I didn't want to leave my office, but I needed my damn green tea.

After putting on a fake smile and engaging in conversation that I didn't want to be a part of, I headed back to my office to sit and prepare myself mentally.

"Glad to see you came in."

That was Rod. He was in my office, waiting for me. I knew I'd be seeing him before Kenny arrived.

"I'm here," I said, sitting in my chair.

"Yeah, but are you *here*?" Rod asked, watching me closely.

I took a sip of my tea and looked up at Rod. "It's a struggle, but I'm here. I'm a professional, remember?"

Rod nodded then closed the door behind him and sat down in the chair that Kenny would soon be sitting in. We looked at each other. "Look," he said, "I want to apologize for the way I threw my weight around before you took your leave."

I looked at Rod and smiled. He'd thrown his weight around, but he knew he had every right to do so. His apology had been given more as an attempt to get rid of any tension between us and get our relationship back to where it normally was. I appreciated his gesture. "No need to apologize," I said. "You were right. I don't have the option of saying that I will or won't take on a client. And if I want that option, then I would have to work somewhere else."

Rod nodded. "So . . . you're going to be okay?"

I took a sip of my tea. Was I going to be okay? Or better yet, would I be able to handle this? I let out a slow sigh. "This is by far one of the toughest things I have to do, Rod. Without going into details, my history with Kenny is one I've been doing my damndest to escape. My experience with him changed me and made me the woman you've come to know. Working with Kenny is absolutely the last thing I want to do, but I'll do it because as you said, you hired me to be a professional. Whether I like it or not, Kenny is a big opportunity for this company, and I am the best designer here, hands down. Will I be okay? I'm honestly not sure. You'll have to ask me that after I finish his site."

Rod smiled, and as he did, my phone rang. I looked at the ID; it was Rhonda. I hit the speaker button. "Yes, Rhonda."

"Mr. Heart is here."

I looked at Rod. He at me. "Send him in," I said. I disconnected the call.

Rod stood, looked down at me, and flashed an affectionate and caring smile. "Do your thing," he said.

I sighed. "Don't I always?"

Rod gave me a reassuring smile then opened the door. Kenny was standing on the opposite side looking as fine as he always did in a pair of black slacks, a baby blue turtleneck, and a three-quarter-length leather coat. While he and Rod exchanged handshakes, I reached into my purse and removed the stress ball I'd bought the day before. I set it on the desk, and when Kenny walked in and closed the door, I wrapped my fingers around it and squeezed.

"It's nice to see you again, Erica," he said.

I squeezed the stress ball even harder, not giving a damn that he could see. "Believe me, the feeling is not mutual," I said coldly.

Kenny lifted an eyebrow then sat down. "So how was your Thanksgiving?"

I exhaled, grabbed the stress ball, and dropped it back into my purse. "Cut the act," I said, giving Kenny a very direct stare.

"What act? I just asked how your Thanksgiving was. It's called making friendly conversation."

"There's nothing friendly about us, so save it. Let's get down to business." I grabbed a pen and opened my notepad.

"So how does it feel knowing that you inspired my book?"

I looked up. "What?"

"How does it feel—"

"I heard the damn question."

"So?"

"So what? What do you want me to say, Kenny? That I'm flattered? Touched?"

"Are you?"

"Am I what?"

"Are you touched?"

"What?"

"Did you read any of the book at all?"

"I already told you, fuck you and your book. Now, can we please get down to business?"

"Damn it, Erica, to hell with business!" Kenny snapped, surprising the hell out of me. He slid forward in the chair. "You and I both know that's not my main reason for being here. Damn it, I love you, Erica. I always have. I know I fucked up and hurt you. And I know I don't deserve a second chance, but I want one. Shit, I can't get over you. Not a day has gone by where I haven't looked at an old picture of us together and wondered what life would be like now if I hadn't made the mistakes I did. Two years have passed, and I still need you. I need the sunshine you used to bring to me. I need to see that smile. I need to look into those brown eyes. I need to feel those hands wrapped in mine. Losing you was the worst thing that's ever happened to me. Life has been miserable for me without you, and I'm tired of being miserable." Kenny stopped talking and locked his eyes on mine.

I waited for a moment then said, "Are you done?"

Kenny raised his chin a bit. "Am I done?"

"I mean are you finished with your bullshit, because I really would like to get working on this site so that you can get the hell out of my face."

"Erica—"

"Goddamnit, Kenny!" I said, slamming my hand on the desktop. "I don't want to hear any more of your bullshit, okay. No more bullshit about you loving me. No more bullshit about how your days have been or how many fucking pictures you look at. No more bullshit about what you need. And goddamnit, no more bullshit about you wanting a second chance. The only thing I want to hear coming from your damn mouth is what you want on this website. That's it." I slammed my hand down on my desktop again. I was sure my banging could be heard outside my door, but I didn't give a damn. How dare Kenny bring his ass in my office and start saying the things he was? How dare he talk about needing me? Asshole. He didn't just hurt me, he broke my fucking heart.

"So you're not even going to give me a chance, huh?" Kenny asked, leaning back in the chair.

"No chance in hell."

"Just tell me one thing."

"I don't have to tell you shit."

"Do you still love me?"

I opened my mouth to reply with another snappy comment, but his question caught me completely off guard. "What?"

"I asked if you still love me."

"I hate your ass," I said.

Kenny folded his arms across his chest. "You didn't answer my question."

"Look up the word *hate*."

"Do you still love me?"

"Why don't you try *can't stand*? Look that up."

Kenny unfolded his arms and leaned toward my desk. "Do you still love me?"

"What's the definition for *detest*?"

Rising from the chair, his palms on my desktop, Kenny asked again. "Do you still love me?"

"Go to hell."

Leaning toward me, his cologne wafting into my nostrils, he said again, "Do . . . you . . . still . . . love me?"

My heart beat heavily, and my palms were wet; I breathed out slow, deep breaths. I tried to move but couldn't.

"Do you still . . . love me?" Kenny asked, coming closer.

I opened my mouth. "No," I said softly.

His lips inches away from mine, Kenny said, "I don't believe you."

And then he kissed me.

And as much as I hated him, I kissed him back. Parted my lips to let my tongue meet his. Closed my eyes to enjoy the softness of his lips. Let out a subtle moan as the kiss brought back memories from the past when his kisses were the norm and his loving was the bomb.

And then I stopped. Opened my eyes and moved back. "Leave," I said, averting my eyes from the stare I could feel him giving me.

Kenny stood straight. "We were good together, Erica, and I know you can tell by that kiss that we still are."

"Leave," I said again, fighting a rising lump in my throat.

"I'm not giving up on us," Kenny said, backing toward the door. "I messed up once, but I won't again. You'll see."

"Please leave, Kenny."

"I'll make an appointment with Rhonda for our next meeting," Kenny said.

I didn't say anything as he opened the door and walked out. I just turned my chair around, stared out of my office window overlooking the parking lot, sought out my car, stared at it through tear-filled eyes, and thought that I should have turned the damn key.

Carmen

"So what changed your mind?"

I was sitting across from Jordan when he asked me that. We were at a Spanish restaurant having dinner. I was eating *arroz con gandules*—rice with beans—with stewed chicken, Puerto Rican style, of course. Jordan was having *parrillada,* a sampler platter of spicy chicken breast, three varieties of sausage, and a serving of steak. He also had coconut rice with black beans on the side.

What changed my mind? That's what he wanted to know. What made me say yes when he came to my desk earlier during the week and asked me out to dinner? What made me lie to Anthony and put on my spaghetti-strapped black dress and black pumps and agree to meet Jordan at the restaurant at seven-thirty? What made me change my mind?

Anthony did.

He did that Thanksgiving night when he embarrassed the hell out of me at his mother's house. We were eating his mother's nasty turkey when it happened.

"So, Carmen," his mother said, watching me, "maybe next year we could have your turkey for Thanksgiving. But you'll have to cook it the normal way."

"Normal way?" I said with an excuse-me tone, staring at Anthony's mother. It was no real secret that we had a strained relationship. Although three years had gone by, Anthony's mother never warmed up to my being a Latina, and whenever she could, she'd slip in offensive and off-the-wall comments. Most of the time, I'd be an adult and just ignore her ignorant ass, but with me questioning my feelings and my relationship with Anthony, I wasn't in the mood for taking shit. "What do you mean by that?"

Anthony's overweight mother gave me a fake smile. "Oh I just know how you people like to put funny spices in your food. My blood pressure couldn't handle any of that."

I stared at the woman across from me. "My people?" I said, putting my fork down. "What the hell do you mean, 'my people'?" I know I was being disrespectful with my outburst, but damn it, going there when it was just her, Anthony, and me was one thing, but going there with everyone else around was out of line.

Obviously not liking my outburst, Anthony's mother looked at me with indignation. "You know what the hell I mean, Jennifer Lopez."

"Jennifer Lopez?" I stood. Oh, she'd definitely crossed the line with that shit. "You know what," I started, but before I could finish, Anthony jumped up and placed a hand on my shoulder.

"Hold on, baby. Relax, all right?"

I turned to him. "Relax? How the hell am I supposed to relax with your fat-ass mother's racist ass?"

"Come on, ba—"

"Oh, hell no!" his mother said, rising from her seat. "I know Charro didn't call me fat ass!"

I slit my eyes at her. "Charro? *Tu puerca! No puedo crear tu me hablas asi!*"

"Excuse me?" his mother said, throwing her hands on her wide hips. "We speak English in this house!"

"Then I guess I better leave!" I said. "Let's go, Anthony."

"Anthony's not going anywhere," his mother said. "He's welcomed here."

I faced Anthony. "Let's go," I said sternly.

Anthony looked from me to his mother, then back at me. "Baby . . . "

"Let's go!" I said.

Anthony looked from me to his mother then back to me again. He grabbed my hand. "Excuse us, please." Before I could snatch my hand, he pulled me away from the table and practically dragged me off into the kitchen. As soon as the door closed behind us, I let him have it. "I can't believe you just let your mother disrespect me like that!"

Anthony looked toward the door then to me. "Carmen, will you calm the fuck down and lower your voice?"

"Lower my voice?" I yelled. "Hell no, I won't lower my voice. Bitch! I want to leave now, Anthony." Puerto Rican curse words rolled off my tongue as I clenched my fists.

"Come on, Carmen. Don't call my mom a bitch."

"What?" I said. "Please tell me you're not defending that *puerca!*"

"Chill with that, goddamnit!" Anthony said. "Look, you know how my mom is. I know she's wrong for saying what she's saying—"

"Then tell her ass that!"

"—but that's how she is. You gotta just let her comments go in one ear and out the other."

"In one...? Oh, hell no! I've done that too many times before. I want to fucking leave now, Anthony. Go and get our damn coats."

"Baby, it's Thanksgiving."

"I don't give a shit. I want to leave."

"Look, just come back out there, will you? I'll straighten my mom out, okay? But I have family here, and I don't feel like adding to the drama and giving them even more to talk about by us leaving."

"I don't give a shit what they talk about!"

"Yeah well, I do," Anthony said. "And we're not leaving."

"Anthony—"

"I said we're not leaving, Carmen. Shit. We're gonna go back inside, and you'll apologize to my mother—"

"I'm not apologizing for—"

"—after I make sure she apologizes to you." Anthony stared at me. I stared back at him. "Come on, Carmen."

"This is some real bullshit, Anthony."

"I know. And I'll straighten it all out."

I took a deep breath to try to calm down, and stared at Anthony. "You better put her in check," I said.

"I will. Now, let's go back in there."

I gave Anthony another you-better-put-her-ass-in-check glare then said, "Fine."

I reluctantly followed him back out to the dining room, and doing my best to ignore the disapproving stares from the other family members who'd had more than enough time to listen to Anthony's mother talk bad about me, I sat down.

"Mom," Anthony said after a few seconds of tense, uneasy silence, "you know you went a little too far, don't you?"

"Baby," his mother said, looking at him, "I didn't mean to disrespect you. I just don't like being disrespected that way."

Disrespect him? I opened my mouth, but Anthony butted in before I could get a word in.

"I know, Mom. And believe me, Carmen's sorry for going off the way she did."

What?

"This is a time to be giving thanks," his mother said. "All I want to do is praise the Lord for this blessed day and the gathering of family."

"I know, Mom," Anthony said, grabbing my hand underneath the table as I again prepared to say something.

"I don't want to be arguing. I don't have time for it."

"I know, Mom."

I bit my tongue as Anthony squeezed my hand.

"I don't like all this tension in my home."

"I know, Mom. And there won't be anymore tension. I . . . we promise. Let's just enjoy this meal."

Anthony's mother smiled then gave me a quick, evil, cutting look. Very quick.

"Well, like I was saying before," Anthony's mother said, "maybe next year we can have turkey at your place, son."

Anthony swallowed a slice of the dry-ass turkey then made a comment that blew me away. "I don't know, Mom," he said, drinking some apple juice. "Carmen's not exactly the best cook."

"No you didn't just say that!" I said. I stood and looked down at Anthony. "I can't believe you just said that."

"Well, he's only speaking how he feels," his mother butted in.

I eyed her. *"Vete para mierda!"* I pushed the chair away from me. "I don't need this shit!" I walked away from the table, not caring who I offended, grabbed my coat, and stormed out of the house. When Anthony came running behind me, I was on my cell calling a cab.

"Anthony, get the hell away from me!" I said, snatching my hand back as he tried to grab it.

"Carmen, what the fuck was that all about back there? Things had calmed down. Why'd you have to act a fool like that?"

"Act a fool? I don't believe you! How could you embarrass me like that back there? Talking about I'm not the best cook. *Pendejo,* I cook for your ass every night, and I never hear any complaints."

Anthony tried to take my hand again, but I wasn't having it. "Carmen, damn, will you chill? I was just trying to lighten the mood and get a laugh."

"At what? My expense?" I yelled out loud.

"Will you calm down, Carmen? It's bad enough that you made one inside, but you're making a scene out here too."

"I don't give a shit," I said, angrily dialing the number for Yellow Cab. "Your mother just completely disrespected me in front of your family, and instead of properly putting her in check, you went and pacified her ass then disrespected me too. And you want me to calm down and not make a scene?"

"Come on, Carmen—"

"Come on, Carmen, nothing," I spat. "Yes," I said to the dispatcher who'd finally answered. "I need a cab."

Anthony tried to grab my hand again. "Carmen . . . "

"Fuck you and leave me alone," I said, pulling my hand away. "No, not you, sir. *Perdoname.* I'm talking to my asshole of a boyfriend. . . . Yes, I know. Thank you." I gave the dispatcher the address, and he assured me a cab would arrive in ten minutes. I thanked him, ended the call, and stared at Anthony as he stewed and shivered with his hands shoved in his pockets. He'd come outside without his coat.

"Carmen," he started again after a while.

I cut him off. "Leave me alone and go back inside, Anthony," I said, slipping my phone in my coat pocket.

"Damn it, Carmen, stop acting stupid."

"Excuse me?"

"Stop tripping and come back inside."

"There's no way in hell I'm going back in that damn house with that woman. As a matter of fact, there's no way in hell I'm *ever* stepping foot in there again."

"Damn," Anthony yelled out loud. "Why are you acting like this? It's not like you didn't take things too far either."

I squinted. "What?"

"Look, whether you admit it or not, you were out of line a couple of times. You didn't have to react the way you did. Yeah, my mother didn't say the nicest things but you didn't have to raise your voice the way you did and then start flipping out in Spanish."

"You know what, Anthony—"

Honk!

I looked to the street. The cab had arrived. And just in time, too, because if Anthony thought I'd made a scene before, I was truly about to give a performance. I shook my head. Going off wasn't even worth it. I gave Anthony a venomous look then walked off to the cab.

"So you're really gonna leave?" Anthony asked as I got to the cab. "You're just gonna embarrass me like this, right? Make me go back inside alone so that my mother and everyone else will have something to gossip about for the rest of the damn night. Carmen!"

I opened the door.

"Carmen!"

I put one foot inside.

"Carmen! This is some bullshit!"

I paused with my one foot in and half-turned to look at him.

"Real bullshit!" he said as I stared at him.

Yes, I thought, not saying a word. This was some real bullshit. I curled my lips into a sneer then got in the cab, closed the door, and gave the driver my address. I slept in the bedroom alone that night. Threw Anthony's pillow on the couch along with a blanket and locked the bedroom door so he couldn't come in.

I called my mother and told her what had happened. Told her a bunch of things, actually. She'd never really cared for Anthony. Not because he's black, but just because she didn't like his personality. We had a long, in-depth conversation, and that night, before I fell asleep, is when I changed my mind.

I smiled at Jordan. He smiled back.

"So you really told your parents about me?" I asked.

Jordan nodded and folded his hands on the table. "Yes, I did."

I smiled and reached across the table and rested my hands on his. "So did I."

Erica

"Girl, where the hell have you been?"

I smiled as Carmen's voice came through the phone. I hadn't spoken to her since just before Thanksgiving. "I've been here," I said.

"No you haven't. I've called a couple of times. And I've left messages."

I sighed. "I know you have. And I've gotten them."

"And why didn't you ever call me back?"

I sighed again and spun my chair around so that I could see the parking lot. "I've just had some issues I've been dealing with," I said softly.

Carmen sighed. "Same here," she said.

"Man problems?" I asked, knowing of course that hers were Anthony problems.

"Yeah, something like that."

"I've got them too."

"You do?"

"Yeah. My ex is back in my life in a major way."

"Kenny? Really? When did that happen?"

I groaned and watched as employees on their way out for lunch scurried quickly from the building to their cars to get out of the cold air. "Remember when you left me at the Olive Garden to go and help your sister out?"

"Yeah."

"Well, right after you left, Kenny showed up."

"What?"

"Yeah," I said, turning my chair back around and leaning my elbows on my desk. "And get this. He had the nerve to try to have a conversation with me."

"I bet that didn't go over well."

"Hell no, it didn't. Without even mincing my words, I told him to go to hell, leave me alone, and never think about speaking to me again. And then I threw my lemonade in his face."

"You didn't!"

"Hell yes, I did. And then I walked off and told the waitress that his ass was taking care of the check. By the way, I have your half of the bill you left."

Carmen laughed out loud. "You ain't right."

"He's lucky that's all I did to him. Shit. For real, girl, after the way he hurt me, he should have known better than to think we could have had a civil discussion."

Carmen laughed out loud again then after a few seconds, quieted down. "So anyway, you said he was back in your life in a major way. What did you mean?"

I rested my hand on my forehead as though I was trying to keep the glare from the sun out of my face, and closed my eyes as the recollection of my meeting with Kenny and the kiss between us appeared in my mind. He was still the best kisser I'd ever known. Damn.

"Erica?" Carmen called out. "You still there?"

"I'm here," I said, squeezing my temples with my thumb and middle finger. "Just thinking."

"So how's Kenny back in your life? Did you see him again?"

I chuckled sarcastically. "Oh, did I. Have you ever heard of some book called, *A Man and Happiness: Why He Can't Have It?*"

"Oh yeah!" Carmen said, a little too excited as far as I was concerned. "That book is the bomb. I read it in like two days."

I rolled my eyes. Had I really been the only woman on the planet not to have read that damn book? "Anyway," I said, "believe it or not, Kenny is the author."

"Author of what?"

"That book."

"Get out of here. You're lying."

"Girl, I wish I was. Believe me."

"He did not write that. His last name is Owens."

"He's using his mother's maiden name."

"No way."

"Girl, I told you he wrote it."

"Dayum!" Carmen whispered.

"Yeah, damn is right. And the good news doesn't stop there."

"Hold up. I need to sit down." There was a slight moment of silence as Carmen did just that. "Okay . . . give me all of the good news you got."

I gave my temples another squeeze, exhaled, then gave Carmen the complete low-down on the drama of my life since Kenny reappeared. I told her everything: why Kenny wrote the book, the way he showed up at my office, the things he said, described the Thanksgiving dinner I ate, told her about the kiss Kenny and I shared. Everything.

When I finished filling her in, Carmen let out another whispered "Dayum."

I sat back in my chair and breathed in and out slowly. Although it was still incredibly heavy, the weight on my shoulders had actually eased a bit since I'd opened up and spilled my guts.

"Dayum," Carmen said again.

"I know," I replied. "Girl, this has me so stressed."

"I can imagine."

"I hate him, Carmen," I said, tears beginning to well in my eyes. "I really, really do. Moving past the way he hurt me wasn't the easiest thing to do. I literally had to become a different person, both physically and emotionally. It was hard, but I did it. I survived. And now . . ." I paused as tears spilled over and ran down my cheeks. I didn't want to cry, but I couldn't help it. "Now he's back in my life." I paused again and broke down.

Carmen waited for a few minutes then softly said, "You still love him. You have admitted that to yourself, right?"

I squeezed my eyes shut tightly as tears fell harder. God, I wanted her to be wrong. I wanted that kiss between Kenny and me to mean nothing. I wanted the dreams I'd had since that kiss to mean nothing. "I'm trying not to, Carmen," I said quietly.

"Spare yourself the emotional turmoil and admit it, Erica. Then you can figure out what to do next."

"Why the hell did he have to come back in my life? I moved past him."

"Yeah, but he obviously has never moved past you."

"What should I do, Carmen?"

She sighed. "I wish I had the answer for you, girl, but that's something you're going to have to ask your heart."

I took a deep breath and let it out very slowly through my slightly parted lips. I knew she was right, but after having walked through the fire, my heart was the last thing I wanted to have a conversation with, because as much as my mind was telling me one thing, my heart, whether I liked it or not, was saying something completely different. I took another deep breath and blew it out quickly, this time through puffed cheeks. I grabbed a tissue and wiped my tears away. "Sorry to unload my problems on you," I said, pulling a mirror from my desk drawer. I was looking very scary at the moment with my puffy eyes and my flushed, tear-stained cheeks.

"You know you don't have to apologize for that," Carmen said. "I'm your girl. My shoulder and ear are always here. Besides, I actually called to unload on you."

Applying some makeup on my cheeks, I said, "So what did Anthony do now?"

"Well," Carmen said, dragging out the word. "I'd love to say that he's causing me all this drama right now, but I really can't. Although he did act a fool on Thanksgiving, but I'll save that for another time."

"Okay. So what do you need to unload about?"

Carmen exhaled heavily into the phone. "I'm falling in love with another man."

I was about to reapply my lip-gloss when she said that. Needless to say, I paused and I said, "What? Another man?" I put my burgundy-colored lip-gloss down and cleared my throat. "Okay, you definitely have to unload now."

Carmen chuckled a bit. "Believe it or not, I've been seeing someone."

"Seriously?"

"Yeah."

"Who?" I was shocked; she'd actually seen past the blinders. "And where did you meet him? And when? And why am I just now finding out?"

"You're now finding out because you finally answered your phone," Carmen said. "Anyway, his name is Jordan, and I work with him."

My turn to whisper, "Dayum. So how did all of this happen? I mean, just a few weeks ago, you were all into Anthony. Now you're talking about falling in love with another man. I mean, damn, girl. What's the story? Wait, let me guess. You and Jordan went out for drinks one night after work, umm, you must have gotten pissy drunk and ended up at some hotel with him, where he gave you the dick so good that you were seeing stars afterward. And now you're sprung and in love. Am I right?"

"Hardly. First of all, I didn't sleep with him—yet. Second of all, even if I had, it wouldn't have been at a hotel. Not all of us can do that. And third, yes, I'm sprung."

"Damn, Carmen. You've really got to fill me in. And I didn't appreciate your hotel comment, by the way."

"Hey, just keeping it real. And I will fill you in, but I can't right now. I have to run and do something. How about happy hour after work? We haven't been out since we all went to Silver Shadow."

"I don't know," I said. "My hours aren't too happy right now."

"Just come on and hang for a bit. I'll fill you in on everything. Besides, I think we could all use the time out."

"We?"

"Shay and Reesa are coming too. I called them before I called you."

I frowned a bit. "Carmen, Shay I have no problem with, but you know Reesa and I don't really get along."

"That's only because you always start an argument with her."

"Yeah well, tell her to stop putting on a front as if Simon was actually worth something, and I wouldn't have to."

"Hey, she's free to put on whatever front she wants about Simon. Anyway, you won't have to worry about that tonight."

"Oh, and why is that?"

"She's not with Simon anymore."

"She's not?"

"No. She broke up with him on Thanksgiving."

I raised my eyebrows. First Carmen and now Reesa. They'd finally come to their senses. "It's about time," I said.

"So will you be able to just hang out and relax now?"

I sucked my teeth. "Sure, sure," I said.

"Good. We'll be at the Shadow again."

"Can't we go somewhere else?"

"Well, I would say meet me at Latin Palace, but I know you all don't do the Latin thing, so I figure Silver Shadow is mature and laid-back enough. Besides, it's closer to Jordan's house, and I want to stop by there after we leave."

My eyes widened. "Girl, you really have to fill me in."

Carmen laughed. "I will."

"You better."

Carmen laughed again, and I have to admit, I did too. And it felt good to do that. "So you feeling any better now?" Carmen asked.

I smiled. "Yeah, girl. Thank you for lending me your ear."

"Anytime. I'll see you after work."

"Okay." I hung up the phone and smiled. I really was feeling better. I should have talked to Carmen a while ago. I spun around in my chair and looked out to the parking lot again. The worker bees were all returning to their hives from their lunch breaks. I'd worked through mine all week—or maybe I should say I sulked through lunch. Eating was hardly something I'd been doing a lot of.

I turned back around to my PC, tapped the mouse, and stared at my monitor as the preliminary work I'd done on Kenny's website appeared. There wasn't much to it since he and I hadn't discussed the site at all, except for one brief phone conversation when he called me. Thankfully Rod had been in my office at the time, so Kenny had no choice but to keep our conversation on a business level.

I looked at the skeletal layout and sighed. I'd finally started to work on it because I just wanted to get Kenny out of my life as quickly as possible. His re-emergence had truly upset the balance I'd found, and admitting that I still loved him was just making things even worse. I still needed wording and pictures from him, but at least I had something. Had the site been for anyone else, I would have smiled at how well it was coming along. That was hardly the case now.

I minimized the screen, leaned back in my chair, and closed my eyes. I was meeting with Kenny the following Monday. It would be the first time seeing him since our kiss. Rod wouldn't be there to run interference like he had been when Kenny called. It would just be Kenny and me. *Mano a mano.* I released a slow breath of air. Happy hour was really starting to look a lot better.

Reesa

"I cannot believe I was keeping myself from all of this fun!" I just had to say that. I shook my rear end to the classic song "Just Got Paid" by Johnny Kemp and sipped on my apple martini. Fun. I was having it. Enjoying it. Reveling in it. All since I'd finally and for good kicked Simon's ass out. "Just got paid. Friday night!" Shit, I couldn't sing, but I was singing anyway. Carmen, who was shaking her tail beside me, laughed.

"You better stop before the deejay kills the music."

I elbowed her playfully. "Whatever. Don't hate because I could give Mariah a run for her money."

"Oh, she'd be running all right. Straight to the police to come and arrest you for disturbing the peace." Carmen laughed again and took a sip of her drink. I laughed, too, and rolled my eyes. "So did you ever hook back up with Mike?" she asked.

I looked around quickly then glanced at her. "Shh," I said, putting my index finger to my lips. "I told you not to talk about him with Shay around."

"Don't worry about it," Carmen said, waving her hand. "Shay can't hear you. She's out on the dance floor. See?"

I looked toward the direction of Carmen's pointing finger and saw Shay getting her groove on with a fine, husky, cocoa-brown brother. "Aww, shit," I said with a smile. "Shay better not forget she has a husband."

"Please," Carmen said. "That ain't happening. She only comes out once in a while, so when she does, she likes to have a good time. But make no mistake about it, she loves her man and wouldn't step out on him."

I nodded. "Yes, she does."

"So, back to my question. Did you hook up with Mike again?"

I put my attention back on Carmen and smiled. Mike. Ahmad's friend. Shay's eyesore. My protector. We'd spoken several times over the phone after the Thanksgiving fiasco at Shay's house, flirting with each other big time. Even without Shay's warning, it would have been impossible not to know what Mike was about because he had absolutely no shame in his game whatsoever.

Before I'd come to my senses over Simon, I would have turned my nose up at a man like Mike in a heartbeat. But once I finally made the decision to liberate myself, I saw a man like Mike in a whole other light. He was a playa, yeah, but he was fine. And smooth. And built. And I could tell by the arrogance in his speech that he knew how to work it in the bedroom.

After a few phone conversations, I knew that Mike was going to be my first sexual partner after Simon. Of course I didn't know that it was going to happen the night Simon came and took what little of his shit he had at my place. Just as he said he would, Mike came over to make sure that Simon didn't act a fool. He had just gotten off duty when he came over, and he was looking damn good in his uniform. So good that twenty minutes after Simon walked out the door, Mike and I had our clothes off and were enjoying some very intense and almost poetic sex. "Mmm," I said, remembering the way Mike's girth filled me up.

"Mmm what?" Carmen asked. "Did you or did you not hook up with him again?"

I smiled then shook my head. "No," I said.

"You didn't?"

"Nope."

"I'm surprised. After the way you called and told me what went down with you two, I was sure you'd be enjoying another ride."

I shrugged. I'd called Carmen right after Mike left my place. The sex had been so good that I had to tell somebody. And since Shay was out of the question, Carmen was my next choice. "That was just a one-time thing," I said. "Mike and I had some adult, consenting, no-strings-attached sex, and that's all it was."

"I see."

"Besides, after the shit with Simon, the last thing I want to do is get attached to any man right now."

"I feel you."

"I'm having fun, girl. These past couple of weeks have been great. I'm enjoying my life the way I should have been."

"I'll drink to that." Carmen downed the rest of her drink.

"I should have gotten rid of his behind sooner."

"Yes, you should have."

I turned my head. Erica had been the one to say that. My smile quickly disappeared.

"How's it going, Reesa?" she asked after giving Carmen a hug.

"Not bad," I said evenly.

"From the sound of it before, it seemed like things were going great for you," Erica said.

"Yeah," I replied. "Not bad."

"Oh, please, you two," Carmen said. "I'm going to get another drink." Without saying anything else, she walked off, leaving Erica and me alone in uncomfortable silence.

I turned and looked out at the dance floor. Erica did the same. We stood side by side that way until two songs later, I broke the silence. "How come you're not out there?" I asked, staring straight ahead.

"Not in the mood to party," Erica replied, looking forward also.

"That's a surprise," I said.

From the corner of my eye I saw Erica look at me. "Excuse me?"

I faced her. "You're usually always out on the floor with a drink in hand."

"And your point?" she asked, her voice laced with an edge.

"No point. Just surprised, that's all."

Erica gave me a slit-eyed look then turned back to the floor. "Yeah well, like I said, I'm not in the mood to party."

I hmphed then turned back to the sea of gyrating hips also. Silence again passed between us until I broke it. "Where's Carmen?"

"I don't know," Erica said. "But if she doesn't reappear soon, I'm leaving."

"So soon?"

"Like I said before, I'm not really in the mood to be here."

I faced her. "So why'd you come?"

"You know," Erica said, meeting my gaze, "you're asking a whole lot of questions."

"Just making conversation."

Erica eyed me skeptically. "Mmm-hmm. So when did you finally wake up and decide to get rid of your dead weight?"

I ran my tongue across the front of my top teeth. "Thanksgiving," I said. Erica nodded but didn't say anything. I don't know why, but I kept talking. "He came to Shay's house with my car, late and high. Then he threatened to hit me—well, he was about to hit me until an acquaintance of Shay's stepped in. I demanded my car and apartment keys right there on the spot. I'd finally had enough of the bullshit."

"It's about time," Erica said.

I stared at her for a long second.

"What?" she asked. "You'd rather I soften my words? Point blank, you were too good for a nigga like Simon."

"Is that why you always gave me such a hard time? Or is it that you just don't like me?"

"Look, I don't really have anything personal against you, okay? I just couldn't stand listening to you put on a front about a nigga that was no good."

"So what was I supposed to do, sit and complain about him all night long?"

"No. You were supposed to do what you finally did: drop his ass. There's no way a female of your caliber—educated, successful, independent—should waste your time on a punk like Simon. You should have left his ass to the chickenheads that don't have shit going on for themselves."

I nodded but didn't respond right away. She'd actually had some nice things to say about me, and that surprised me. "You're right," I admitted with a sigh. "Hell, if you really want the truth, you've always been right. I should have never been with an ass like Simon."

"So why were you?"

"You want the truth?"

"Sure."

"Let's get a drink then I'll tell you."

Erica shrugged. "All right."

We made our way through the growing crowd and walked over to the bar, ordered a couple of Margaritas then grabbed a table as a couple got up to dance.

"So," Erica said, moving her head to "Milkshake," the new Kelis song. "Why'd you settle?"

I sipped my Margarita, licked some extra salt from the glass then gave her the rundown I had given to Shay. As I expected, she said the same thing Shay had said to me. This time, instead of rebutting, I sat and listened and agreed; I was crazy to ever think that having a baby with Simon was the right thing to do.

"Just be glad you didn't have any slip-ups," Erica said with raised eyebrows.

"Yeah, I know. I was lucky."

"Damn lucky. That would have been drama and headaches for real. And he was already giving you enough of that."

"More than enough."

"Hey! You two are still alive!"

Erica and I turned our heads in unison as Carmen appeared. She was wiping her forehead with a napkin in one hand and fanning herself with the other. Erica spoke first.

"Where have you been?"

"Sorry, girls," Carmen said, sitting down. "I went to get a drink, and on my way there I was taken hostage by this fine Usher look-alike. So . . . like I said, you two are alive. That's a good thing."

"So what, we're supposed to be arguing or something?" Erica asked, giving me a look and a subtle smile.

I followed her lead. "Yeah. You act like we don't get along," I said.

"Like we're always at each other's throats," Erica added.

"Snapping at each other like two bitches waiting to be unleashed," I said.

"Yeah—" Erica started before Carmen cut in.

"Yeah, yeah! Very funny! You're just a regular pair of girlfriends from back in the day. I got you."

We all laughed out loud then screamed as the old school classic "O.P.P." was played. No words needed, we all jumped up from our seats and hit the dance floor.

Fun. I was having it. We were having it. And when Shay came over and joined us, we made our way to the middle of the dance floor and let everybody in on it. The deejay must have been feeding off our energy because he kept the old school hits coming one right after the other. We danced until our feet demanded that we quit.

Tired and buzzed, I decided it was time for me to head home. "All right, ladies," I said, gathering my purse, "I'm out of here."

"I'm right behind you," Shay said. "It was fun, ladies, but I have a little alcohol in my system, and my mother is watching Nicole tonight. I'm going home to get me some. Mind you, I don't need the alcohol, but it helps."

"I ain't mad at you," Carmen said.

"You guys are staying?" Shay asked.

"Yeah. I'm gonna hang for a little while then head out."

"Wow. Anthony must be out of town," Shay said. I had to laugh at that.

Carmen rolled her eyes. "Whatever. I am my own woman, thank you very much."

"Excuse me, blondie?" Erica said. "Don't you even go there."

With another eye roll and a sucking of her teeth, Carmen said, "Shut up."

We all broke out laughing again. I looked at Erica. "You're staying too?"

"Yeah. I'm gonna hang with Carmen for a little while."

I smiled. "Okay. Well it was fun, girl."

Erica smiled back. "Yeah, it was."

I reached in my purse and pulled out my cell phone. "Why don't we exchange numbers?"

"Works for me."

As we entered each other's numbers into our phones, Shay and Carmen stared at us as though we'd lost our minds. Erica and I exchanged glances and rolled our eyes. "You'd think we didn't like each other or something," I said.

"I know, right," Erica responded.

"Okay," Shay said. "You two definitely had too much to drink. Carmen, don't let her have another drink. Reesa, I'm calling a cab for your behind."

I laughed. "You're stupid."

"Stupid is as stupid does," Shay replied.

I turned to Erica. "Umm, I think I'll be calling a cab for her ass."

We all broke out into laughter again then hugged one another good-bye. When Shay and I stepped out into the cold, Shay said, "How the heck did that happen?"

I shrugged. "Guess we finally took the time to get to know each other."

"It's about time."

I smiled. "Yeah, it was."

Shay and I said our good-byes then went our separate ways, she to her husband to get her swerve on, me to the solitude of my apartment. And that was just fine with me. I turned the radio on in my car as I headed home down 29N. Ironically enough, "Milkshake" was playing, which made me think of Erica. I smiled. Something told me that we were going to end up being good friends.

Carmen

I couldn't believe what I was about to do. It was crazy . . . No, it was the alcohol. I'd had too much to drink, and I'd lost all ability to think straight. That was it. I was drunk. Pissy drunk. And that's the only reason why my index finger was just inches away from pressing Jordan's doorbell.

Right?

Wrong.

Damn.

I lowered my hand and let out a long breath. I wasn't drunk at all. Not even close. My head and mind were as clear as the wind was bitterly cold. "This is wrong, Carmen," I said to myself. "This is just wrong."

I stood still for a few seconds.

Wrong, wrong.

I raised my hand, extended my index finger again, and this time I pushed it into the glowing doorbell to Jordan's home. I let out another breath as I took a step back. Seconds later the door opened. Jordan, who'd been expecting me, stood on the inside of the door dressed in a pair of black sweatpants and a white T-shirt. On his feet he wore a pair of black leather slippers.

God, he looked fine.

"I'm glad you came," he said, smiling.

I smiled back. "So am I."

Jordan stepped back and held the door open. "Come out of the cold."

I hesitated for a second then quickly stepped past him into the warmth of his home as the wind whipped at my legs. Jordan closed the door. "You have a beautiful home," I said, admiring the warm, stylish décor before me. This was my first time coming to his house.

"Thank you. But I can't take any credit. Terry was the designer of the house. I haven't done anything to it but clean it since she passed. Decorating's just never been my thing."

Peering into the burgundy-colored dining room, I said, "She had very good taste."

"Thanks. Here . . . let me take your coat."

I unzipped my leather coat, slipped out of it, and handed it to him. Jordan took a moment to admire the black skirt and low-cut lavender silk blouse I was wearing then went to hang up my coat. "So," he said coming back, "how long can you stay?"

"For a while. I told Anthony that I was going out with the girls."

Jordan took my hand in his and pulled me toward him slowly. "I'm really glad you came."

"So am I," I said again.

And then we kissed. Slowly. Gently. Passionately. This wasn't our first, but it was our first one without having to worry about other eyes. Our tongues danced as our bodies pressed into each other. I felt Jordan harden against me, and that made my body heat rise. Jordan caressed the small of my back then his hands made their way down to my rear end. I moaned softly from the gentle way he touched me. I think we could have kissed forever had his tea kettle not broken our moment with its whistling. I pulled away from Jordan, wiped my lips, and smiled.

He sighed. "I forgot I had that on. Would you like a cup? I have regular or herbal."

"Do you have peppermint?"

"I do."

"Then count me in."

I followed Jordan into the kitchen and sat down at an island with enough room to accommodate at least fifteen people. "Very nice," I said, admiring the space, the marble countertops, and warm marigold color of the walls.

"Terry picked out everything. It cost an arm and a leg for some of the things she wanted, but it was worth it."

"She should have been a designer."

"Interior decorating was always a hobby of hers. She loved all of those home repair and home decorating shows."

"She should have pursued it full time," I said, admiring the oak cabinets.

"I think she would have, had she not been so good at being a lawyer."

"Talented and blessed . . . she must have been something."

"She was," Jordan said, his voice lowering slightly.

"I'm sorry," I said softly.

Jordan walked over with two cups of tea in hand, set them down, and sat beside me. "No need to apologize. For the first time in a very long while, I am actually able to talk about her without breaking down. And that," he reached out and caressed my cheek with a finger, "is because of you, Carmen. You're a special woman, and I'm happy that you decided to take a chance on us."

I smiled slightly but didn't say anything. Instead, I looked down, picked up my cup of tea, and stared at my reflection in the water.

"Did I say something wrong?" Jordan asked.

I shook my head. "No," I said, allowing the soothing peppermint vapor to fill my nostrils. "You didn't say anything wrong at all."

"Then why can't you look at me? And why the silence? Are you regretting being here?"

I shook my head again. "No, I'm not. Not at all."

"Look at me, Carmen," Jordan said quietly. I did as he asked and met his gaze with my own. "Talk to me."

I took a slow, deep breath and let it out easily. Jordan's gaze was focused on me. I studied his eyes. Looked past his long lashes that most women wished they had. Looked past the deep brown color. Looked past all that to the gentleness of the soul behind them and saw all of the joy and pain he'd been through; saw all the love he'd given and had to give still. "How can you be happy with all of this?" I asked.

Jordan furrowed his brow. "What do you mean?"

"I mean how can you be happy with our situation? Anthony's still in the picture."

"I know that."

"And you're okay with that?"

"Honestly, no. I'm not."

"So why am I here? Why are you continuing to be with me this way?"

"Is this your way of trying to end things between us?"

"No. I just want to know how you can be okay with being the man on the side."

Jordan took a sip of his tea then put down his mug. He reached out to touch me again, but my guilt made me pull away. He sighed. "Carmen, what do you want me to say?"

"I want you to tell me the truth about how you feel."

"I love you."

"As nice as that sounds, that's not what I want to hear."

"But that's the truth."

"Damn it, Jordan. I'm being unfair to you, and that has to bother you."

Jordan frowned, stood, and took his mug to the sink. After placing it down, he turned around, leaned back against the counter, and stared at me. Tears were welling in the corners of my eyes. I fought to keep them from falling. *This is unfair,* I thought. I was being unfair.

"I hate this situation, Carmen," Jordan said after a few seconds of silence. "I hate the fact that we have to see each other on the side. That we have to be careful about expressing any type of feelings for each other out in the open. I hate the fact that the first and last thing Anthony gets to see each day is your beautiful face. I want you to drop him so bad and be with me it hurts."

"So why go on with me this way?"

"We were meant to be together, Carmen. That's why. I know it. And you do too."

"But Anthony and I—"

"At some point, you and Anthony will be history."

"But how do you know that? I don't even know that."

"Yes, you do. One day you'll wake up and decide once and for all that you've had it with getting second-class treatment. Until that day, I'll be the man on the side. I told you before, I'm not going anywhere."

The tears I'd been fighting fell slowly from my eyes. "How can you be so sure that day will come?" I asked, wiping them away.

"Because I am," he said, walking toward me.

"But what if . . . what if I can't end things with him?"

Standing directly in front of me, Jordan cupped his hand underneath my chin. "Why would you want to stay with him?" he asked.

This took me back to my conversation with Erica before we left Silver Shadow.

"Dump Anthony and move on to better things, Carmen," Erica had said after I told her about how Jordan made me feel. "Stop wasting your time in a relationship that's not doing anything for you."

"But Anthony's been really good to me lately."

"So?"

"So maybe he's changing. Maybe he's ready to be a real man."

Erica had sucked her teeth. "Maybe my ass. So he's been on good behavior lately. So what? Leopards can't change their spots, girl. The old Anthony will return soon."

"But shouldn't I give him the benefit of the doubt?"

"For what? How did you say Jordan made you feel again?"

I had smiled. "Like I'm the only thing that matters."

"You said you were falling in love with him. Is that true? Are you?"

I had thought about her question for a moment then nodded. "Yes."

"Then get rid of Anthony's ass and be happy, Carmen. Seriously . . . why would you want to let a man like Jordan go to stay with a sorry ass like Anthony? Damn, *chica,* your decision to be happy shouldn't be this hard."

I looked up at Jordan. Why wouldn't I want to end things with Anthony? Erica had asked, and now Jordan was too. After all of the ups and too many downs, why wouldn't I want to just be happy with Jordan? I was ready to after Thanksgiving. That had been the last straw for me. So why didn't I get rid of Anthony? Was it because since then Anthony had been extra attentive with me? Was it because he'd been showering me with affection the way he used to when we first started dating? Perhaps it was because on more than one occasion since Thanksgiving, he'd told me how much he loved, cared, and needed me. Or was it simply because despite how strongly I felt for Jordan and despite how true his words were, I couldn't deny or ignore the fact that Anthony, whether I liked it or not, still had a hold on my heart?

Why would I want to stay with Anthony? Erica couldn't understand it, and now Jordan wanted an explanation.

"I don't know," I said, unable to tell him the truth.

"I don't know either," he replied. "So I'll wait because it's only a matter of time."

"But how do you—" Before I could finish my next question, Jordan pressed his lips against mine. I wanted to resist. I wanted to talk some more, because my guilty conscience had been beating me up the past couple of days, but I couldn't utter a word. His kiss had me silenced and weak. I was powerless to do anything but kiss him back. After a few minutes, Jordan pulled back and extended his hand.

"You're here, Carmen. And you'll be leaving soon."

"Jordan . . ."

"I don't want to sleep with you, Carmen. Not yet. I just want you to sit with me. I want you in my arms until you have to leave." As he watched me and waited patiently, I couldn't help but sigh. He was a beautiful man. Gentle. Genuine. Caring. He was the kind of man I'd always hoped for. A man who was everything Anthony wasn't. *Why would I want to stay with Anthony?* I thought again. I took a quick glance to the time illuminated on the microwave on the counter behind Jordan. It was going on eleven P.M. I turned my gaze back to Jordan. God, he was a beautiful man. Beautiful on the inside and out.

I took his hand. "Let's go up to your room."

A few hours later, my internal clock woke me up. I was in Jordan's bed, with him spooned behind me, his arm draped around my waist. We fell asleep that way, fully clothed, shoes still on. When I took Jordan's hand and asked to go to his room, my intent was for us to make love. I wanted to feel him inside of me, pleasuring me the way I knew he could. I wanted my body to be adored, my curves to be savored; I wanted to be made love to, something I wasn't accustomed to. Not anymore, at least. But in the midst of our kissing and caressing, my conscience got to me. Told me that what I was doing was wrong. My feelings for Jordan were real and intense, and I can't lie, I wanted him, but until I could figure out what I was doing with Anthony, I knew that sleeping with him wouldn't have been fair. He wouldn't have been getting all of me, and as special a man as he was, he deserved to get just that. So I stopped with the heated tongue-of-war that we had going on, put an end to the walking that our fingers were doing, and explained why I couldn't give him my sweetness just yet. Jordan never complained. Instead, he moved behind me, slipped his arm around my waist, and held me until we fell asleep. We didn't even talk much. Just enjoyed each other's silence and the soft jazz he had playing from a shelf system in the room.

I didn't want to get out of the bed. Didn't want to move his arm from around me. Everything felt too right. But it was close to two in the morning, and I knew Anthony would be looking for me soon. Hell, I was surprised he didn't call my cell phone the way he normally did.

Shit. My cell phone.

That's when I remembered I'd turned it off before I got to Jordan's.

Damn.

Reluctantly, I moved Jordan's arm from around me. I was trying to do it slowly so that I wouldn't wake him, but that didn't work. He stirred. "Are you leaving?"

I sighed. "Yeah."

"I wish you could stay."

"So do I." I got out of the bed, smoothed my skirt and blouse, re-fastened my bra. Jordan stood and watched me as I neatened my hair in his dressing table mirror. "I had fun," he said, folding his arms across his chest.

I smiled. "So did I." I was sincere, but my mind was on my cell phone, which was in my purse downstairs. If Anthony called like he usually did when I went out, and didn't get me the first time, then he'd called fifty thousand times after that. If that was the case, I was in for a hell of a lot of voice mails and a headache when I got home.

I turned around. "I better get going."

Jordan nodded. "Okay."

He led me downstairs, grabbed my coat and purse, and handed them to me. I slid my coat on, zipped it up, and adjusted the collar. Did all of that in slow motion.

"Guess you couldn't say you spent the night at your girlfriend's house, huh?" Jordan asked with a handsome but sneaky smile.

I frowned. "I wish I could, but it's better to be safe, you know."

"Yeah. I understand."

I leaned toward him. "Thank you for a great time," I said, kissing his cheek. I kissed him there because had I done it on his lips, I don't think I would have been able to leave.

Jordan must have understood. He nodded. "Anytime." Then he opened the door, allowing the biting December wind to invade the warmth. I looked at him. He at me. We smiled, then I stepped outside and hustled to my car. I turned on the phone after turning on the ignition. Just as I thought, I had voice mail messages waiting for me. Ten to be exact. I didn't even listen to them. I just hit the gas and thought about how I wouldn't have to be coming up with any lies if Jordan were my man.

Erica

Silence.

That's what hovered in the air of my office. That's what escaped from my lips as I stared at Kenny, who didn't say a word either, but rather sat with a smug look on his face. I knew why he wasn't saying anything, and he knew I knew why. The move was mine to make. He'd made his. Made it successfully, too. If we were playing checkers, he jumped all of my pieces and claimed them, leaving me with one piece on the board. That's how successful his damn kiss had been.

Asshole.

I averted my gaze from him to the yellow notepad I had sitting on my desk, ready to scribble notes down about what other things Kenny wanted for his website. On my monitor, I had the skeleton site I'd done so far. Of course I knew that what was on my screen and the yellow pad I was staring at didn't mean anything. I glanced back up at Kenny. He was looking good in a navy blue sweater, a pair of black slacks, and black shoes. His leather coat was draped on the back of his chair. Leather gloves were in his hands. He was clean shaven, save for the goatee around his full, Malik Yoba-like lips. He appeared to be every bit the successful, fine author that he was. I exhaled the breath I'd been holding in.

I was tense. My shoulders. My neck. All over.

I inhaled and exhaled again. It was my move now. "Okay," I said. I paused. *My move,* I thought again. *Shit.* "Yes . . . I still love you." I hated admitting that, but had no choice. I'd already given the answer when I couldn't pull my lips away from his. I was just making it official now. Kenny smiled and stroked his goatee. His smugness worked my nerves. "Don't get too happy," I said quickly. "I still love my hamster, too, and he died when I was seven."

Kenny laughed and shook his head. "Erica, Erica," he said with a chuckle. "You're funny."

With a scowl, I said, "I don't remember telling any jokes."

Kenny laughed again, which really pissed me off. "Stop it," I said, forcing the tone in my voice to stay low. I didn't want any more attention than I'd already had. "This isn't funny." I was on the verge of tears again, which made me even angrier because that was the last thing I wanted to do in front of him. This, of course, made it even more difficult to keep my tears from falling. "This is a fucked-up situation, Kenny."

He stopped laughing and sighed. "It doesn't have to be, Erica."

"What do you mean it doesn't have to be?"

"I mean now that you've admitted your feelings, we can move on to the next step."

"The next step? And just what would that be?"

"Lunch. Dinner. Maybe both."

My turn to chuckle. "Lunch and dinner, huh? Now you're the one who's being funny."

"What's wrong with my suggestion?"

"A whole hell of a lot," I said.

"Erica, why are you making this so damned hard? We're still in love with each other."

"No . . . you're the one who's in love."

"You just said—"

"I just said I still love you," I snapped. "I didn't say anything about being in love."

"Come on, it's the same damn thing."

"No the hell it isn't. There's a big difference between the two. Loving a person means you care about them. That person is in your thoughts. Being in love means you not only care about that person, but you want to spend the rest of your life with them too. They mean the world to you. You would give anything to marry them, have children with them, and grow old with them. I used to be in love with you, Kenny. Used to. But my feelings changed the day the paternity test showed that you were a father. I had to let go of the false hopes and the lies I'd been telling myself when those results came. You were a father. I didn't have your baby, because you fucked someone else." I stopped talking and stared at Kenny intently. I needed him to believe my words. I needed him to believe that I wasn't in love with him. I needed him to believe my lies.

Kenny leaned forward and rested his elbows on his legs, rubbed his palms together, and stared down at the floor. I watched him and waited. I'd taken my turn on the checkerboard and jumped and claimed several of his pieces. At least I hoped so.

"You're not in love with me, huh?" he said, standing.

I folded my arms across my chest. "No . . . I'm not."

"I'm sorry I have to pull this card, Erica, but you're leaving me with no choice."

I looked at him skeptically. "Pull what card?"

Kenny gave me a you-asked-for-it look. "Do you swear on your grandmother's grave that you're not in love with me?"

Oh no he didn't!

"I don't have to answer that," I said, flustered.

"Why not? You said you weren't in love with me. I just want you to swear that on your grandmother's grave. What's the big deal?" Kenny gave me another smug look, folded his arms across his chest and waited for me to say something.

Asshole.

My grandmother. The woman who was just as responsible for me being the woman I am today as my mother was. Gram. That was the nickname I'd given way back when. My Gram. My heart. I tried to ask God to keep her around forever, but I guess He had other plans and took her away from me when I was sixteen. Losing her was hard on me. I locked myself in my room and cried for two weeks straight. Gram was special. One of a kind. She had a way of making you feel warm inside with her smile alone. And there wasn't a problem that Gram couldn't solve with some hot chocolate sprinkled with nutmeg, bits of marshmallows, and an ear waiting for you to unload on. Kenny truly pulled the trump card. I'd been swearing on her grave since she died. Did that when I was absolutely, positively telling the truth. Kenny knew that, and now he was waiting for my answer.

Goddamn him.

I was in a no-win situation. Don't answer the question and he'd know I was lying. Answer the question and he'd know I was lying. Catch fucking twenty-two. "Why did you come back?" I asked.

"That's not an answer," he said.

I let out a frustrated exhale. "Do you really need one?"

"Yes."

"Why?"

"Because I need to hear you say it."

"Why?"

"Why ask why?"

"Don't answer my question with a question. Why do you need to hear me say it?"

"Because."

"Because what?"

"Because I need to know that I still have a chance."

"I told you before you didn't have a chance in hell."

"That's not what your answer would say," Kenny said, eyeing me.

"I didn't give an answer," I said.

"I'm still waiting."

"Keep waiting then."

"On your grandmother's grave, Erica. Do you swear?"

"Keep waiting," I said again.

Kenny and I stared at each other, him waiting, me stalling. Damn it, this wasn't fair. I was supposed to hate him for what he did. I was supposed to detest the sight of him. This just wasn't fair.

Kenny cracked his knuckles. I always hated that habit. He must have read my thoughts because he cracked them again. "Erica," he started, his voice low.

"I told you to keep waiting," I cut in.

"Have dinner with me."

I snapped my head back slightly. "Excuse me?"

"Have dinner with me," he said again. "Tonight."

I took a deep breath and shook my head slowly.

"Please, Erica. Let's quit the back-and-forth banter. Have dinner with me tonight. We'll talk. Really talk. No holding back. No sugar-coating. We still love each other. We're still *in love* with each other."

I opened my mouth to protest, but then closed it and damned him for being right.

"Seven-thirty," Kenny said. "I'll pick you up. We'll go to Copeland's. What do you say?" He watched me with gentle eyes and waited for my answer. Dinner. With him.

God, I wanted to hate him.

I breathed out slowly. He'd made his final move and jumped my last piece on the checkerboard and claimed it. The game was over. I lost. I was still in love with him, and he knew it. "Okay," I said softly, "but I'll meet you there."

Kenny nodded. "Fair enough." He gathered his coat and slipped it on. Pulled his gloves over his fingers. "Don't stand me up, Erica," he said, moving to the door. "If you do, I'll be back here every day, appointment or no appointment, until we go out."

"That's not very businesslike," I said.

His hand on the door handle, Kenny replied, "I don't care about business. I never did. Don't stand me up."

"Seven-thirty," I said, rolling my eyes. "I'll be there."

Kenny gave me a long stare then opened the door and walked out. I watched him walk away, and when he disappeared, I sat down. Seven-thirty. Dinner. Damn. This website was never going to be completed.

Reesa

For the first time in three years, I was shopping for Christmas presents, and Simon wasn't on my list. I thought that not having him to shop for was going to bother me and somehow make me regret kicking him out, make me miss his company. Hell, any company. But it didn't. I was just fine. In fact, instead of feeling lonely or regretful for not having a man in my life, I felt free. Simon was no longer my headache to stress over or waste money on. Cecilia could do that shit if she wanted. The only thing I wouldn't get to do, which I was a little sad about, was buy Jabari a gift. I always looked forward to seeing the big smile on his face when I got him gifts that he wanted. Unfortunately, the close relationship I had with Jabari was lost. Hopefully he wouldn't forget about me.

Oh no. Not again.

I stopped walking and put one hand on my stomach, the other over my mouth, and didn't move as my stomach did flip-flops and a lump rose in the back of my throat. I was about to throw up again. Damn.

"Are you okay, miss?"

That was an older gentleman. He was standing to my right, holding a bag of Popeye's chicken. He had a worried look planted on his jovial face. I gagged as the scent from his fried chicken wafted into my nostrils. Without saying anything to him, I turned and sprinted toward the restrooms, which were thankfully in the same wing of the mall that I was in.

I bumped into someone on my way into the bathroom and knocked them down, but I didn't stop to see if they were all right. I just ran straight for an empty stall, bent over, and threw up into the toilet bowl. Oh my God, I felt awful. My stomach retched over and over again. Felt like I was going to throw up my insides.

"Reesa?"

I heard my name being called, but couldn't turn around to see who was calling me. I threw up some more of my breakfast. In between dry-heaves, I felt a hand on my back. "Girl, are you okay?"

I took a slow breath and placed the voice. It was Erica. I retched again, but didn't throw up anything. I stood straight when the churning in my stomach finally subsided. I wiped tears away from my eyes with the back of my hand and turned around. "I'm fine," I said. Erica stared at me with skeptical eyes. "I'm fine, really," I insisted. "I just need to wash out my mouth."

Erica nodded then stepped out of the stall. I flushed the toilet, went to the sink, turned on the faucet, doused my face, and gargled water. When I finished getting rid of the tart taste in my mouth, I wiped my face with a paper towel then said, "Damn, I need some gum."

"I got you, girlfriend."

Erica handed me a piece of Wrigley's spearmint Eclipse. I popped it into my mouth, chewed, then did like the commercial and breathed out as the vapors cooled and freshened my breath. "Thanks."

"No problem. Are you sure you're okay?"

I nodded. "Yeah."

"So what happened? Did you eat something that didn't agree with you?"

I shook my head. "No. I think I have a stomach virus."

"Really?"

"Yeah. For the past week, off and on, I've been dry-heaving. Today was the first time I actually brought anything up."

"Have you gone to the doctor to get checked out?"

"I've been meaning to, but I haven't had the time. I've been really busy with work. Doing a lot of overtime the past couple of weeks. A lot of stress right now."

"Well you better make time and go and get checked out. I don't want you running me over anymore." Erica smiled.

My mouth fell open. "Oh my God! That was you?"

Erica nodded. "I was about to go off until I realized it was you."

I grabbed Erica's hand. "Girl, I am so sorry. I didn't even see you."

"Please," Erica said with a smile. "I would have done the same damn thing."

"I feel so bad, though."

"Don't. Now, if you would have thrown up on me, we might have had to fight." Erica laughed and so did I. I really felt bad, but like she'd said, at least I made it to the toilet bowl.

"So anyway, are you feeling good enough to walk out of here? Now that the ordeal has passed, the smell in here is starting to get to me."

I nodded. "Yeah, I'm good. Let's get out of here." We headed out of the restroom and started walking.

"So what are you doing here?" Erica asked.

"Christmas shopping," I said, looking at a cute outfit that would be perfect for my nephew, displayed on a mannequin in the window of The Children's Place. "I got a late start this year."

"Please," Erica said, rolling her eyes. "I'm a habitual last-minute shopper. I probably won't start until the middle of the month."

"Oh, so you're not here to get presents?"

Erica frowned. "Unfortunately, no."

"Why the frown? Is this trip not a good one?"

Erica frowned again then sighed. "Not really. I'm here to buy an outfit for a dinner date tonight."

"Oh, I see. From the look on your face, it must be a business dinner."

"I wish," Erica said with a strained look. "I'm having dinner with my ex."

"Oh."

"Yeah. We've been apart for a little over two years. Dated for three. We ended on terrible terms. He cheated on me and got his ex pregnant."

"Well, all right then."

Erica raised her eyebrows and curled her lips.

"So how did you two end up with a dinner date?" I must have asked one too many questions, because Erica twisted her lips and rolled her eyes. "I'm sorry for prying," I said quickly.

"Oh, girl, you're not prying. It's just this whole situation is frustrating. Have you ever heard of *A Man and Happiness: Why He Can't Have It*?"

I nodded. "Yeah."

"Let me guess . . . you loved it, right?"

"Well, I had a hard time swallowing some of the things in it, but as a whole, the book was off the chain. Why?"

Erica exhaled. "My ex wrote it."

I stopped walking and looked at her. "Seriously?"

"Yeah."

"And should I assume you are the woman it's dedicated to?"

"Yup. That's me."

"Wow."

"Yeah, wow."

"Have you read it?"

Erica twisted her lips again. "Just half."

"Oh, so you don't know how it ends?"

"Nope. Don't really care either. I don't plan on reading any more of it."

I nodded and raised my eyebrows. "Umm, I think you should finish it. I think you'll find the end interesting."

Erica's turn to stop walking. She looked at me. "Oh, really? What happens?"

"Read it," I said.

Erica hmmed and started walking again. "Maybe."

"So anyway, how did you two end up hooking up again?"

Erica stopped walking again. "Do you think your stomach can take any food?" I took this as a sign to back off with my questions. Erica must have seen the look on my face. "Oh, I'll tell you all about how Kenny came back into my life. I'm just hungry. And honestly, I don't think I'll be doing too much eating tonight."

"I understand. Umm, I should be able to hold some food down."

"Okay. Let's head over to the food court. I'm in the mood for some chicken."

"Okay. I think I'm going to have Chinese."

We went to the food court and split up to get our meals. Since my line was shorter, I got something then luckily found a free table in the middle. I hustled to it before someone else could grab it and kept my eye out for Erica. The mall was packed with holiday shoppers out in full force, all searching for that perfectly expensive gift.

As I waited for Erica to join me, I took a cautious bite of my lunch. I was a little worried about my stomach turning again. I let out a sigh of relief when I tolerated the vegetable fried rice with ease. I was about to take my second bite when I saw Erica looking around for me. I stuck my hand up and called her name. She saw me and smiled. As she came toward me, I smiled and thought how it was funny that just a few days ago we couldn't stand each other.

She sat down. "I hate when the mall is this packed."

"It'll be like this until after the new year."

"Yeah, I know. That's why I shop late. I can only take the crowds but for so long."

I laughed. "I understand," I said, taking another couple of bites. I chewed then took a sip of my Diet Coke. "You got your food to go?" I asked, noticing Erica's closed bag as she prayed.

"Yeah. Just in case I can't eat. This dinner has me stressed."

"I can imagine."

Erica sighed then opened her bag. As the aroma of the chicken hit my nostrils, my stomach turned. "Oh shit." I leaned to the side and gagged.

"Again?" Erica said.

I couldn't answer. I just gagged again. Because I didn't have much in my stomach, I did more dry heaving than anything. After a few minutes, the queasiness subsided. I sat up and was about to speak when the Popeye's fried chicken aroma hit my nostrils again. "The chicken," I said, dry heaving again.

"Huh?" Erica asked.

In between heaves I managed to say again, "The chicken. Get rid of it."

"My chicken?"

I nodded and dry heaved again. "Please."

Erica got up, went to throw away her chicken, and came back. With the aroma gone, the queasiness subsided after a few more minutes. I hung my head low as I wiped my mouth with a napkin. I was completely embarrassed and could feel everyone's eyes on me. "Damn," I whispered. "I really need to go to the doctor and get this virus checked out."

"Are you okay?" Erica asked.

I finally worked up the nerve to look up. As I did, people tried to pretend they weren't watching. "I'm fine," I said. "I'm just embarrassed as hell. Damn, I don't know what happened. The aroma from the chicken just made my stomach turn. It's a good thing you didn't eat it. I think it was spoiled." Erica stared at me and didn't say anything. Stared so hard it made me uncomfortable. "What? Do I have throw-up on my face?" I wiped around my mouth and my cheeks frantically with a napkin.

Erica shook her head. With her eyes still on me, she said in a very low, very serious voice, "Reesa, my chicken wasn't spoiled and you don't have a stomach virus. You're pregnant."

Carmen

"No."

I shook my head.

"No."

I bit my nails.

"No."

Tears trickled slowly from my eyes.

"No."

I sat on the rim of my bathtub and stared at the E.P.T. pregnancy test I'd just taken. Stared at the two pink lines indicating a positive test result.

"No!"

I was pregnant. I shook my head. Said "No" again, then covered my face with my hands.

Pregnant.

"Oh God. Not now. *Por favor.*" I stared at the results again, somehow hoping that the result would only show one pink line. But it didn't. I was pregnant. Anthony was the father. Damn it.

I shed more tears and cursed out loud in both English and Spanish. This was the worst thing that could have happened. The worst. All day long I'd been praying. Praying that I'd been two weeks late with my period because I was stressed over work. Stressed over my decision to break up with Anthony to be with Jordan. Praying that by some miracle, I hadn't actually been late with my period; that somehow I'd slept through it, or that my body was just fed up with the cramping, the bloating, the bleeding, and had had enough of its monthly-on-time-seven-day-exactly visit and decided I didn't need to have it anymore. I looked at the results again through teary eyes. Goddamnit.

Pregnant.

With child.

Con un nino.

However you said it, it was still the same. Anthony's sperm had invaded my egg and that was that. But how?

And then I remembered one of the good nights I'd had with Anthony a few weeks back. He'd surprised me and picked me up from work and taken me out for drinks and dancing. We had a lot of fun that night. He didn't like salsa too much, but he took me to the Latin Palace where we danced and put a good amount of alcohol in our systems. After the club, we went home and had sex. Good sex. Sex with no condom. Sex with no diaphragm. And I don't take the pill.

Damn. I was pregnant.

"Carmen?"

Shit. I looked up. Anthony was home. I got up from the tub, went to the sink, turned on the faucet, and wet my face. I couldn't let him see the tears. I turned off the water, dried my face, and looked at myself in the mirror. Damn. My eyes were slightly swollen from crying. I smiled to see if that would make a difference in my appearance. It didn't.

"Carmen?" Anthony called out again.

He'd come knocking on the bathroom door soon. I let go of my smile and looked at the E.P.T. test. I had to hide it somewhere. But where? Not in the garbage; couldn't take the chance of him spotting it somehow. Obviously I couldn't put it in the medicine cabinet. And since I only had a towel wrapped around myself, I couldn't sneak it out. Damn.

"Carmen?" Anthony said, knocking on the door. He tried to open the door. Thank God I'd locked it.

"One sec," I said. "Just finishing up." I flushed the toilet. *Think, think.* Under the sink was my only option. I opened it and found a spot in the back and buried the test and the box there. Buried them under my pads. No reason for him to look there. I closed the cabinet and looked at myself in the mirror one last time. Eyes were still a little puffy, but I figured I could pass. I'd just say I had a rough day and was tired. I adjusted my towel, took a deep breath, let it out slowly to calm my nerves a bit, then opened the door. "Hey, baby," I said in a fake voice with a fake smile.

Anthony looked at me in my towel as though he suspected something. My heart beat heavily as he stared past me into the bathroom. Beat so hard that I was worried he'd see the movement. He settled his gaze back on me. Seconds of silence seemed to last for hours before he smiled, and said, "Hey, you." Then he kissed me on my lips. I didn't kiss him back, though. Just let go of the nervous breath I'd been holding when I opened the door.

"What are you doing home already?" I asked. "I thought you were going to the mall."

Anthony moved past me and stepped into the bathroom. "I went during my lunch break," he said, lowering his zipper. "How come you took a shower already?"

"I . . . was tired. Had a rough day. I just needed to relax a bit."

Anthony moaned as he pissed into the toilet bowl. "Oh, okay. Hey, what's for dinner?"

"Leftovers," I said, walking to the bedroom.

Anthony flushed the toilet and came into the room. "No leftovers," he said, removing his pants. "I took what was left to work and ate it before I hit the mall. You're gonna have to cook something."

With my back to him, I squeezed my eyes shut tightly. "You mind cooking tonight? I really just want to relax."

"Cook?" Anthony asked. "Come on, baby, you know that's not my thing."

"Anthony," I said, struggling to keep my voice normal, "just give me a break tonight, please. Cooking for one night's not gonna kill you." I removed my night clothes from under my pillow and put them on.

"Come on, Carmen. You know I don't do the cooking thing. Just whip something up real quick like you always do."

I exhaled. Damn him and his chauvinistic ass. "I'm not cooking tonight, Anthony," I said firmly.

"So what am I supposed to do then? I'm fucking hungry."

"Either cook or order something. You're not a fucking child."

"What's up with the attitude?"

"I had a rough day, Anthony, and I just want to relax. But I can't do that because you're acting like an ass."

"Hey, you're not the only one who had a rough day," Anthony said. "Damn, you know the routine."

"To hell with you and your routine," I snapped. "Either cook or order something." I climbed into bed and pulled the covers over my head. "Whatever you do, just leave me the hell alone." I squeezed my eyes shut tight again as tears threatened to fall. Anthony hadn't walked out of the room yet and I didn't want to let go of the tears until he did.

"You know it's real fucked up that I work all damn day and when I come home, instead of getting a hot meal, I get a fucking bitchy-ass attitude."

I slammed my hand on the mattress, threw the covers off me, and sat up. "Goddamnit, Anthony, why don't you leave if you don't like my bitchy-ass attitude? I'm your girlfriend, not your maid."

Anthony glared at me and clenched his jaws. "I don't know what the fuck's your problem, but you need to get a grip. I'm not in the mood to be stressed at home after being stressed at work."

"I told you I just wanted to relax. If you would just let me do that like I asked, neither one of us would be stressing right now."

Anthony threw his hands in the air. "Fine. I'm outta here." He went to the closet, pulled out a pair of blue jeans, and slid them on. "You'll get to relax all you want to now," he said, slipping on a black sweater.

I threw the covers back over my head. "Good."

"I'm going to my mother's. At least I know I'll get a hot meal there."

"Whatever."

Anthony mumbled something about shit being ridiculous then walked out of the room. Five minutes later I heard the front door slam shut. That's when I let my tears fall.

Goddamnit. I was pregnant.

I cried heavily until my head hurt. Then I fell asleep. Two hours later, I woke up and cried some more. Did that several times over the course of the night. Anthony never came home, which I was thankful for.

I cried. I slept. I cried and slept some more.

I also forgot to get up and get rid of the E.P.T. test.

Erica

"You look incredible."

I didn't say anything to Kenny. I just took my time to sitting to let him admire the form-fitting black slacks, which accentuated my hips and ass, and the black V-neck cashmere sweater I wore, which fit snug enough to accentuate my breasts. I had on a simple teardrop diamond necklace to set off the black. My hair was Kelised out, of course, but contained; my makeup was done just right: black eyeliner and maroon eye shadow, maroon lip-gloss to match, blush lightly brushed on. I wanted Kenny to see—really see—what he'd fooled around on. That's why I went to the mall to buy a new outfit. I figured since I'd agreed to the dinner, I should make sure to look my best. Of course my mall excursion hadn't exactly gone the way I'd planned. I felt bad for Reesa. Even though she denied being pregnant and swore that she'd just had her period, I knew she was lying. I could tell by the look of despair in her eyes. Her world had been flipped upside down.

My heart went out to her and her situation. She had some tough decisions to make: Tell Simon or don't tell him. Keep the baby or have an abortion. I didn't envy her. If she would have only gotten rid of Simon's ass from the start, she wouldn't be in the predicament she was in. I wanted to tell her that, but I didn't. No need to state what I knew she was already saying to herself over and over. But of course, according to her, she wasn't pregnant.

Once her queasiness subsided, she went with me to pick out my outfit. Before we parted ways, I promised to give her a call to check on her. She swore that she was fine, but I knew better. She was going to need a friend. A brutally honest friend who'd been through something similar. I'd make sure to give her a call the next day.

But until then . . .

I looked at Kenny. His hair and goatee freshly groomed, he was looking as stylish as ever in a pair of black slacks, a form-fitting black shirt, and a black blazer. He accentuated the black with a simple platinum necklace with a cross hanging from it, and a platinum bracelet. For a brief moment, my mind went back to the days when I used to get so hot for him. No other man had ever made me pool the way Kenny did so effortlessly.

I cleared my throat and slid into the booth. As I did, a waiter approached with a glass of wine for Kenny. "Hello. My name is Andrew. Will you be having a glass of wine also?" he asked, looking at me.

I looked at Kenny. "No thank you," I said to Andrew. "This water will be just fine."

"Are you sure you wouldn't like a glass?" Kenny asked.

I looked at him. Wine always loosened me up and made me horny. I knew that's why he wanted me to have some. "I'm sure," I said, sending a clear message.

We stared at each other for several silent seconds until Andrew, who must have sensed some tension, cleared his throat. "Are you ready to order appetizers?"

"Yes, we are," Kenny said. Without asking me what I wanted, he ordered the spinach-and-lobster dip, a favorite of mine.

When Andrew walked away, I said, "How do you know I wanted that?"

Kenny gave a smile that made my skin tingle. "Don't even try it," he said.

"Don't even try what? I just asked a simple question."

Kenny gave me a yeah-right smirk then picked up his glass of wine. "Do you remember the first time we ever shared a glass of wine?" he asked, taking a sip.

Touching the condensation on the outside of my glass of water, I said, "Yeah."

"That was a funny moment, wasn't it?" he asked with a chuckle.

I tried not to smile, but I couldn't help it. Already an infrequent drinker, wine had been the one alcoholic beverage that Kenny rarely touched. It was New Year's Eve when he made the suggestion that we open a bottle of red wine. We were at his place, cuddling in front of the fireplace with the TV muted. He was wearing a pair of silk boxers, I was wearing a silk chemise—gifts we'd bought each other for Christmas. Will Downing was crooning softly in the background. The plan was to cuddle then make love as midnight approached. We were going to share a toast after we shared our love, but forty-five minutes before the New Year came, we decided to open the bottle for an old year's sip.

Two.

That's how many glasses we each had.

Two.

A drop in the bucket for me, a sedative for him.

Twenty minutes after our second glass, I got up to use the bathroom. When I came back, Kenny was fast asleep. No, not just asleep. Passed out. Snoring. I couldn't believe it. I didn't even hesitate to wake him up. The wine had me horny, and I wanted some. Unfortunately, the wine had kicked his ass, and he fell back to sleep minutes later. Twenty minutes after the ball dropped, he woke up.

"How much time do we have left?"

"Time's up," I said, not in the best of moods.

"Shit. Did I really sleep through it?"

"Snoring and everything."

"Damn."

"Yeah, damn."

"Happy New Year," he said with a please-forgive-me smile.

"Too late," I replied.

Kenny put his hand on the inside of my thigh. "Can I make it up to you?"

"Don't know. Can you?"

Sliding his hand up toward the pool gathering between my legs, Kenny said, "I'm sure I can."

148

We may have missed the big apple dropping and the fireworks, but believe me, the fireworks and explosions we created more than made up for his momentary episode of narcolepsy.

I let out a slow breath as the memory went through my mind of the way Kenny had taken his time to satisfy all of me.

"What are you thinking about?" he asked.

I looked at him. I know he damn well knew what I was thinking about, but I wouldn't give him the answer he wanted. "Bills," I said.

He smiled, shook his head, and took another sip of wine.

"Better be careful," I said. "You don't want to pass out here."

Kenny laughed. "Don't worry. I'm schooled now. I'll be up all night."

"I'm happy for you," I said, sipping my water. "I'll be sleeping."

Kenny licked his lips. "Is that right?"

"Definitely."

We grew silent and watched each other again. Although I was doing my best to put up a defiant front, I was extremely nervous and uncomfortable. Because I had admitted that I still had feelings for him, I was left with my wall completely gone and vulnerable. A position I didn't like being in.

Breaking our silence, Andrew returned with our appetizers. "Do you need a few minutes before ordering your entrees?"

I looked at Kenny; he knew what I wanted. "She'll have the linguini with shrimp. I'll have the roasted chicken. And bring a whole bottle of wine."

Andrew smiled then walked off. When he was out of earshot, I said, "What if I wanted something different?"

"Then you would have said something."

I gave him a you-got-me-there look and played with the condensation on my glass again.

"So," Kenny said, dropping the volume in his voice a bit.

"So," I repeated.

Kenny intertwined his fingers on the table and sat back. He looked at me with intense eyes. Already uneasy, I tried to look away but couldn't. His gaze demanded that I give him attention, and I had no choice but to give it. I cleared my throat. Didn't say anything. Just cleared it because of the uneasiness.

"Do you know why I'm able to drink wine now?" Kenny asked. He waited for me to say something. I didn't. His eyes grew even more intense. "After I lost you, I tried to kill myself with alcohol. Every day, didn't matter the time or day, I drank. Beer, hard liquor, wine—everything. I'd drink before work, sip on a flask during work, and after work, I'd go home and drink until I woke up the next morning not remembering much of what had happened the night before. I got so good at being drunk that at one point I couldn't function or do my job properly without alcohol in my system. I was that way for five solid months. Drink, eat, and sleep; that was my routine. Sometimes I'd just skip the eating."

He paused as the waiter returned with the bottle of wine he'd requested, chilling in an ice bucket. "Your food should be ready soon," Andrew said.

Neither Kenny nor I responded. We just stared at each other. I don't even know when Andrew left.

"I wanted to forget about you," Kenny continued. "I wanted to forget the hurt in your voice when you said good-bye. I wanted to forget the pain in your eyes. That's why I drank the way I did. I figured if I could be drunk, or at least close to it, twenty-four hours a day, then my guilty conscience would leave me the hell alone. But that didn't happen. No matter how much liquid poison I threw down, the sight of you crying and walking away from me, the sound of your voice telling me not to talk to you ever again and to stay the hell away from you, went everywhere with me: work, the store, my dreams. Everywhere. I couldn't escape it. I couldn't escape you. And that only made me drink more."

He stopped talking again and took a sip of his wine. I still didn't say anything. Just sat quietly and watched him. I could see a lot of pain in his eyes, and for a second I actually found myself feeling sorry for him. But then I remembered that I was the victim, and the feeling went away. I opened my mouth to go off. Wanted to tell him to spare me the story of his "pain," but he spoke before I could say anything.

"One night I had a dream. I was at home drunk out of my mind, my body and breath reeking. Suddenly there was a knock on the door. Somehow, I managed to get up from the couch I was slouching on and stumbled over to the door. It took me three tries to get my hand on the knob. Anyway, I finally opened the door to see you standing on the other side. You were beautiful. Your hair was done, makeup tight. You had on this banging dress that clung to your body. Beautiful." He paused and cracked a slight smile. Obviously his mind was still on that image.

"Is there a point to this?" I asked. I did that to break him from his trance.

He cleared his throat, took another sip of wine, and nodded. "You were there to forgive me and take me back. You were there to talk about the letter I'd never sent. You were going to tell me how much it touched your heart. How it made you think. Made you realize that despite your pain and my wrongdoings, our love was worth working on and worth keeping. You were going to say all of these things until I opened that door. Everything changed after that. The sight of me repulsed you. The scent coming from me made you gag. You backed away into the wall and stared at me with the most foul look, like I was the most disgusting thing you'd ever laid eyes on. How could you have ever thought of being with a man like me? That's what you wondered. How could you have ever thought that coming back to me would be a good thing? I tried to talk to you, but you turned and ran away from me. Ran fast. I screamed out your name, but you never turned back. I woke up screaming your name.

"I stopped trying to kill myself with alcohol after that. The dream really got to me, and I figured that if by some miracle you did come back, it'd be better for you to see me sober and with my shit in order. Of course you never did come back." Kenny took another sip of wine. "Doing all of that drinking really brought my tolerance level up."

I gave an oh-please look and said, "I'm so happy for you."

Kenny let out a breath. "Erica, can you please just drop the act? It's tired."

151

"Excuse me?" I said, snapping my head back in shock. "Drop the act?"

"Yes. All this attitude you're giving me. It's unnecessary. I know how you feel about me. You know how you feel about me."

"So what? I'm supposed to jump up on your horse and go riding off into the sunset with you? Drop my act? Nigga, let me help you understand something. I love you, yes. I'm still in love with you, yes. But by no means am I letting you back into my life any more than you already are."

"Erica—"

"This is my time, Kenny. You had yours, so shut up and let me speak. You must really think I'm a fool. Either that or you are definitely living in a fantasy world to think that you can win my heart back so damn easily. Do you have any idea what you put me through emotionally? I may not have written a fucking book, but I went through the wringers too. I gave everything to you. Everything. My body and soul were completely yours. You could have come home one day and told me that you took a job offer in Kingdom Come, and I would have gone in the room and started packing. No worries, no complaints. Where you went, I went. What you wanted, I wanted. I'd never loved any man as hard as I loved you. I'd never given my all. You had me, Kenny. You had me, and you abused me physically and mentally."

"Erica, I never laid a hand on you in any kind of disrespectful way."

"Oh yes, you did. You abused me physically every goddamned time you touched me, kissed me, put your dick in me. Every time. Because while you did that to me, you were doing the same shit to your ex."

Kenny looked around. He was obviously a little self-conscious because of the rising volume in my voice. He breathed out. "Erica, I know what I did was wrong, but I still never physically harmed you."

"Nigga, you didn't bother to use a fucking condom! Who knows who that bitch could have been sleeping with besides you? Did that ever even cross your mind? Abuse. Physical abuse. You had no regard about giving me some disease or possibly sending me to my deathbed."

NEVER SAY NEVER

Kenny dropped his head. "Erica, I'm sorry. Believe me, I regret ever hurting you. If you read the book, you'll see—"

"I told you I don't give a fuck about that book. So you wrote it. So the fuck what? I'm supposed to feel sorry for your ass now? You repented and admitted that you fucked up on paper, and I'm supposed to give you another chance?"

In a low voice, Kenny had the balls to say, "Yes."

"Oh please." I grabbed my purse and coat and stood. "It doesn't work that way, Kenny. You don't shatter a woman's heart, write a tell-all book then get the woman back. This isn't some fucking movie."

I was about to walk away when Kenny reached across the table and grabbed me by my wrist. "Erica, please. Don't leave. You're still in love with me, and I need you."

I looked down at his hand then back up at him. "The only thing you need is to let go of my damn wrist before I yell out rape."

"Please, Erica," Kenny said, his grip loosening.

I snatched my wrist away. "Go to hell, Kenny. I may still be in love with you, but guess what; I still hate your ass." I grabbed my glass of water, threw it in his face, and turned to walk away. Andrew was just arriving with our food as I did. "You may want to give him a doggie bag," I said. "And give him a bone while you're at it."

I left the restaurant. Walked right past all of the diners who'd stopped eating, drinking, laughing, and talking to watch my show, and stepped out into the cold. I was so heated I didn't even zip up my coat. I just stormed to my car, got in, turned the key, and burned rubber out of the parking lot. I was pissed. Not because Kenny had left me with bad memories or broken my heart. And not because he'd gotten his ex pregnant. I was pissed because his ploy was working; he just might get me back.

Ain't that a bitch?

I turned on my radio.

I needed to hear Kelis.

Needed to scream.

I never got to, though, because "Un-Break My Heart" by Toni Braxton was playing on the radio. I didn't want to, but I

153

turned up the volume and sang the chorus with Toni.

"Un-cry these tears I cried so many nights. Un-break my heart. My heart."

My heart.

Goddamnit, he still had it.

I lowered the volume and picked up my cell phone. Tears poured from my eyes as I dialed a number I hadn't called in so long. I never knew I still had it memorized until my fingers started pressing the buttons.

"Erica?" he answered.

"You never changed your number."

"No."

"Why not?"

"If I had changed the number, you never would have had a way to contact me."

"I was never going to try," I said.

"I know. But I still had hope."

"I see."

"Listen, Erica, I'm—"

"Come over."

"Huh?"

"I assume you know where I live. Come over. But give me thirty minutes."

"Erica, I—"

"Good-bye, Kenny." I hung up the phone, raised the volume, and cursed Toni all the way home.

Reesa

This wasn't fair. Why me? Why now?

I stared at the pregnancy test that I should have taken two weeks ago when I realized that my ever-reliable period was five days late. I stared at it and cursed God and myself. I wanted to deny the results the same way I'd denied it when Erica said that I was pregnant. I wanted to deny the results the way I'd been denying that I was pregnant. But I couldn't. My predicament was real, and I couldn't live in denial anymore.

I covered my face with my hands and let my tears fall. My body shook from the hard crying I was doing. In the midst of my sobbing, I laughed. This was a cruel, sick, twisted joke. A little over a month ago, as wrong as it would have been, the news of pregnancy would have made me happy because I would have satisfied my goal: babies or at least a baby before my thirty-fifth birthday. Good man or not, that was what I wanted. Now this was the worst thing that could possibly be happening to me. *Why now?* I thought again, my tears flowing harder. Why now when I'd finally figured out what it was to be happy without settling?

I shook my head and lay down on my bed, bringing my knees to my chest. Damn it. What the hell was I supposed to do now? My head hurt from the painful reality of my situation; it hurt from the confusion. My biological clock was ticking, and I did want to have a baby. But not this way. The desperate and scared woman I was before—the woman who didn't care whether she had a good man at her side or not—wouldn't have cared about having a baby under these circumstances. The cut-off age was thirty-five, and that was what mattered. But that woman no longer existed. A strong and brave woman had replaced her, and she couldn't imagine having a child under these circumstances.

I laugh-cried again and slammed my hand down on the mattress. I wanted a baby, but at the same time I didn't. I squeezed my eyes shut tightly as the pressure behind them increased. "Why me?" I whispered. "Why am I being punished like this?" I opened my eyes to allow the flood of tears to fall.

Punished. This was a punishment. Had to be, right? But weren't children supposed to be blessings? Wasn't childbirth the greatest gift God could bestow on a woman? Wasn't I wrong for thinking that I was being punished? That this was the worst thing in the world?

I was blessed. Not punished.

Right?

It was an honor to bring life into this world.

Right?

I dropped my chin to my chest. Why were my answers to those questions all no's?

Carmen

"You're three weeks pregnant."

My shoulders dropped as Donna, the OB-GYN I'd been going to since I was fifteen, confirmed what I already knew. Even though the E.P.T. test is pretty accurate, I still had hopes that its results could have been wrong, so I made an appointment with Donna the next day. The hope was gone now. I was definitely pregnant. Three weeks at that.

"Are you sure?" I asked anyway.

Donna nodded. "Very sure."

My shoulders dropped a little more.

"I get the feeling that this isn't the news you were hoping for."

I sighed. "No. I knew you were going to say that."

Donna came from behind her cherry desk, sat in the chair beside me, and took my hand. "What's wrong, Carmen? Why aren't you happy about this?"

The tears I'd been trying to hold back fell from my eyes. "The timing's just all wrong," I said.

Donna handed me a tissue from her desk. "Why? You and Anthony have been together for a while now, and you both have good jobs. It would seem to me like the timing couldn't be any better."

I wiped the tears away with the tissue and took a deep, calming breath. "It could be a lot better," I said, wishing I'd ended things with Anthony before the shit hit the fan. "Everything could be better."

Giving my hand a slight but gentle squeeze, Donna asked, "Are you and Anthony having problems?"

157

"You could say that."

"Does he know yet?"

"No. I haven't said anything to him."

Donna put her hand to my cheek and pulled my face easily so that my eyes could meet hers. She gave me a look that reminded me of my mother. "This is his baby, isn't it?"

I nodded. "Yes."

Donna let out a sigh of relief. "When are you planning on telling him? You are planning on telling him, right? Or are you thinking about possibly having an abortion?"

A wave of hard tears fell with her last question. "I don't know," I said. And then I cried harder. I was just torn up inside and didn't know what to do. I wanted to be with Jordan, but I knew that was going to be impossible as long as I had Anthony's baby inside of me. Wasn't it? Damn it, what was the right thing to do? Have an abortion and leave Anthony to be with Jordan? Tell Anthony, keep the baby, and end my relationship with Jordan to continue with Anthony? Or keep the baby, end things with Anthony, and hope that Jordan would be willing to be with me despite having a baby that wasn't his? I covered my face with my hands. I never imagined that I would be in this position.

Donna wrapped her arms around me and let me lay my head against her shoulder. "Don't make any rash decisions, okay?" she said softly. "Just go home and think about what you want to do. Think about what the best thing for you to do would be. You have time. This isn't a decision that you have to make right away. Okay?"

I sniffed and lifted my head. "Okay," I said, wiping my eyes with a fresh tissue. "I'm sorry for breaking down like this. This is just not the best time right now."

"Carmen, I've known you since you were fifteen. My shoulder is yours whenever you need it. You know that."

I smiled weakly. "Thank you."

"No need to thank me. But I do want you to try not to cry anymore, okay? I know it's hard, but try not to be so down about this. The timing may be bad, but you never know, this could be a blessing in disguise."

I nodded and stood. "I'll try."

"Call me anytime, Carmen. And remember—don't make any rash decisions that you'll regret later on."

"I won't." I gathered my purse, blotted my eyes again, and left Donna's office. Before driving home, I let more tears fall. I wanted to believe that my being pregnant could be a blessing, but it was hard to. Like I'd told Donna, the timing was just all wrong.

I started the car and was about to pull off when my cell phone rang. I pulled it out from my purse and looked to see who was calling. It was Anthony, and he was calling me from home and not his job. Damn. If he was calling my cell phone that meant he'd tried calling me at work first. I never told him that I was taking the day off. I thought about not answering the call, but decided against it. If I didn't answer, that would just make him suspicious, and that, of course, would just increase my stress level. "Hello?"

"Baby," Anthony said in a much too cheery voice.

"Hey, Anthony," I said, trying to match his joviality with my own. "What are you doing home?"

"The system crashed, and it's gonna take our IT department all day to fix the problem, so they let us all go a little while ago."

"Oh," I said, trying to keep him from hearing the deflation in my voice. I really just wanted to go and lay down. With Anthony there, I knew that was going to be impossible. "So you've been home for a while?"

"Yeah. I stopped by your job to see you, but they told me that you called off today. How come you didn't tell me you were taking the day off? Are you feeling okay?"

"I didn't plan to take the day off. I just wasn't feeling too well this morning, and I decided to stay home and lay down. It was a last-minute decision."

"So why are you out now?"

I rolled my eyes. "I felt a little better and decided to run out to the mall to get something."

"Oh yeah? What?"

"A sweater. But it was sold out. Why are you asking me so many questions? You don't trust me or something?"

Anthony laughed, which surprised me. "No, no. I trust you, baby."

"Why are you laughing?"

"I'm just a happy man."

"Happy? Why?"

"You coming home soon?"

"Yeah," I said reluctantly. I don't know why, but I didn't have a good feeling about his unusually happy mood.

"Good, good. I have something I want to talk to you about."

"What?"

"Just get home and we'll talk."

"I'm tired, Anthony. I just want to lie down when I get home."

"You will, baby. After we talk. I promise."

"So tell me what you want to talk about," I said, agitated now.

"When you get home."

"Fine. Whatever."

"Don't get all worked up, Carmen. It's not good for you to do that."

"Huh?"

"Are you hungry? I'm cooking just in case you are, so don't stop for anything to eat. The food should be done by the time you get home."

"Uh . . . okay," I said. Now I really didn't have a good feeling.

"Well, I have to stir the pot. Get home safely, baby."

"Uh . . . okay."

"You have your seat belt on, right?"

"Uh . . . yeah."

"Good. Well, I'll see you soon. Love you. Bye."

I was too stunned and too worried to respond. Thankfully I didn't have to, because Anthony hung up without giving me a chance.

Did I have my seat belt on?

Was I hungry?

He never asked me things like that. I pulled out of my parking spot, my stomach doing flips.

When I got home, I couldn't speak because my bottom lip was too busy hovering just inches from the floor. The place had been cleaned—vacuumed, dusted, magazine stacks on the coffee table in the living room neatened, furniture rearranged, cushions fluffed, glass wiped, air freshener sprayed and tickling my nostrils along with the scent from food coming from the kitchen. Cleaned. I swear it was like being in a different house. I put my purse down.

"You're home!"

Anthony came over to me, threw his arms around me, and kissed me on my lips. I was so shocked I couldn't even kiss him back. I just stood frozen and a little scared by the display of affection with which he was showering me. When he pulled back, he looked me up and down and smiled.

"What?" I asked. He was really freaking me out.

"Nothing. I'm glad you're home."

"You are?"

"Yeah. Really glad."

"Okay. So what did you want to talk about?" I'd been thinking about it the whole way home.

Anthony smiled. "Give me ten minutes."

"Ten minutes?"

"Yeah."

"Why?"

Anthony flashed a smile again. "Just give me ten minutes. I need to check on the food." He gave me another kiss, which I didn't reciprocate, and hurried off. I didn't know what to make of the spring in his step or the delight in his voice. Ten minutes? What was he up to?

I went to the bedroom and flopped down on the bed. Anthony's good mood was the last thing I felt like dealing with. I put my hand on my stomach and sighed. Life was inside of me; growing and developing with each passing second. I was going to be a mommy.

If I kept it.

My bottom lip quivered, and tears welled in my eyes. *If* I kept the baby. The tears were about to fall when Anthony suddenly appeared in the room.

"Hey, you," he said, coming on the bed beside me. "How are you feeling?"

"Fine. Just tired."

"Same here," he said, stretching. "I cleaned the whole place in like an hour and a half."

"Yeah, I see. It looks good," I said with a weak smile. "What brought that on?"

"Nothing. Just wanted to give my baby a much-deserved and much-needed break."

"Oh, well, thank you."

"No problem. It wasn't that tough. Well, maybe just the bathroom."

"The bathroom? What was so . . . " And then I paused.

The bathroom. He cleaned the bathroom.

I looked at him. "Did you say you cleaned the bathroom?"

Anthony flashed a huge Kool-Aid smile that made my heart pound. "Yeah. I got rid of a lot of garbage from under the sink."

Shit.

I couldn't speak, couldn't move. He'd been under the sink.

I looked at him. Studied his eyes for the answer running through my mind. Stared at his smile and the gleam of his pearly whites. My eyes opened wider as his smile broadened.

No, no, no!

He knew. Goddamnit, he knew.

"Excuse me for a moment," I finally said. I got up and went to the bathroom as quickly but calmly as I could. I shut and locked the door behind me, turned the faucet on full blast, said a short prayer in front of the mirror, then opened the cabinet under the sink. Did all of that in one move. I had to pause for a second; under the sink was certainly nice and neat. My hands trembled as I made a mess of things to get to the back to my hiding spot. "Please let it be there. Please let it be there," I whispered over and over.

I finally spotted my pads. They were still there. In the same spot. Good. "Please let it be there." I moved the pads, my breath short, my heart pounding African drum rhythms. "No," I whispered as all of the breath sighed out of me. "No!" I fumbled around, searching, praying, pleading for the E.P.T. test that I'd forgotten to get rid of. But I found nothing. I was pregnant. Going to be a mommy, Anthony a daddy. And he knew it.

I closed the cabinet, not even bothering to fix the mess I'd made. I got up and frowned at myself in the mirror. This wasn't fair.

"Carmen?" Anthony said, knocking on the door.

"Coming." I flushed the toilet then wet my hands and face. I closed my eyes and forced myself not to cry. Damn it, this wasn't fair. I went to the door and put my hand on the knob. God, I didn't want to go out there, but I had to. I had no damn choice. I opened the door. Anthony was standing, waiting for me, holding the E.P.T.

"When I came home, I went to use the bathroom. My stomach was bugging me. I think it was from the cup of coffee I had this morning. Anyway, I was reaching to turn on the faucet to wash my hands when my arm accidentally hit a pair of your earrings that were sitting to the side of the sink. I tried to grab them before they fell in, but I only managed to grab one. And just as luck would have it, the stopper wasn't there and the other one fell down the drain. It's the pair that your mother bought you a couple of years ago from Puerto Rico—the ones with the emeralds. Anyway, knowing how much you love them, and knowing that you could only get them in Puerto Rico, I couldn't let you only have half a pair, so I went and got my tools and went under the sink to unscrew the pipe to get your earring back. That's when I found it. Why'd you hide it?"

Anthony watched me with intense eyes. The smile he'd been wearing since I'd come home was gone as he waited for my answer. I stared at him for a long, hard second then looked at the pregnancy test and cursed myself for forgetting to throw it away. I wanted to yell out so bad, but I couldn't. Why did I hide it? He wanted to know. Why did I hide it?

I opened my mouth, not knowing what the hell I was going to say. "I-I-I wanted to surprise you." *Surprise him?*

Anthony flashed a huge grin. "I knew it!" he yelled out, startling me. "You were gonna tell me on Christmas, weren't you?"

I nodded and said weakly, "Yeah."

"I knew it," he said again. "I told her that's what you were going to do. I told her you weren't hiding it with any bad intentions."

"Told her?" I said. "Told who?"

Still cheesing from ear to ear, Anthony said, "My mom."

"Your mother! And what do you mean by bad intentions?"

"She was just tripping, talking about you hiding the test because you were never gonna tell me that you were pregnant and that you were gonna have an abortion."

"What?"

"Don't worry. I put her in check. I knew you wouldn't do some shit like that. Damn. I'm gonna be a dad!"

"I can't believe you went and told her," I said angrily. I gave him the most screw-faced look and stormed past him and went to the bed.

Anthony came behind me, wrapped his arms around my waist, and kissed me on the back of my neck. "Awww, don't be mad, Carmen. I didn't mean to spoil your surprise. I was just so excited and happy when I found the test that I had to talk to someone about it. Who better than my mom?" Anthony kissed me again. "I'm gonna be a dad," he said again, squeezing me.

"Ouch!" I said. "Let go of me." I removed his hands from around me and moved a couple of steps away from him.

"I'm sorry, baby. I'm just so happy."

With my back to him, I rolled my eyes and shook my head. Damn it, as if being pregnant wasn't bad enough, now I had to deal with his bitch of a mother. "You shouldn't have said anything, Anthony."

"I told you I was just happy. Damn, Carmen, what the fuck is up with your attitude? Aren't you happy with my reaction?"

I sighed. This was just so fucking unfair. "Yes," I said. "I'm happy. I-I'm just pissed that you told your mother. You know how we feel about each other."

"I wasn't thinking, Carmen. Don't crucify me for being a happy man. Shit, maybe this baby will be just the thing to bring you two together."

"I don't think so," I said.

"You never know."

"No, I do know," I said, turning around and looking at him. "Your mother's a racist bitch, and I can't stand her ass. And you damn well know she can't stand me. Baby or no baby, nothing's going to bring us closer together."

"We'll see at Christmas."

"At Christmas?"

"My mother invited us for Christmas dinner. She said she'll believe that you were really gonna tell me about the baby when you talk about it in front of everyone."

"What? You know we always do Christmas dinner at my parents'! Besides, I'm not setting one foot in that woman's house anymore. I told you that after the bullshit on Thanksgiving."

"Come on, Carmen. That was over two weeks ago."

"I don't care if it was two years ago, Anthony. I'm not going!"

"My whole damn family's gonna be there."

"And so is mine."

"So we'll go over there in the morning."

"Anthony—"

"Carmen, I'm fucking happy! This is gonna be my mom's first grandchild. Your parents already have one from your brother. Don't be so fucking selfish about this. I know you and my mother are always at each other's throats but I'm telling you, things are gonna be different after you announce our baby."

I stared daggers at Anthony as he watched me. Shit. Could my life get any more complicated? I wanted to protest some more about how there was no way in hell I was going over to his mother's house again, but I didn't. I could tell from the determined look in his eyes that Anthony wouldn't give up. He would continue to harass me until I gave in, went crazy, or killed him—whichever came first.

Anthony came closer, took my hand in his, and smiled. "Please?" he begged.

I opened my mouth to protest.

"Please?" he begged again.

I closed my mouth and watched him looking at me with puppy dog eyes. I sighed.

I wasn't a killer.

I was already well on my way toward crazy.

"Fine," I said. "I'll go."

Anthony smiled and swallowed me up in his arms. "Thanks, baby. Believe me, you won't regret this. Things will be cool after Christmas. I guarantee it." I was about to say "whatever," but instead kept quiet, struggled to fight off my tears, and wondered why all of this had to happen. Anthony gave me another kiss then stepped back. "Shit. I almost forgot I have the stove on. Why don't you go ahead and change? I'll have everything served by the time you're done."

"I'm really tired," I said. "And I'm not really in the mood to eat. The pregnancy, you know."

Anthony nodded and smiled. "Right, right. I got you."

"I'm sorry," I said, trying to sound as genuine as I possibly could. "Maybe in a little while I'll feel up to eating. I just really want to lie down right now."

"No problem, baby. I understand. I'll go and turn off the stove and let the food sit. You mind if I eat?"

"No, you go ahead." I was relieved that he'd been so understanding.

"All right." He took my hands in his. "You've made me a happy man, Carmen," he said, his voice as sweet-sounding and sincere as I'd ever heard it.

I struggled to put on a smile. "I'm glad."

Anthony kissed my forehead then hugged me again. "I gotta call my boys and tell 'em I'm gonna be a dad." He flashed his pearly whites again then walked off. When he was out of the room, I removed my jeans and sweater, slipped into a pair of sweats and the T-shirt I usually wore at night, and climbed under the covers. Why did this have to happen? I wondered again as tears spilled from my eyes to my pillow. Why?

I fell asleep asking myself that and one other question: How was I going to tell Jordan?

Erica

I was on Kenny.

Riding him. Shifting my hips. Allowing him to go deeper inside of me. I was in the moment. Moaning. Grimacing with pleasure from the way he filled my insides.

My hands were roaming. Running through my hair. Down my neck. Over my breasts, pausing to squeeze my nipples then moving from me to Kenny's back. Then his shoulders. The back of his head. Pulling him. Guiding him to my breasts. I arched my back as he drove deeper inside of me and enjoyed the fullness of my C cups with his mouth; savored the feel and growth of my nipples.

I was lost. Out of control. Dripping. On my way toward an orgasm that would make me gasp, buck, scream, curse, call out God's name, call out Kenny's. An orgasm that would make me cry and yearn for his dick all over again.

Ring.

I opened my eyes. I was in my bed, my legs sprawled, my fingers dancing inside of me as my mind took me back to the intense sex Kenny and I had. The door had barely even slammed shut before our hands were all over each other. We didn't speak as we removed clothing and made our way to my bed. We didn't speak as our bodies molded to become one. We didn't speak after eruptions were created. Kenny wanted to talk, but I didn't. Eventually he got the hint from the silence I was giving him as I lay with my back to him, and he stopped trying and just spooned with me, his nakedness against mine. We didn't speak when, an hour later, I reached for him, stroked his manhood to life and took him from behind.

We didn't speak.

We just fucked.

Well, I fucked. Kenny made love. I could tell by the way he moved. The way he caressed. The way he kissed. He was gentle—strong, forceful, hungry, but gentle.

Okay, okay, I'm lying.

I made love too. That's why I didn't speak. Not just because I was so lost in the sex, but also because it had been hitting me hard that after what he'd done to me, and after all the anger I held inside, I was actually making love to him.

Ring.

I removed my hand, closed my legs, and reached for the phone with my dry hand. I looked at the caller ID and thought about not answering, but before my thoughts could go too far, I pressed the talk button and put the phone to my ear. "What?"

"Damn, Erica. Hello to you too."

I let out a breath. "What do you want, Kenny?"

"I want to talk. I miss you."

"Yeah well, I don't want to talk, and I don't miss you," I said pointedly.

"What?"

"You heard me."

"Come on, Erica. I can't believe you're going to act like this after what happened the other night."

"What happened was nothing," I said, thinking about the something it really was. "We fucked. End of story."

"Fucked?" Kenny said, sounding as though I'd truly hurt his feelings. "That's what you called what we did? Fucking?"

"Nothing more."

"That's bullshit, and you know it. We did a hell of a lot more than just fuck. Why can't you just admit that what happened was special?"

"I can't admit what I don't believe," I said defiantly.

Kenny laughed. "You're a real trip, you know that?"

I rolled my eyes. "Is there a reason for your call?" I needed to get off the phone because I had no idea how much longer I was going to be able to keep up my charade.

"Erica—" Kenny said.

"Erica what?"

"Just admit that the sex meant something. That it wasn't just fucking."

"I told you—"

"Do I have to pull the Gram card again?" he asked, cutting me off.

I closed my eyes and shook my head. Goddamnit. Goddamn him. I slammed my hand down on the mattress. "Fuck you, Kenny," I said then hung up the phone. It rang seconds later. I knew he would be calling back. I should have thrown the phone, but instead I hit the talk button. "What do you want from me, Kenny?" I asked softly.

"I want all of you, Erica."

"I gave you all before."

"And I fucked it up. I'm human, and that means I'm going to make mistakes. That's what we humans do. But with every mistake that's made, there's a lesson to be learned, and whether you believe me or not, I've learned my lesson. I fucked up, but I want a second chance at us."

"Kenny—"

"Erica, a few days ago we made love that was as intense and as real as it gets. Why do you insist on fighting this so hard?"

"Because I can!" I yelled out loud. "I can make this as hard as I fucking want to because your ass was the one fucking around! Not me. Shit. Yes, yes, yes, I am in love with you still. And yes, we made love. Good love. The kind of love that has me sitting here with my fingers inside of me, pretending to be your dick. Damn good love, Kenny. But one night of great sex doesn't erase the past. One night of great sex doesn't mean that my arms are open wide and waiting for you. This is real life, not a fucking movie. You don't just sex me good and make all my walls tumble down. You have to chisel away at it piece by fucking piece before you can get to grab hold of my heart again. And just so you know, your chisel better be made out of steel, because my walls damn sure are!"

I paused and wiped away a few tears, which had been falling, with the back of my hand. The outburst had taken a toll on me emotionally, so much so that I actually felt a little exposed and vulnerable. I should have never answered the damn phone. More tears fell, and even though Kenny couldn't see them, I quickly wiped them away as though he were standing in front of me, watching me.

"You really messed things up for me," I said, fighting the rising lump in my throat. "I was doing so well until you came back into my life."

"I wish I could say I'm sorry, Erica, but I can't, because I'm not. I'm so determined to have us back together for good that if it takes steel to break down your walls, you may as well call me Superman. Because I'm here and I'm not going away. I love you too much."

"Kenny, we're . . . we're . . ."

"We're what? Meant to be?"

"Yes . . . no . . . Damn it, I don't know."

"Yes, you do, Erica. You do know."

Unable to keep up with my tears, I lay on my side and sobbed openly, no longer caring that he knew. He was right. I did know. We were meant to be together. I knew that before and after he broke my heart.

"I love you, Erica," Kenny said softly. "I love you, and as hard as this may be for you, I won't leave you alone until you give us a second chance."

Silence claimed the conversation as Kenny stopped talking. I didn't say anything. I just lay on my side and cried. There was so much sincerity in his voice, so much determination. He wasn't going to give up. He wasn't going to leave me alone, because he loved me. I don't care who the woman is; any woman that's been hurt by a man she truly loved has fantasized about that man crawling back to her on his hands and knees, bearing gifts, ready and willing to do whatever it takes to make things right again. Every heartbroken woman has thought about and yearned for that Jerry McGuire, "You complete me" moment to happen.

I put the phone down, got up, and went to the bathroom. I used it, washed my face and hands then paused to stare at myself in the mirror for a few seconds. When I was done, I went to the kitchen and poured myself a glass of wine. I took a few sips before going back to the bedroom. I stood beside my bed and looked down at the phone.

Call him Superman.

I bent down and slid my hand underneath the mattress, removing the picture of Kenny and me that I had ripped up. I'd thrown the pieces into the garbage can in my room, not realizing that the can was empty at the time. The day after Kenny and I made love, I went to the garbage, retrieved all of the pieces and taped the picture back together. I had truly intended to throw that picture away, but after that night, I couldn't.

I looked at the picture. Looked at myself standing beside him. Looked at the sparkle in my eyes. Although they were a little swollen and red from crying, I'd seen a hint of the same sparkle in the bathroom mirror a few minutes ago.

Call him Superman.

I slid the picture back under the mattress then grabbed the phone. "Still there?"

"Told you I wasn't going anywhere."

I smiled. "I don't know what's going to happen, but whatever happens, it won't happen overnight."

"However long it takes."

My smile widened. "Come over."

"I'm on my way."

Reesa

"Shay, I don't know what to do."

I'd just finished telling her about my dilemma and my inner turmoil. God, forgive me, but I didn't know what to do about the baby inside of me. Shay put her hand on mine. Her gentle contact unleashed the flood of tears from my eyes. I lay my head against her shoulder. Damn it, I didn't want to cry. I'd been doing so much of that.

Shay wrapped her arm around my shoulders and gently stroked my hair. "Don't worry," she said softly. "We'll work this out."

"Why? Why did this have to happen to me now?"

"I don't know."

"It's just not fair. I was just beginning to enjoy my life. Really enjoy it. No more Simon. No more settling. No more cut-off age. I was just living to enjoy life to the fullest. Why did I have to become pregnant now?"

"I don't know," Shay said again. "I guess it was just your time."

I lifted my head. "What if I don't want it to be my time?"

Shay shrugged. "Then I guess you have a decision to make."

I broke down after she said that, the weight and seriousness of her words just too much for me to bear. My head back on her shoulder, I cried until I couldn't cry anymore. "I need a tissue," I said finally. Shay excused herself and returned with a box of Kleenex. I grabbed one and blew my nose. "I'm sorry," I said. "I didn't mean to unload on you like this."

"Apology not accepted, girl," Shay said with a smile. "My shoulder is yours whenever you need it."

"Thanks," I said, truly appreciating her friendship.

"I have to admit you floored me. When you called me and said that you needed to talk, I figured you were going to tell me that you and Simon were back together. You being pregnant was the last thing I thought you'd say."

"Believe me, it's the last thing I ever thought I'd say too. I was really so damn happy with my life. I was doing things, meeting new people."

"Sleeping with Ahmad's best friend," Shay said.

I looked at her. "You know about that?"

Shay pressed her lips together. "Mmm-hmm. He told Ahmad all about you two. And of course you know Ahmad told me."

I shook my head. "I can't believe he told."

"I told you he was a dog."

"What all did he say?"

"We know about the fruit, girl," she said suggestively.

I blushed. "You mad?"

Shay shook her head. "You're grown, and I'm not your mother."

I smiled and raised my eyebrows. Knowing how she felt about Mike, I was glad she wasn't upset.

"You did make sure he wore a condom, right?"

I nodded. "Of course."

"Good."

"I can't believe he told."

"Dogs always kiss and tell. They do that to stroke their egos. Besides, I think he took pleasure in sleeping with one of my girls just to spite me."

My smile dropped as I suddenly felt really bad. "Damn, I'm sorry," I said, feeling as though I'd betrayed her somehow.

"Like I said, you're grown. Anyway, enough about Mike and his hoeing ass. Girl, this is a real bind you're in."

I frowned. "I know."

"I hate to say I told you so, but I told you to get rid of Simon before he brought more drama to you."

"I know."

Shay shook her head disapprovingly, which made my frown drop even lower.

"I really don't know what to do, Shay. I wanted a baby so badly before, but in these past couple of weeks, I've really changed. My mind-set is different. I don't know if I'm willing to give up my carefree life just yet and assume the responsibilities of motherhood." Shay shrugged but didn't respond. "But at the same time, I don't know if I can go through with having an abortion. What the hell am I supposed to do?" My eyes welled with tears again, but I didn't want to let them fall. I blotted my eyes quickly with a tissue.

"I really don't know what the best advice to give you is," Shay said. "I mean, as a mother, I can only say that having a child is one of the greatest joys you'll ever experience in life. Not a day goes by when I don't look at Nicole and just think how blessed I am to have been chosen to give birth to her. I couldn't imagine my life without her. I live to see her happy. Being a mother is everything to me. But . . . " Shay paused and sighed, and looked at me with very serious eyes. "I had Nicole when I was ready. I'd had enough of the carefree, childless life. I was ready to begin a new phase. My clock was ticking, and I listened and made the decision to have a baby. I know that I wouldn't have made that decision if I wasn't ready."

"So you're saying I should have an abortion?" I asked.

"No. I'm saying you need to really think about what you want in your life right now. Do you want responsibility that will never end? And believe me, it won't. Or do you want to go on having fun and meeting new people, and enjoying life as a single, unattached woman? Which is more important to you right now? That's what you have to decide."

I wiped the corners of my eyes again and breathed out slowly. I looked away from Shay to the beige-colored carpeting. Responsibility that never ended: Was I ready for that? A little over a month ago I would have probably said yes, thinking that I was. But now . . . Now, could I go through with having an abortion? Wouldn't that be a selfish thing to do? I put my hand on my flat stomach. "I don't know. Damn it, I just don't know. I do want to be a mother, but . . . but . . . this is just so hard. God, I'm going to go to hell for this, aren't I?"

"No, you're not going to hell, girl."

"Yes, I am," I insisted.

"If you are, then a whole lot of people are going with you," Shay countered.

I sighed. "Am I wrong for considering an abortion as one of my options?"

Shay shook her head. "No, you're not wrong. You have to do what you have to do for you. No one else. Having a baby is a life-changing event for only you. No one else is going to raise your child. No one else's life will be affected as dramatically. If you aren't ready for the change, then how could having an abortion be the wrong thing for you?"

"But to have an abortion means I could be preventing a future Martin, Malcolm, or Oprah from changing the world. I could be getting rid of the next President of the United States."

"True. But you could also be preventing the horrible actions of a rapist, drug lord, or serial killer."

"Rapist and drug lord—maybe. But we don't do the serial killing thing," I said.

"I thought that too," Shay said with a sneer. "Until those damn Washington snipers."

"Oh yeah. I forgot about those fools."

"Hey, I've got someone even worse than them that you could be protecting the world from."

"Who?"

"The next G.W. Bush."

I couldn't help it. I laughed after that one. Shay laughed too. Minutes later, after we wiped happy tears away from our eyes, we grew silent. "This is the toughest decision I've ever had to make," I said despondently.

Shay put her arm around me. "I'm here for you."

"Thanks."

"Two questions for you."

"What?"

"One: Would you ever consider giving the baby up for adoption?"

I didn't even have to think about my answer. I shook my head vigorously. "No way. I could never do that."

"Okay. Just thought I'd ask. Question number two: If you decide that you want this baby, are you going to tell Simon?"

The answer to this question I had to think about. It was actually one that I'd been asking myself. If I kept the baby, telling Simon would mean that he would become a permanent part of my life. For good or bad, we'd be joined at the hip. That was not something I wanted. But if I kept the baby . . . "Yes," I said finally. "As much as I'd hate to have him know, he would have a right to know."

"Okay. That's a good answer. Now you're definitely not going to hell."

"Don't be so sure," I said. "I haven't made up my mind yet."

"When your time comes, you'll be walking through the pearly gates."

"We'll see. Anyway, I've taken up enough of your time with my drama. I'm going to head home."

"You sure? We can talk for as long as you want."

"Thanks, but I've shed enough tears. Besides, I need to get home and clean up. I've been wallowing in my pity so much lately, my place looks like a hurricane blew through it."

"Okay. Well, I'm a phone call away if you need me."

"Thanks." I stood and gave Shay an appreciative hug. I still had a heavy weight sitting on my shoulders, but I felt a little better. I paused at the door and gave Shay another hug then headed home. I'd only been there for ten minutes before my stomach turned and I had to sprint to my bathroom, just making it to the toilet bowl to throw up. I didn't even get up from the floor when I was done. I just flushed the toilet and cried. My mind was made up. Right or wrong, I wasn't ready for the change.

Erica

"You're what?" *Oh Lord,* I thought, *not her too.* "Carmen, are you serious?"

Carmen frowned. "I wish I wasn't."

"Oh, girl." I ordered another Cosmopolitan for myself and another ginger ale for Carmen, which I now understood why she was drinking. "How many weeks?"

"A little over three."

"Damn."

"Don't say anything to the girls when they get here, okay? You're the only one who knows."

I sighed. "Okay. Have you spoken to Reesa lately?"

"No. Why?"

"No reason. Just wondered." I sipped my drink. Obviously Reesa hadn't told anyone about her situation either. Of course she didn't exactly tell me. I just knew the signs. "So anyway, when did you find out?"

"About a week ago. I was late with my period and decided to take a home pregnancy test. I confirmed the test results with my OB-GYN last week."

"Damn. Did you tell Anthony yet? Or is it not his?" She'd told me that she hadn't yet taken it to the next level with Jordan, but still—you never know.

"It's Anthony's," Carmen said, sighing. "And as far as telling him . . . " Carmen paused and groaned. "I never had a chance to."

"Huh?"

"Anthony never comes straight home after work. He always goes to the gym or stops at his mother's or runs some errand.

Something. Anyway I took the test right after I got home from work, figuring that I'd be alone for a little while. Just my luck, Anthony decided he wasn't going to the gym or anywhere else that day, and he came straight home. I was in the bathroom, stressing over the positive results when he called out my name. Not knowing what the hell I was going to do, I hid the test beneath my pads underneath the sink, just knowing that Anthony would have no reason to look there. Especially since they're all the way in the back."

Carmen paused to sip some of her ginger ale.

"Anyway, I hid it there with the intention of throwing it away later on, but I was so down about my situation and what I was going to do that I just forgot all about it."

She paused again, took another sip of her soda, then let out a breath.

"You see these earrings?" she asked, tugging on them.

"Yeah."

"They're the reason Anthony knows I'm pregnant."

I looked at her curiously. "Huh?"

Carmen inhaled and exhaled. "My mother got these for me from Puerto Rico. They're my favorite pair and can only be bought in Puerto Rico. Most of the time, these are the earrings I wear because they go with everything. But every now and then I'll switch it up and wear a different pair. Last week I decided to do that." Carmen paused to drink some of her ginger ale again. I was tempted to ask her where she was going with the earring story, but kept my mouth shut and decided to be patient.

"Normally when I take off my earrings, I'll put them in my jewelry box. But with everything going on and me not being in the right frame of mind, I took them off and left them by the sink. Well, of course last week, the system at Anthony's job just had to crash so bad that they let everyone go home early. This just happened to be the same day I took off from work and went to confirm my test results at my OB-GYN. Anyway, to make a long, frustrating story short, Anthony went home, went to the bathroom, and accidentally knocked one of the earrings into the sink, sending it down the drain. And because he knew they were my favorite pair, my wonderful boyfriend got his tools and went under the sink to disconnect the pipe to get it back."

Carmen paused, said a curse word in Spanish, and looked at me. My mouth was hanging partly open as I whispered, "Damn."

"But wait, it gets better," Carmen said.

"Really?"

"Really. I was just leaving the gynecologist's office when Anthony called me all lovey dovey, wanting to know when I was coming home, if I was hungry, and if I had my seat belt on."

"Oh no," I said.

Carmen groaned. "Erica, the house was spotless and he'd cooked. That's how happy his ass was."

I tried not to, but I had to laugh a little. "So what did he say?"

Carmen rolled her eyes. "He didn't say anything until after I went into the bathroom and saw that the test was gone. That's when he broke his discovery down for me. After he was done, he asked me how come I didn't tell him about the test."

Chuckling now, which was the wrong thing to do, I said, "What did you say?"

"The only thing I could say. That I wanted to surprise him."

It was so, so wrong, but my chuckling turned into all-out laughter. "And his response?"

"Girl, the idiot jumped up and down like he'd won the lottery, yelling about how he knew that was why I had the test there, and how his mother was wrong about me hiding it because I wasn't going to tell him."

I stopped laughing. "His mother?"

With a dissatisfied look on her face, Carmen said, "Yes."

"He didn't."

"He did."

"Damn."

"Yeah, damn. And it gets even better."

"Hold on a moment," I said, putting my hand up. "Let me take a sip." Her predicament was so terribly funny that I didn't want to spit any of the drink out while laughing. I took a couple of sips of my Cosmopolitan and shook my head. "Okay. So how much better does this get?"

Carmen twisted her lips. "We're going over to his mother's for dinner tomorrow so that I can announce my pregnancy in front of everyone, so his mother can truly believe that I wasn't planning on keeping the pregnancy a secret, which of course I was." Carmen slammed her palm down on the bar counter. "Isn't that just the most wonderful story?"

I raised my eyebrows. "Damn, girl. That's terrible."

"*Terrible*'s not the word. This is the worst thing that could have happened to me. I had finally worked up the nerve to leave Anthony so that I could be with Jordan, and now this happened."

"I'm really sorry, Carmen," I said.

"So am I."

"What are you going to do about Jordan?"

Carmen shut her eyes tightly and took a deep breath then let it out heavily. When she opened her eyes, they were glazed with moisture. "I've done nothing but agonize over that question since this all happened, trying to figure out a way out of this situation. I truly feel like Jordan's the one for me. He makes me feel so special and so necessary. I'm the most beautiful woman in the world when I'm with him. I'm also the happiest. Before Anthony found that test, I was seriously considering having an abortion. I know it may not have been the most righteous decision, but I was thinking about it. It was either that or have the child, drop Anthony, and pray that Jordan would still want me."

I nodded. "True. But that would be a big risk. You know how men can be when it comes to being with a woman who has a child that's not his."

"I know. But Jordan isn't like most men, and I know he truly cares about me. I think I would have been willing to take the chance. But, Erica, Anthony is so damned happy that he's going to be a father. He's been telling everyone the news. Even strangers."

"Really?" I said, shocked. "I honestly wouldn't have expected him to be that way."

"I didn't either," Carmen said softly.

We got quiet for a few minutes as the activity in Clyde's Bar and Grill increased as more people came in to celebrate for Christmas Eve. "So," I said after a while. "You and Jordan?"

Carmen sighed. "Jordan and I are going to have to end. There's no way I could be with him now. Not after the way Anthony's reacted. I couldn't do that to him."

"So you'd rather end things with a man who makes you happy and be with a man who stresses you out?"

"I really don't have a choice, Erica."

"Yes, you do."

"No. I really don't. Anthony hasn't always been the best, but he's not the worst. Who knows? Maybe having this baby will really change him. I mean, he's already changed."

I looked at her with skeptical eyes. "I don't know, girl. This change could just be a temporary thing."

"Or it could be a permanent one. I've lasted this long with him. Shouldn't I give him and us a chance?"

I shrugged. "After the things you just said about the way Jordan makes you feel, do you really want to give you and Anthony a chance?"

Carmen frowned. "I think I have to."

"Why?"

"Because . . . because it's the right thing to do. I am carrying his baby."

"So?"

"So . . . I don't want a baby daddy."

"So you'd rather settle with a man who you can't stand?"

"I never said that I couldn't stand him. Those are your thoughts."

I smiled. "Oops."

"Anyway," Carmen said. "If Anthony's change is for good, I really couldn't say that I'd be settling. Not if he becomes a better man."

"Better than Jordan?" I asked, staring at her.

Carmen shrugged but didn't say anything and looked down at her glass.

"Ladies!"

Carmen and I turned around. Shay and Reesa had just arrived.

"Hey sistah-girls," Carmen said, the frown gone from her face and now replaced by a beaming smile. She gave me a look that said not to say anything as she got up from her barstool.

I gave her a reassuring nod then stood. "It's about time y'all got here," I said.

"Hey, blame Reesa, not me," Shay said.

I looked at Reesa. This was the first time we were seeing each other since the mall. "Hey, girl."

"Hey yourself," she replied.

We hugged then pulled away. My eyes on hers, I said, "How's the stomach virus?"

Reesa looked at me then looked down. "Uh . . . getting better," she said. "Excuse me, ladies. I need to go to the bathroom." She turned and walked away. When she was gone, Shay was staring at me.

You know, don't you? That's what she said with her eyes.

Yes, I do, my eyes answered.

"Reesa's sick?" Carmen asked.

"Yeah," I said, looking at Shay. "She's not feeling that great. Right, Shay?"

Shay nodded. "Right indeed."

"Aww," Carmen said. "Right before Christmas too. I hope she feels better soon."

I raised my eyebrows. "I'm sure she'll be okay," I said.

Shay smiled at me. "If she's not, we'll be there to help her."

"Yes, we will," I replied.

Shay and I exchanged knowing glances before I turned away and looked at Carmen. I had to give it to her. Knowing how down she was about her situation, she was putting on a hell of a front. "Why don't we order some more drinks?" I suggested.

"Good idea," Shay said.

"How about some wine?" I said.

"Another good idea," Shay answered.

"Order another ginger ale for me," Carmen said. "My stomach's not feeling right either."

"I'll order one for Reesa too." I looked at Shay. "We better be careful. A bug must be going around."

Shay's eyes widened a bit.

I said, *Yup,* with my eyes then got the bartender's attention and ordered two glasses of wine and two glasses of ginger ale for our Christmas Eve celebration.

Carmen

"Will you marry me, Carmen Maria Jimenez?"

You know how in the *Matrix* movies when everything moves in slow motion and you can see bullets flying through the air, raindrops falling, sweat dripping, eyelashes blinking, etc?

Well, while my bottom lip fell to the floor and I stared down at Anthony, who was kneeling in front of me, holding open a tiny black box with a marquise diamond gleaming from inside of it, everything—and I do mean everything—was moving in ultra-slow motion around me. People's mouths as they opened in shock. Anthony's eyes as they blinked while he waited for me to answer. His mother's face as it contorted into a twisted mask of absolute disgust.

He proposed to me.

I couldn't believe it.

Didn't want to believe it.

He proposed.

I was dreaming. Having the worst nightmare that I'd have ever had. Had to be dreaming. Please let it be a dream.

"Carmen?" Anthony said, snapping me out of my *Matrix* moment.

I blinked. "Huh?"

"Will you marry me?" Anthony flashed a nervous smile and looked from side to side without moving his head.

I blinked again and looked from him to the ring, then back to him. "Anthony . . ." I started out slowly.

"Don't marry her ass!" his mother said. "She's not good enough for you. And I don't care if she said anything, she didn't really want to tell anyone about that baby."

183

I turned my head and glared at Anthony's mother. *Bitch.* Making the announcement of the baby in front of her and the rest of his family had been agonizing and extremely hard to do because I knew that once the words escaped from my lips, there would be no turning back. I tried to back out of having to do it by pretending that my stomach was upset from the pregnancy, but Anthony begged me to make the announcement.

"Just do it then we can leave, baby. Please? I just want to get my mother off my back. I'm tired of her insisting that you weren't going to tell me. Please. Just tell everyone then we can go home and I'll take care of you."

That's what he said. Over and over and over. I didn't want to give in, didn't want to make any announcement, but Anthony wouldn't give up. I finally did it at the dinner table, right before the food was served.

"Before we all eat, I would just like to say that contrary to the opinions of some people here—" I said that with my eyes on his mother—"I am indeed pregnant with Anthony's child and I am very . . . very . . . happy about the new addition to our lives."

Everyone at the table congratulated Anthony and me, as they were all ecstatic over the news.

Everyone but one person.

Anthony's mother stared at me with deadly, hate-filled eyes. "I hope you don't plan on giving my grandchild some Mexican-sounding name," she said.

Silence shrouded the festive mood after her ignorant-ass comment.

"Mom," Anthony started.

Whether I wanted the festive moment or not, how dare she disrespect it like that? I cut Anthony off. "First of all," I said with an edge sharp enough to cut steel, "I'm Puerto Rican, not Mexican, so get it right. And as far as my child's name goes . . . a Latin name is one that he or she will have, so you better brush up on your pronunciation."

Anthony's mother twisted her lips into a snarl. "Well, he or she will be half black, so I think he should have a black name."

"I don't care what you think," I snapped, my skin getting hot with anger.

Anthony's mother rose from her seat. "I hope you don't plan on disrespecting me like that in front of my grandchild."

I stood also. "I'll show you the same respect you show me."

Anthony's mother scowled then looked at Anthony. "You better make sure my grandchild knows he's black."

"Come on, Mom!" Anthony said.

"Half black," I said. "And believe me, he'll know it."

"Mmm-hmm."

"Ladies!" Anthony yelled out while the rest of the family members watched in entertained silence. "It's Christmas, and this is supposed to be a special moment. Do you have to do this now?"

"Stop bringing Shakira's disrespectful ass to my home, and there won't be any problems."

"Oh, hell no!" I yelled. "Did she just call me Shakira?" Enough was enough. I was too through with her shit. I was about to go into overdrive with a Spanish arsenal of every curse word under the sun when Anthony pulled the rug from underneath all of us.

"Marry me!" he yelled out.

My mouth opened to begin my verbal assault. I paused and looked at him. "What?"

Sliding from his seat and crouching down on one knee, he presented a small black jewelry box.

Oh God, no.

He opened the box, revealing the diamond. And as everyone oohed and ahhed, he proposed. Damn it, he really proposed.

You all know the rest from there.

Anthony's mother and I cut our eyes at each other. *Bitch,* I thought again. And I know she thought the same about me.

"Mom, please," Anthony said. "This is my woman. Respect her and let her speak." My mouth dropped a bit; I'd never heard Anthony talk to her like that.

His mother sucked her teeth, cut her eyes at her son, and folded her arms tightly across her chest. She did all of that and didn't say a word. I gave her a smirk then looked back to Anthony who was still on his knee, still holding the ring, still waiting for my answer.

Would I marry him?

He waited.

I debated.

Thought all about the conversation I'd had with Erica the night before. Thought about the things I'd said about Jordan and the way he made me feel. Then I thought about my rationalization about Anthony. He wasn't the best man all the time. Truth be told, he could be a real ass a lot of the time. He wasn't the most sensitive; he wasn't the most passionate.

But he was my baby's father.

And now he wanted to be my husband.

I looked at him. Looked at his eyes. I could see genuine love in them, just like I had seen over and over in Jordan's. Erica said I didn't have to stay with Anthony. But could I leave him now?

I directed my gaze to Anthony's racist bitch of a mother. She would be my mother-in-law. She stared at me with poison in her eyes. The suspense was killing her. She would be my mother-in-law. I would hate that.

But she would hate it more.

I apologized to Jordan in my mind then looked at Anthony.

"Yes . . . I'll marry you."

Erica

"You what?" I pulled the phone away from my ear and stared at it for a quick second, then put it back to my ear. "You did not say yes. Tell me you're joking."

Carmen let out a long breath. "I'm not joking," she said.

"Carmen!" I yelled. I couldn't believe it. "How could you do that?"

"What do you mean how could I do that? I had no choice. He asked me in front of everybody."

"So?"

"So? What was I supposed to do, say no?"

"Yes."

"Erica, we talked about this the other night. I'm having his baby. How could I say no to his proposal?"

"You could say no because you don't love him," I said, my palm pressing on my forehead.

"Ye, I do," Carmen insisted.

"Not as much as you do Jordan," I countered.

Carmen didn't say anything for a couple of seconds. No matter what she said, she knew I was right. Finally she sighed. "Look, Erica, I know you don't agree with my choice, but I feel like I made the best decision I could. Anthony is the father of my child. Not Jordan. Anthony is the man I've been with for more than three years. Not Jordan. Like it or not, Anthony, not Jordan, is the man I should be marrying."

"The words sound good coming out of your mouth, Carmen, but I know you don't believe them." Whether she would admit it or not, I was speaking nothing but the truth.

"Yes, I do," Carmen said.

187

"No, you don't. I don't care what you say. I know you don't really believe you should be with Anthony and not with Jordan. I saw your eyes the other night. I saw the truth in them. I love you, but I have to be honest. You're really making a mistake by not following your heart."

Carmen exhaled, and in a more subdued voice said, "I'm just trying to do the right thing, Erica."

"I feel you, girl. I really do. But like I said, I saw the truth in your eyes. Marrying Anthony—"

"Marrying Anthony is what I'm going to do."

Both Carmen and I grew silent after her declaration. Even though her tone was strong, I could hear the doubt in her voice. She understood where I was coming from. I was sure of it. "Carmen, drop the act and tell me why you're doing this. This isn't what you want."

"Erica . . . I-I'm just trying to do what's right, okay?"

I shook my head. "But Carmen—"

"Erica please," Carmen pleaded, cutting me off. "I've gotten enough of this from my mom. Please give it a rest. Look . . . you're right, okay? I do believe that I should be with Jordan. I do think he is the man for me, but no matter what I feel for him, it's not his baby I'm carrying. Believe me, saying yes to Anthony wasn't the easiest thing to do because doing that meant that whatever I had with Jordan would have to end. And that was hard for me to accept. But I had to. I had to accept that my future is with Anthony and the baby I'm carrying. Do you understand where I'm coming from?"

I held the phone loosely against my ear and bowed my head and frowned. "Yeah, I understand," I said.

"Good. Because I need your support, girl. I need for you to be happy for me."

"I may not agree or like it, but you have my support. And I am happy for you."

"Thank you."

"Tell me something . . . did you tell Jordan anything at all?"

Carmen sighed. "No," she said softly.

"Carmen," I dragged in a disappointed tone.

"I know," Carmen said.

"Girl, the man cares about you. You can't do him like that. You need to talk to him before he falls any deeper."

Carmen exhaled heavily again. "I know, Erica. And I'm going to. I just don't know how to tell him."

"You just have to be as straightforward as you can. That's the only way."

Carmen groaned. "I wish I didn't have to say anything at all."

"So when are you going to talk to him?"

"I don't know. Soon."

"Soon like when?"

"I don't know."

"What about tonight?" I know I was pushing her, but she needed it.

"I can't tonight. Anthony wants to go out and shop for things for the baby. Then he wants us to sit and start picking baby names."

"Damn. Already?"

"Yeah. I told you he was ecstatic. Of course his mother's not happy."

"Don't worry about that bitch," I said. "She doesn't have to be happy."

"You should have seen her face when I said yes to Anthony. I thought she was either going to have a heart attack or run and grab a steak knife and come after me—or both." Carmen laughed.

I smiled. It was funny, but I couldn't help but wonder. "Carmen, you didn't say yes to Anthony just to spite his mother, did you?"

Carmen didn't answer right away, which was leading me to think that she had. Finally, she said, "I won't lie to you, Erica, saying yes and watching his mother's reaction was very satisfying for me. I truly can't stand her ignorant, racist ass, and in a way, accepting her son's proposal was the ultimate payback for all of her comments, her attitude, and her disrespect. I couldn't have gotten under her skin any better. So saying yes was kind of like me having the last laugh on her, but it wasn't the main reason I accepted."

"Are you sure?" I asked skeptically.

"I'm sure. Even though it feels good to get to her in this way, ultimately, this isn't about her. It's about doing what's right."

"All right. Just thought I'd ask. Anyway, you need to talk to Jordan as soon as you can, girl. If you plan on moving on with Anthony, then you really need to close that door right away."

"I will," Carmen replied.

"Please do. I've never met the man, but I really feel bad for him."

"It wasn't my intent to do something like this to him," Carmen said, her voice sounding as though she was crying.

"I know it wasn't," I said sympathetically.

"Getting pregnant was the last thing I wanted to happen."

"That's the way it is, girl. Shit always happens when you don't want it to."

"It's not fair."

"Life isn't fair."

"I don't want Jordan to hate me."

"He won't."

"How can you be so sure?"

"I'm not," I said honestly. "I just have a feeling that he won't hate you. I think he'll understand somehow."

"I don't want to hurt him."

I sighed. "I think that's unavoidable."

Carmen groaned again. "Yeah, I know."

"I'm here for you, Carmen."

"Thanks. You want to be there when I talk to Jordan?"

"No thanks," I said. "You got that one."

"I thought you said you'd be there for me."

"I will be, girl. In spirit." We laughed, which was a good thing, because the conversation was really depressing. "Well, let me hop off this phone, girl. I have some things I need to take care of."

"Okay."

"Call me after you talk to Jordan, okay?"

"I will."

"You better."

"I will. I promise."

"Okay. Oh, and make sure you talk to him in person. Don't do some high school over-the-phone breakup."

Carmen chuckled. "I would never do that."

"Just checking. I'll talk to you later, girl."

"Okay. Bye."

I hung up the phone and sighed. It was amazing how in just a couple of months all of our lives had been so completely upended. Reesa was suddenly single and pregnant. Carmen was pregnant, engaged, and in love with another man. As for me . . . well as for me, I was in love again and confused as to whether that was a good or bad thing. I wanted it to be a good thing. I really did. I was just scared. By allowing Kenny back into my life, there was the potential for him to hurt me again. Of course that all depended on how deeply I let him back in.

Something I could control, right?

My phone rang suddenly. I looked at the caller ID and tried not to smile. I was unsuccessful, though. I hit talk and put the phone to my ear. "Hello?"

"Hey, beautiful."

I blushed. "Hey yourself."

"Were you busy?"

"No. I just got off the phone with Carmen."

"You guys have plans?"

"No."

"Did you tell her about us?"

"She knows you're around, but that's it. There's nothing more for me to really tell her since *us* is not an official thing."

"Yet," Kenny said.

"We have a lot of talking to do before that can happen. *If* it happens."

"I know."

"How's Tyson?" I hadn't seen Kenny over the Christmas holiday because he had to fly to California for business. He also went to visit his son, Tyson, who lived in Pasadena with his mother. Spending Christmas with Tyson was a promise he'd made before anything happened between us.

"Tyson's fine. I spent some good quality time with him. Took him to the amusement park and—"

"Spare me the details, Kenny. *Fine* was good enough." Tyson's existence was one barrier that was up between us, one that I wasn't sure could be knocked down. His ex's existence was the next barrier. And that barrier was like the Berlin Wall—it was going to take years before that fell.

"Sorry about that."

"Whatever. Like I said, we have some talking to do."

Silence fell between us for a second or two before Kenny spoke again. "I have your Christmas gift. Is now a good time to come over?"

I smiled again. "Now's fine."

"Okay. I'll be over in an hour."

"Okay."

"Erica."

"Yes?"

"I missed you."

I bit down gently on my bottom lip. I wouldn't admit it, but I missed him too. "I'll see you when you get here, Kenny." I hung up the phone before what I felt could slip out.

An hour later, after scrubbing all of my necessary areas and throwing on a pair of sweats and a T-shirt, I was opening the door for Kenny. At first I was going to put on something semi-sexy for his pleasure, but as I was scurrying about, looking for something to put on, I caught a glimpse of myself in the mirror.

What are you doing?

That's what my reflection asked me.

You're going to put on something sexy for him? Have you forgotten what he put you through? Don't you remember all those nights you spent crying over his ass?

"I remember," I said.

So then what are you doing? Okay, so you're still in love with him. And yes, what he does to your body is unexplainable and unmatchable. But, Erica, the fool went behind your back for four damn months. And now he has a son that he just saw, which means that he just saw that bitch's ass too. If he slept with her when you two were "official," don't you think the chances of him sleeping with her now would be greater?

"I-I never thought of that."

You mean you didn't want to think about it. Erica, you spent too much time building your wall brick by brick for it to be broken down so easily. He has a son, and that means that no matter what you do with him, his ex will always be in the picture. And as long as she's in the picture, your heart is in danger of being broken again, and I know you don't want to deal with that shit again.

"No. I damn sure don't!"

That's when I threw on my sweats and T-shirt. I'd almost let my guard down, but luckily for me, my subconscious mind's words had gotten through. I wasn't going to be anybody's fool ever again.

"Hey, sexy," Kenny said. He leaned toward me to give me a kiss, but instead of my lips, I gave him my cheek. Kenny looked at me curiously. "Something wrong?" he asked, stepping inside.

"No," I said, closing the door. "Everything's just fine again."

Kenny slipped out of his coat. "Again? What do you mean by that?"

I shook my head. "Nothing."

Kenny gave me another curious look then stepped to me and tried to take my hands in his. I wouldn't let him, though, and stepped back.

"Erica," he said, watching me, "what's wrong? Why are you acting like this?"

"Like what?" I asked, folding my arms defiantly across my chest.

"Why are you giving me the attitude?"

"This isn't attitude," I said.

"Well, whatever it is, what's up with it? You weren't acting like this over the phone a little while ago."

"That's because I didn't have a chance to think."

"Think about what?"

I cut my eyes at him as the words from my subconscious whispered in my ear. *Pig. Four months and we were official then.*

"Did you sleep with her?"

"What?" Kenny asked, his face a mask of absolute confusion.

"Did you sleep with that bitch?"

"What bitch?"

"Your ex."

"My ex?"

"When you saw your son, did you sleep with her again?"

"Huh?"

"Don't 'huh' me. Did you or didn't you sleep with her ass? It's a simple damn question."

"No, it's a ridiculous one that doesn't need to be answered," Kenny said.

"So then you did sleep with her?"

"I never said that."

"Your non-answer said enough."

"Erica, why are you tripping out like this? I thought we were going to exchange gifts and spend some time together. I missed you. This is not the homecoming I had in mind."

"Yeah well, this isn't your home," I said bitterly. The more I looked at him, the angrier I found myself becoming. He called my question ridiculous, and he never gave me an answer. "Get out," I said.

Kenny's eyes widened as he stood frozen. "What?"

"You heard me. Get out."

"But I just got here."

"And now you can leave."

"You're kidding, right?"

I gave him a hard glare then stormed past him to the door and opened it. "Do I look like I'm kidding?" I asked, showing him the way.

"But . . . but what about the gift I have for you? I really want to give it to you."

"I don't want your gift," I snapped. "I just want your trifling, non-answering ass to leave now!"

"So that's what this is about? My not answering the question."

"That among other things."

"Other things? What other things?"

"Leave, Kenny."

"Erica, I didn't sleep with her."

I pointed to the hallway. "Out."

"Did you just hear what I said? I didn't sleep with her. And just so you know, the thought never even crossed my mind."

194

"I don't care," I said. "You did it before."

"Yes, before. But not now. I thought we were past this."

"Why wouldn't you sleep with her, Kenny? She has your son."

"So?"

"So that's all the reason you need to be in the bed with her."

"But I don't want her, Erica. I want you. Can you please just chill with this and let's enjoy our time together? I have a present that I think you'll like."

"I told you I don't want your present," I said. "I just want you to take your ass out of my place."

"So it's like that?" Kenny asked. "After what's happened between us recently, you're not even going to try and take my word for what it is?"

"I did that before, and it didn't get me anywhere, so yeah, it's like that."

"But Erica—"

"Leave, Kenny."

Kenny stared at me for a few seconds without saying a word. He didn't know it, but I was wringing the hell out of my subconscious's neck for reapplying the mortar between the bricks of the wall that had been slowly coming down. I wanted to be happy. Hell, I deserved to be happy. And I thought Kenny could bring me that happiness. But, like it or not, the things my subconscious mind said to me were valid, and the fact of the matter is that Kenny lied to my face a countless number of times before and betrayed my trust when we were an item. I said it before, and I'll say it again. I wasn't going to be played for a fool again. "Leave!" I said as Kenny stood unmoving.

"This wasn't necessary, Erica."

"It wasn't necessary for you to fuck her either."

"Why won't you let that go? It's keeping us from being together. It's keeping us from being happy."

"I was happy before, and you screwed that up for me."

"Let me stay, Erica."

"Leave."

"Let the past be the past. Give me a chance."

"Get out, Kenny."

"I didn't sleep with her, Erica. I need for you to believe that. Do you?"

"Kenny . . ."

"Just tell me if you believe me and I'll go," Kenny said, staring at me intently. So intense that I had to look away from him.

"Please leave, Kenny," I said, looking out into the hallway.

"Do you believe me, Erica?"

"Kenny . . ." I paused. Did I believe him?

Did.

I.

Believe.

I wanted to, but I couldn't.

"No. I don't. And don't even think abut pulling your card again, because I'm not playing that game."

Kenny pressed his tongue against his cheek and looked at me with hurt eyes. He didn't say anything and neither did I. I didn't believe him. I said it. Had a lot of conviction in my voice. I didn't believe him. Too bad I didn't believe that either.

"So it's like that, huh?" Kenny finally said.

I wanted to look at him and answer his question, but I couldn't. "It's like that," I said, still focused on the hallway.

"And what about us?"

"There never was an us." I didn't need to look at him to know that my answer had stung. I could tell by his silence.

"You win, Erica," he said in a defeated tone. "You win." He walked past me with his coat in hand and stepped into the hallway. "I love you, Erica," he said with his back to me. "No matter what you think or say. And no matter how many lies you tell yourself or me, I love you. Good-bye." Just like that, he walked away.

I leaned back against the door and watched him walk to the elevator and press the button.

Good-bye.

It was so final. So tragic. And so not what I wanted.

I opened my mouth to call out his name, but paused as the elevator dinged, signaling its arrival. I'd won, but that wasn't true, because the minute he stepped into the elevator and the doors closed, I would have lost everything. Damn what my subconscious would say.

"Kenny!" I called out.

I was too late, though. The doors had closed.

Reesa

"Are you sure you want to do this?"

I took a slow, deep breath. I was about to walk into the Women's Medical Center and have the abortion. I'd made up my mind to have it done when I went home and threw up after confiding in Shay. But then I changed it when I went to visit my parents in California over the holiday. I'd flown out to see them after my get-together with Shay, Carmen, and Erica on Christmas Eve. The trip home had been a much-needed and much treasured one. Being around my parents brought up a lot of feelings and memories from my childhood. Although I'm an only child, I never wanted for anything because my parents did whatever they could to provide me with all the necessary material things I wanted and needed, and their love and support was never-ending. With their guidance, I enjoyed every second of my adolescent and young adult life.

Being around them reminded me about how important and special a family could be, and that's when I decided to keep the baby. I didn't break the news of my pregnancy to them because I didn't want to have to see the disappointment in their faces. Although they would have been happy, I knew they would have given me some minor hell because neither one of them cared for Simon. To spare myself the looks and lectures, I decided to let a couple of weeks pass before I said anything. I just wanted to enjoy my time with them and the decision I'd made.

But during the flight home, I changed my mind again. I have Kara to thank for that. She was a fifty-five-year-old woman who was finally enjoying her life for the first time.

"Being a mother is a blessed thing," she'd said. "God knows I love my three girls, but I can't tell you how good it feels to be on the plane traveling someplace you've never been before but always wanted to go to. Although I don't regret a minute of my life with the girls, I had to sacrifice a lot—friendships, relationship with men, and of course leisurely activities. If I had to do it all over again and I was still guaranteed to have the same kids, I think I would have waited before becoming pregnant. I'm having fun now, but it's not quite the same as being in my twenties or thirties. Hell, even my forties! But I am having fun now, and that's what matters. Do you have any children?"

That's when I changed my mind. After listening to everything she'd said, I realized right then and there that although she was happy, I didn't want to be in her position when I reached her age. I smiled and told her "No."

"I'm sure," I said to Shay. We were standing at the door about to go inside. I'd asked Shay to come with me because even though I'd made up my mind, I was still nervous and needed some moral support. Ahmad dropped us off because he needed the car. He didn't know what I was about to do. That's why we had him drop us off a couple of blocks away at a clothing store that we pretended to want to go to, and braved the January cold and walked to the center.

"Are you sure you're sure?" Shay asked again, holding my hand. "You don't have to do this if you don't want to. You know that, right? You still have a couple of weeks to think about it."

I breathed out slowly. "I know," I said, "but I really don't need any more time. Like I told the counselor when I met with her, I'm sure about this. I'm not ready to be a mother. Maybe in another year or so, but not now."

"Okay. As long as you're sure."

"I am. I just want to start the New Year off fresh," I said.

I pushed the door and walked in with Shay behind me. I was surprised by the center's immaculate and inviting interior. Instead of the drab and dreary environment I expected to walk into, the center's waiting area was pleasantly warm and inviting with mint-green walls surrounded by a lavender border. Several serene paintings of different flowers along with a warm painting of a desert hung on the walls, giving the area a living room feel. I turned and looked at Shay. "This is the right place."

I stood just inside the center's doors and looked around at several of the patients as they all sat silently, waiting to see the doctor. A teenage girl sat next to a woman I assumed was her mother. I looked at the teenager, whose face was filled with anxiety, and sighed; I couldn't imagine going through this experience at her age. My heart went out to her. I looked from her to the mother. Like the daughter, she was silent and sat with a pained expression. She'd brought her daughter to the medical center to have an abortion. How were you supposed to cope with something like that?

I looked away from the mother and her child and glanced at a woman who appeared to be in her mid twenties. With a magazine in her lap, she sat alone quietly with her hand covering her face, and every now and then she'd sniffle. Seeing her silent inner struggle with what she was about to do made agonizing bumps rise from my skin. I looked around at a few of the other patients and trembled. With the exception of one woman who appeared to be close to my age and who seemed far too comfortable, they all shared the same tortured demeanor.

"Reesa?"

I blinked as Shay called out my name, breaking me from the trance I hadn't realized I'd fallen into. I turned to her. Giving me a look, but not saying a word, she asked me yet again if I was sure about the decision I'd made. I looked back to the women in the room and closed my fists tightly. As I did, my mind went back to the airplane with Kara and the way she smiled when she talked about how much fun she had been having. She'd put everything on hold for her girls, and now at fifty-five, she was living. I turned back to Shay and nodded. I was still sure.

I walked to the receptionist's counter while Shay took a seat. An older white woman with a Brady Bunch smile said, "Hello. Can I help you?"

I cleared my throat. "I-I . . . have an eleven o'clock appointment," I said softly.

The woman flashed another happy smile, which was a little irritating, considering the fact that as each second passed, I was feeling more stressed and uncomfortable. "Okay. Your name?" she asked.

I leaned forward a bit, and in an almost inaudible voice said, "Reesa Nichols."

The receptionist looked down at an appointment book, put a checkmark beside my name, then grabbed a clipboard with papers attached to it. "Here are some forms for you to fill out," she said, handing the clipboard to me. "The first is for your medical history. There's a front and back to that. Just answer the questions as best as you can. The second is a consent form for the anesthesia that will be used. The third is the H.I.P.A.A form, and the last page is the consent form for the actual procedure."

"What does H.I.P.A.A. stand for?"

"Health Insurance Portability & Accountability Act. It's basically to protect your privacy."

I nodded. "Okay."

"Just bring them all back when you're finished. And how will you be paying today?"

"With cash," I said.

"Okay. I can take that when you bring the papers back."

"Thank you," I said, taking the papers and going to sit beside Shay, who was thumbing through the pages of an *Essence* magazine.

She looked up at me as I sat down. "Hanging in there?"

I gave a half smile. "I'm hanging."

I didn't say anything else for a long while after that. I just sat silently and stared at the forms on my lap. I didn't even read them. I just looked at them until the letters blended together into blurred black lines. I think I could have sat there forever had someone not sneezed, breaking me again from another trance. I opened and closed my eyes a few times then grabbed the pen. My heart was beating so quickly I felt as though everyone could hear it above the silence. I took a deep breath, put the pen to the paper, and exhaled as I moved it across the paperwork.

When I was finished, I let out a breath and momentarily stared at my Joan Hancock on the page giving my permission to have the procedure done, then took all the forms back to the receptionist's counter. The woman with the Brady Bunch smile was gone, replaced now by a younger black female. "Here you go," I said, laying the paperwork on the counter.

The receptionist looked up from a magazine she'd been skimming through. She opened her mouth to say something, but paused and stared at me.

Feeling uncomfortable with her gaze, I said, "Is something wrong?"

She closed her eyes a fraction and took a second more to look at me then very slowly said, "No. There's nothing wrong. Is that *your* paperwork?" Something about the way she said *your* made me feel as though she were saying "You're having and abortion at your age?"

I nodded. "Yes, it is."

She looked from me to the clipboard then shrugged ever so slightly. "How are you paying for this?"

"Cash."

"Okay. It's three hundred and fifty dollars."

I reached into my purse, removed the cash I'd taken from the ATM, and handed it to her. As she took the money, she asked, "Have you brought someone with you or will someone be picking you up? You won't be able to drive yourself home afterward."

"My friend is with me," I said.

"Okay, well have a seat, and we'll call your name when the doctor's ready."

I nodded and went to sit down.

"Everything all right?" Shay asked.

"I guess," I said. I leaned my head back against the wall and took a breath and released it as slowly as I could to calm my nerves.

"I have to admit, girl, you're holding up better than I thought you would."

I turned my head toward Shay and shrugged. "I'm just not ready to have this baby," I said evenly. "That's all there is to it." I didn't say anything else and neither did Shay. I turned my head then closed my eyes. Honestly, I was holding up far better than I thought I would too. I thought that the minute I walked into the center I was going to break down and change my mind, but surprisingly, that didn't happen. Although I was feeling anxiety, I wasn't feeling nearly as much as I thought I would feel, and in a way, that worried me.

Why wasn't I crying?

Why didn't I have one foot out the door, ready to take me away from the center?

Was I just being heartless and extremely selfish?

Was I just more ready than I thought?

Listening to the silence around me, I dozed off until my name was called twenty-five minutes later. The time had come. Relieved to be getting it over with and a little terrified and nervous at the same time, I stood. Shay gave my hand a gentle but strong squeeze. "You sure?" she asked me one final time.

I looked to the doctor's assistant waiting for me and said, "I'm sure."

Shay squeezed my hand again. "You want me to go with you?"

I smiled and shook my head. "No, that's okay. This is something I need to do by myself. Besides, I don't think they'd let you go back there with me anyway."

Shay gave my hand a squeeze again and let go. "Okay, well, I'll be here."

I bent down and gave her a hug. "Thanks, girl." I flashed as confident a smile as I could then followed the assistant to the back.

Was I sure? Was I sure? Was I sure?

As I followed her, that question replayed itself in my head over and over.

Carmen

My heart was beating so quickly my body seemed to shake. I was so nervous and scared that I couldn't even seem to take a proper breath. I was standing outside of Jordan's home, poised to knock on the front door. I was there to tell him that things between us had to end. That I was pregnant and getting married. I didn't have anything rehearsed or pre-written, so I didn't know how the words were going to come out. I was so stressed about having to tell him that I hadn't even called to tell him I was coming over.

Hopefully he didn't have company. I'd finally worked up enough courage to do what I should have done before things got really complicated, and I just really wanted to get the deed over with. But as much as I didn't want him to have anyone over, a part of me hoped that he did, preferably female company. A female that he was seeing on the side for comfort and satisfaction when I couldn't be there. It would hurt to see, but at least then I wouldn't have to tell him anything. I could just curse him out and end things between us, placing the blame squarely on his shoulders. "Please let there be another woman," I whispered as I rang the bell. "Please let there be another woman."

A minute or two passed, and I smiled and imagined Jordan and another woman scurrying around, trying to gather their clothing. *Yes,* I thought. *I'm going to get off easily.*

But when the door opened and Jordan, who was wearing a flannel pajama pants and white T-shirt, stood alone and smiled, my smile disappeared. "Carmen," he said, "what are you doing here?"

204

"Is that a bad thing?"

"No. I'm just surprised to see you."

"I'm sorry I didn't call. My mind was preoccupied, and I forgot."

"No need to apologize, beautiful. You don't have to call me before you come over. My door is open to you anytime, day or night."

I smiled and cried on the inside. *God, this man is perfect.*

He stepped back from the door. "Come in."

I stepped past him into the warmth of his home. "I hope I didn't catch you at a bad time," I said, taking a discreet look around for company. I could hear the television.

"No, not at all," he answered, closing the door. "I was just relaxing, watching some television. I was just finishing up a phone conversation when you rang the bell. I'm really glad you're here. I've missed you." He approached me and cupped a hand underneath my chin. "I've really missed you," he said again softly. He pulled me toward him and brought his lips to mine. I should have pulled away. Should have stopped the kiss, but I didn't. Instead, I reciprocated every ounce of passion and tenderness he gave to me. After a few minutes of kissing and caressing, Jordan pulled away. "Do you have to leave right away?" With his eyes, he asked me to say no. I obliged, though not for the reason he wanted me to.

"No."

He smiled. "How about some wine?"

I'd love to, but I can't because I'm pregnant, Jordan. That's what I should have said. Instead, I said, "I'll have water. I'm not really up for any wine right now."

Jordan nodded and moved behind me and helped me out of my coat. "Go ahead and have a seat in the living room. I'll be back in a sec."

I watched him head toward the kitchen and sighed. I went to the living room and sat down, my heart aching from what I had to do. This was the first time in two weeks that I'd been completely alone with him. Since finding out I was pregnant, I'd made sure that one-on-one moments between us were impossible to have. I just couldn't chance being alone with him because I knew that I'd break down and tell him about my situation. Although that would have been the right thing to do, I just couldn't bring myself to do it. I squirmed in the sofa, my entire body trying its best to make me get up and leave. But as much as I wanted to give in, I fought back and stayed put. There was no turning back, no matter how badly I wanted to.

"Here you go," Jordan said, coming into the living room with two glasses in hand—juice for him, water for me. He handed me my glass. I didn't hesitate to take a hearty sip to quench the dryness in my throat. "So," he said, sitting beside me.

"So," I replied, offering nothing more.

An awkward silence fell between us, broken only by laughter coming from the show *Good Times* playing on the new black television channel, TV One. I took another sip of my water—slow this time—and kept my eyes glued to the television screen. I did that to avoid the stare I could feel coming from Jordan.

"Can I ask you something?" Jordan asked, clicking off the TV.

Staring at the now dark screen, I nodded and took another sip.

"Please look at me, Carmen."

I took one final sip then put my glass down on a coaster he'd laid out for me. As my heart skipped a beat, I turned to look at him. His tone had been serious. His eyes even more so.

"Have I done something wrong? Or have I offended you in some way?"

I shook my head. "No. Why would you think you had?"

Jordan's brow furrowed as he clenched his teeth. "Well, if I haven't done anything wrong and I haven't offended you, why does it seem like you've been distancing yourself from me?"

"Distancing myself? Why would you think that?" I asked the question, but I already knew the answer.

Jordan sighed. "Carmen, for the past two weeks, every time I've asked you out for lunch, you've given me an excuse about not being able to go. And every time I've called you, you seem to do your best to rush me off the phone as quickly as you can."

"I don't—"

"You wouldn't even give me some time before I left to spend Christmas with my parents. I mean, I know we agreed that we wouldn't exchange gifts—something I was against—but still, a few minutes alone would have been nice."

I sighed. I was so worried about hurting him, I hadn't even thought about the possibility that I'd already been doing just that. "I'm sorry, Jordan," I said, the apology meaning so much more than he realized. "I just had so much going on. In between work, shopping for Christmas, my friends, and Anthony, I was just stretched really thin."

"I hear what you're saying about being over-extended, but you used to make time."

"Jordan—"

"Your actions aren't the only reason I feel like you're pulling yourself away, Carmen. Your body language is making me feel that way too. You aren't the same around me. You're reserved. Stiff. You almost seem uncomfortable to be with me. And I don't know why. Things were going so great between us. Hell, the only thing keeping us from being together was Anthony, but I'll be honest, I didn't think he'd be a factor for too much longer. Especially after the conversation you and I had a few weeks back about the possibility of you ending things with him. What happened? Have you changed your mind about how you feel about him? How you feel about us? Do you not want to see me anymore? Should I keep pulling myself away from you, which is what I've been forcing myself to do lately?"

"Jordan—" I tried again softly, but he wasn't finished.

"I just want you to be frank with me and tell me the deal, Carmen. You and Anthony have history together. If you've decided that you'd rather add to that history with him than create new history with me, I'll understand. I won't like it, but I'll deal with it. After all, I'm the guy on the side. Although I feel strongly that we belong together, and even more so about you feeling that way, too, I knew the possibility of you choosing to stay and be with Anthony was there. I just want the truth, Carmen. I love you and would love to have you as my woman for good, but if you don't feel the same—if your heart is taking you in a different direction—please tell me. I need to know. Hell, I think I have a right to know."

Jordan stopped talking and watched me with piercing but pleading eyes. I stared at the stress lines in his forehead; the subtle ones at the corners of his mouth. With all the stress he'd already been through with the loss of his wife, I hated that I had been hurting him this way. I should have told him the day after the pregnancy test. I could have avoided all of this. I exhaled, frowned, and did my best to keep my eyes from tearing.

Had I changed my mind?

He wanted to know. And he wanted the truth.

Was I ending things with him?

He deserved nothing but the truth.

I took a slow breath and looked at his gentle eyes. I opened my mouth to speak and released air slowly, preparing to form words.

And then I leaned forward and pressed my lips into his.

It was the wrong thing to do. I knew it. He deserved to hear the truth right then and there. But I didn't stop. I kissed Jordan with all of the passion and intensity I'd been holding back, trying to keep myself from stepping over the line we'd never crossed. I knew that once we did, it would change everything. "I want you," I whispered, my tongue intertwining with his. "God, I want you."

"Are you sure?" Jordan asked as his hands slid beneath my sweater.

I stopped kissing him and pulled back for a moment to look at him. "Yes," I said in absolute honesty. "I want you inside of me. Now." I removed my sweater as Jordan unsnapped my bra. "I want you so bad," I whispered as he ran his tongue around the nipple of one breast and gently squeezed the other. I slid my hand beneath his pants, stroked his erect member, enjoying the way he throbbed in my palm. "I want you, Jordan. I love you and I want you."

Jordan looked at me and smiled. "I have to be honest. After the way you've kept yourself away from me, I was worried that you'd actually come over here to end things between us. I—"

Before he could say another word, I put my index finger to his lips. "Don't talk," I said. "Just take me."

He nodded and stood. "Are you sure?" he asked again, holding out his hand for me to grab.

I took his hand and stood, begging myself to stop.

Don't go up to the room.

Don't do this to him.

He deserves to know.

"Yes," I said, my voice a whisper.

Jordan gave my hand a gentle squeeze then, before I knew it was happening, he scooped his arms beneath my back and legs and carried me upstairs to the bedroom. He lay me down on the bed, kissed me softly on my neck, then went to the window and opened the blinds, allowing the moonlight to illuminate the room. After turning on soft jazz on a small shelf system, he removed his T-shirt and came back to the bed. I breathed in and out slowly as I admired his toned upper body. Jordan smiled and traced his fingers down from my neck, over my breasts, and over my stomach, making bumps rise from my skin. I exhaled from his gentle touch.

"I've thought about this moment for a long time, Carmen," he said softly. "I can't tell you how many times I've imagined you lying on my bed, naked. I've felt your body so many times already. I've caressed you, kissed you, been inside of you. For a while I started to lose the hope that this moment would ever happen. I love you, Carmen. Letting you go home after this is going to be damn near next to impossible."

"Take me, Jordan," I said, ignoring the pleading from my conscience to tell him the truth.

Jordan slid out of his sweats then helped me out of my pants. I lay back on the bed while he climbed over me and kissed me, pressing his manhood against my flesh. We kissed each other slowly and with heated, intense passion as our hands explored the contours of each other's body. I moaned from his touch. I moaned from the feel of his skin beneath my fingertips. I inhaled the sweet, masculine scent of him as his manhood dirty danced with the wetness between my legs, teasing but never penetrating.

"Take it, Jordan," I said breathlessly.

He looked at me, and with his intense eyes, asked if I was absolutely sure about what I was demanding. My conscience screamed at me to stop what I was doing. I hadn't crossed the line. It wasn't too late. I returned Jordan's gaze. Licked my lips as his member pulsed against me again.

Right or wrong, I loved Jordan, and I wanted to be his completely.

Right or wrong, I wanted to cross the line. Needed to cross the line.

I opened my legs wider, grabbed hold of him, and guided him toward my sweetness. His tip at the threshold, Jordan stiffened up. "What about protection?"

"I want to feel you, Jordan," I said, cursing at myself for what I was about to do. "I want to feel only you." I pulled him down toward me and caught my breath as he penetrated me. "Oh, Jordan," I whispered as his girth filled me. I wrapped my legs around his waist as he moved rhythmically in and out of me. I dug my fingers into his back and ordered him to take me faster, deeper, and harder. My skin tingled with pleasure, and I moved my hips to meet his thrusts. Making love to Jordan was everything I thought it would and could be. Everything and more.

Without breaking our stride, I had him roll over onto his back and mounted him. I was going to have an orgasm regardless, but I wanted it as I rode because they were always more powerful that way. I worked my hips downward as Jordan thrust upward. It felt so good. He felt so good. We felt so good. So right. At that moment, I wasn't thinking about the truth that I should have told him. At that moment the feeling of regret for crossing the line had been replaced by a feeling of sheer, incredible, never-felt-before pleasure.

"Right there," I said, rocking my hips faster.

My muscles tightened.

"Right there."

My body tensed.

"Don't stop."

I arched my back.

"I'm going to cum. Oh, Jordan . . . I'm . . . going . . . to . . . cum!"

And then I exploded.

I moaned out loud and yelled out Jordan's name as passion escaped from within me. I slid up and down, begging him to join me, until he finally did.

"Carmen," he said as his body jerked.

"Jordan," I whispered.

And then my tears came.

Unexpected, I couldn't hold them back.

"Carmen?" Jordan said. "What's wrong?" He tried to wrap his arms around me, but I wouldn't let him. I rose from on top of him, grabbed my sweater and underwear, ran into the bathroom, and closed and locked the door. "Carmen!" Jordan called out as I sat naked on the toilet bowl and cried. "Carmen!" Jordan said, knocking on the door and fiddling with the doorknob. "What's wrong? Why are you crying? Did I hurt you? Please answer me."

Tears fell heavily from my eyes as Jordan pleaded with me. I wanted to answer him. Wanted to say something, but I couldn't. Overcome with guilt over what I'd just allowed to happen, I could do nothing but cry.

"Carmen!"

I buried my face in my hands as I listened to the confusion and anxiety in Jordan's voice.

"Carmen! Open the door, please! Talk to me. Tell me what's wrong. Tell me what I did. Carmen!"

I pressed my palms into my forehead as my body shook from sobbing.

"Carmen!" Jordan yelled, pounding on the door again. "Don't make me break the door down. Please talk to me."

I lifted my head and looked toward the door. I wanted to scream so badly. I should have stopped. I should have told him. I closed my eyes tightly as my guilty tears continued to fall. "I'm coming," I whispered. I cleared my throat. "I'm coming," I said, stronger this time. "Just give me a second."

"Are you all right?" Jordan asked. The tone in his voice was still laced with worry, but it was a little less frantic.

I wiped tears away with the back of my hand. "I'll be out in a few minutes. Just wait. Please."

Jordan sighed then said, "Okay."

I waited until I knew he'd moved away from the door before I stood slowly, went to the sink, and turned on the faucet. My hands were trembling slightly, my head aching from all the crying.

I took a glance at myself in the mirror. I looked horrible. My hair was a disheveled mess from the sex, my cheeks were flushed, and lines of mascara ran from my red and puffy eyes down my cheeks. Tears started to fall again, but before I could completely break down, I doused my face with water. When I finished washing it, I put on my sweater and underwear and ran my hands through my hair, doing what little I could to neaten it up. I never looked in the mirror to see how neat I'd made it because I couldn't bear to look at myself again.

I went to the door and put my hand on the knob and paused. My heart beat heavily inside my chest as I thought about Jordan waiting for me to tell him what was wrong; waiting for me to break his heart. I rested my forehead against the door. Tears wanted to fall again, but I wouldn't let them. I took a breath and held it for several seconds, then exhaled and opened the door and stepped back into the room.

Jordan, who was dressed and sitting on the bed, stood and started to approach me.

"Stay there, please," I said quietly as I put up my hand.

Jordan gave me a bewildered look and stayed where he was.

"Jordan . . . I-I just want you to know that tonight . . . what happened between us was so, so special. So magical and so perfect. It was an experience I will never, ever forget. Something that I will always treasure. Something I know I will never experience again."

"What are you saying, Carmen?" Jordan asked, his tone low and apprehensive.

"Jordan, I love you. Do you know that?"

"Yes. I love you too."

"I know," I said, my eyes watering. "That's why tonight . . . tonight . . ." I paused and closed my fists tightly at my sides.

"What, Carmen? What about tonight?"

"Tonight . . ." I paused again as tears cascaded down my cheeks.

212

"Carmen, talk to me please," Jordan begged. "You can tell me."

I trembled with anxiety. "Tonight shouldn't have happened, because . . . because . . ."

"Because what?"

"Because I'm pregnant and engaged."

"You're what?" Jordan asked after a few seconds of dead silence.

My shoulders slumped. "I'm pregnant, Jordan. Anthony knows, and he proposed and I said yes. I came over tonight to tell you that things had to end between us, but—"

"But what?" Jordan said, cutting me off. "You figured you'd get a fuck before you did?"

I don't know why, but the rising anger in his voice surprised me. "No!" I said.

"Then why did you do this to me?"

"I tried to tell you," I insisted, sobbing heavily.

"Bullshit! I gave you the opportunity to tell me the truth. I asked why you'd been avoiding me. You could have told me. But instead, you started kissing me and begging me to make love to you."

"It was hard, Jordan. I wanted to tell you, but it was so hard."

"So it was easier to use me?"

"No! I didn't . . . didn't mean to use you. Please don't feel that way."

"How the hell am I supposed to feel, Carmen? You tell me that you love me, you take me inside of you, and then you tell me that you're pregnant and engaged after you have your orgasm. How the hell am I supposed to feel? How would you feel?"

I shook my head. "Jordan, please . . . it wasn't that way. Everything I said . . . everything I did was genuine. I love you."

"Bullshit!"

"I do!"

"If that were true, Carmen, you would have told me the truth from the beginning. You would have never done me like this."

"I-I wanted to, Jordan. I just didn't know how. I was scared—scared of losing you."

"How do you know you would have lost me, Carmen?"

"Because I knew that once I told you about being pregnant you wouldn't have wanted to be with me anymore."

"How do you know that?"

"Because I do!"

"Well, you know what? I don't know. I don't know what I would have done."

"But I'm carrying Anthony's baby. Why wouldn't you want to end things with me?"

Jordan shook his head with disdain. "You just don't get it, do you? I love you, Carmen. Yes, the news would have hurt me. Yes, it would have probably taken me some time to digest it. And no, I don't know what my ultimate decision would have been. But you never even gave me a chance."

"I was scared, Jordan. I'm sorry."

Jordan looked at me with eyes full of pain, but didn't respond. His silence was making my soul hurt even more than it already was. I never gave him a chance. I never even tried. What if I had? Would I have lost him? Would he have accepted me and the baby? Did he love me that much?

"Say something, please," I begged.

Jordan stared at me for a few more tense seconds. "Say something?" he said finally. "What the hell am I supposed to say to a woman I don't know?"

"What is that supposed to mean?"

"I mean who the hell are you, Carmen? You're not the woman I fell in love with. The woman I fell in love with would have never done something like this. Never. It took me a second, but I now realize that this is a blessing in disguise. Obviously you're not the woman I thought you were, and it's better that this shit happen now than later on down the road when my heart would have really been invested in you. Jesus, I can't believe I fell for a woman like you."

"Jordan, please," I said, his biting words stinging me. "Don't say that. You don't mean it."

"Oh trust me, Carmen, I mean every fucking word I'm saying right now."

"Jordan—"

"Get the hell out of my house, Carmen."

Silence.

That was my response after his last statement—no, not statement, demand. I looked at him as though he'd just slapped me. Honestly, even though I hadn't been physically touched, it was one of the hardest blows I'd ever received. "What?"

"Get the hell out," he said again, his voice as bitter as before.

"Jordan—"

"Get the fuck out!"

I stood unmoving, crying heavily, shaking my head. "Jordan . . . please . . ." I tried again.

But again he cut me off. "Grab your clothes and get out, goddamnit. Get out now."

I stared at him, hoping, praying, needing for him to change his mind. Needing for him to say that he wanted me to stay. But he never said a word. I opened my mouth to speak again, but before I could, he shook his head, telling me without words that nothing I could say would make a difference. I sighed and did as he asked. When I finished dressing, I looked at him. He was sitting on the bed now, elbows resting on his knees, hands intertwined, staring at the bare wall across from him. I wanted to go to him. Wanted to beg for forgiveness. Beg for a chance to make things right.

Sensing my desire, Jordan said, "Good-bye, Carmen."

I wiped tears away with my hand as they flooded from my eyes. Good-bye. He'd said good-bye.

With certainty.

With finality.

Good-bye.

"I love you, Jordan."

And then I left.

I sat in my car crying for I don't know how long before I took one last glance at Jordan's front door, hoping to see it open. But it never did. My heart broken and filled with regret, I slid the diamond engagement ring that I'd slipped into my pocket back on my finger, and started the car. "Happy New Year," I whispered. I took one last glance at his front door then

215

pulled off and drove home to the life I'd chosen to live, for better or for worse.

Erica

"What a way to start the New Year, huh?"

Carmen blotted her eyes with a tissue. "Yeah. What a way."

I sighed and reached across the table and patted her hand. She'd called me on New Year's Eve and told me about what went down between her and Jordan. Because we both had pre-planned events for ringing in the New Year, this was the first chance we'd had since then to get together and talk.

I have to admit, I was shocked when she told me when and how she broke the news of her engagement and pregnancy to him. I never thought she would do something so dirty, intentional or not. Only because she was so broken up inside did I hold my tongue. She's lucky she was my girl. "I'm sorry things worked out the way they did."

Carmen frowned and let out a sad sigh. "I never meant for anything to happen."

"I know you didn't."

"I just didn't know how to tell him."

I handed her another tissue to replace the one she'd soaked up.

"I'm a fool, Erica." I wanted to say "Yup," but I stayed silent and let her speak. "How could I have done that to him?"

I patted her hand again. "Try not to beat yourself up too much over it."

"How can I not? I used him. I didn't mean to, but I did. Damn it, Erica, all the man did was treat me the way I wanted to be treated. The way every woman wants to be treated. He didn't deserve to be used like that. All I had to do was go over there and tell him the truth and then leave. Why couldn't I just do that? After he gave me every opportunity to tell him, why did I have to go and start kissing him? Why did I have to go and have sex with him?"

She finally stopped ranting and slammed her hand down on the table top. Only because she was depressed, frustrated, and not in the right frame of mind did I hold my tongue. My table was all glass with marble columns for the legs, and had been expensive as hell. But if she slapped it again, I'd have to say something.

"Have you tried talking to him?"

"Tried and tried and tried. He won't talk to me. Won't give me the time of day at all. This whole situation sucks because I've lost not only someone I love and care about, but more importantly, I've lost a friend. That's truly what hurts the most." Carmen wiped tears away and sighed. I sighed too. Although I honestly felt that she was getting what she deserved, she was my girl, and it hurt to see her in so much pain.

"I know it's hard, but you've got to try not to let this stress you out. Remember, you're carrying a baby, and you want him or her to be as healthy as he can be."

"I know."

"I know it's easier said than done, but you're going to have to move on. It may not have been the best way to end things with Jordan, but at least now you can focus on the commitment you made."

"Yeah," Carmen said, turning the engagement ring around on her finger.

"How has Anthony been with you? Has he noticed anything?"

Carmen shook her head. "No. It's been hard, but somehow I've managed to fake being normal around him."

"Well, that's good. Keep it up. You don't need any more stress in your life."

"No, I don't. Speaking of stress, what's going on with you and Kenny?"

I frowned at the mention of Kenny's name. "Everything and nothing," I told her.

"Huh? What do you mean?"

I gave her the rundown of everything that had happened between Kenny and me—from the kiss in my office to the dinner to the sex to the way I'd kicked him out.

When I finished, Carmen dragged out a soft, "Damn. Why didn't you tell me anything?"

"You had your own drama to deal with."

"So have you heard from him since you told him to leave?"

I exhaled. "No. And I don't think I will."

"Why not? I thought you had his website to design."

I shook my head. "Not anymore. He pulled the plug on that earlier this week."

"Really?"

"Yeah." I breathed out again as I thought about how pissed off Rod had been over losing Kenny's business. Although Kenny had apparently told Rod that he decided to keep his identity a secret, Rod was adamant that Kenny's decision had to do with me and my attitude. I did my best acting job and insisted that I had nothing to do with Kenny's decision. I even showed him the work I'd done already for the site, but Rod wasn't buying it. Without saying it directly, my status as the company's best web designer was the only thing that saved my job.

"So have you tried calling him yet?" Carmen asked.

I gave her a look. She gave me one back.

"Don't even try it, Erica. You can fake the funk with somebody else. You slept with him, not once but twice, and we both know that wasn't happening if you didn't still have intense feelings for him." Carmen gave me a knowing look. She was right and she knew she was right.

I passed my hand through my hair. "No, I haven't tried calling him."

"So what are you waiting for?"

"What am I waiting for? I can't call him back."

"Why not?"

"Because."

"Because what?"

"Because I kicked him out."

"Okay, and? You still love him."

I sucked my teeth. "I'm not calling him back."

"Why not?"

"Because I'm not. And stop asking me that."

"Come on, Erica."

"Come on, Erica nothing," I said. "After what he did to me, the last thing I'm going to do is call him. That would be like me crawling on my hands and knees. And I don't do that for anybody. Especially a man who's done me wrong."

"So you're going to let your foolish pride get in the way of happiness?"

"Excuse me. Foolish pride?"

"Yes, foolish pride."

"I don't think so," I said, rolling my eyes.

"Whatever. Girl, you love the man. Point blank. Like I said, you wouldn't have slept with him if you didn't. Okay, so over two years ago he hurt you—bad. But from what you've told me, he's been coming correct with his cards out on the table, his heart on his sleeve, and his book in hand. Erica, like it or not, mistake or no mistake, you and Kenny were meant for each other. Why would you let your foolish pride get in the way of happiness? Take it from someone who just had happiness kick her out of his home. The last thing you want to do is let happiness go."

Carmen reached out and patted my hand this time. "Nobody is perfect, Erica. Kenny made his mistake, but we all make mistakes. Some of us worse than others. Stop being so stubborn for once and give him a call. You deserve to be happy, and I know that Kenny brings that happiness to you, whether you admit it or not."

I looked down at Carmen's hand on mine then looked up at her. "I thought I was supposed to be consoling you," I said.

Carmen smiled slightly; something she hadn't done since she'd come over. "I made my mistake, but I'll get over it. Hell, I have no choice. I just don't want you to make one that you'll regret too."

"But he has a son, Carmen," I said, my voice low. "How am I supposed to deal with that?"

"One day at a time, Erica."

"Do you think Jordan would have accepted your child?"

Carmen raised her eyebrows and thought about her answer for a moment then shrugged. "I don't know. Maybe, maybe not.

220

Something in my gut is telling me that he would have, though. I wish I would have given him a chance. Believe me, *chica,* you don't want to feel like I am right now. Call Kenny and talk to him. Put everything out on the table. Your wants, your hopes, your fears—don't hold back anything. Put it all out and then go from there. You never know. The second time around for you two may be it."

I sighed as Carmen gave me a raised eyebrow, just-give-it-a-try look. "I hate saying this, but I really love his sorry ass."

"I know you do."

"I hate him at the same time too."

"I know."

"How the hell am I supposed to trust him after what he did?"

"Ask him."

"How the hell am I supposed to give him my all again?"

"Ask him."

I let out a long and extremely frustrated breath of air. "Calling him is almost like losing to him."

"This isn't a game, Erica. This is about you being happy."

"I know."

"So call him. Tell him what you told me. Ask him what you asked me. Take the chance and see what happens."

"I don't want any baby momma drama," I said.

"Tell him that."

"Are you trying to tell me to shut up?" I asked with a smile.

"Nope. I'm trying to tell you to get off your butt and call the man."

I stuck out my tongue. "I won't do it," I said playfully.

"You better before I do it for you."

"Not possible. You don't have his number."

"You have caller ID, don't you? I'm willing to bet that his number shows up on your call log."

I sucked my teeth and rolled my eyes. "Whatever."

"Yeah, whatever," Carmen said, snickering. "Just make sure you make that call."

"Yeah, yeah, I will."

"You promise?"

I groaned. "Is that necessary?"

"Yes."

I sucked my teeth again. "I promise."

"Good. And on that note," Carmen said, standing, "I'll drag my sorry butt home now."

"Yeah, why don't you?" I said with a big smile.

Carmen gave me an I-know-you-didn't look and flashed me the finger. We both broke out in some much-needed laughter.

"Anyway," I said, wiping happy tears away from the corners of my eyes. "Are you going to be okay?" I wasn't trying to get serious again, but I had to make sure.

Carmen flashed a half-smile. "I'll be all right."

"You sure? You know you don't have to leave now."

"Actually, I do. Anthony and I are going to the mall to buy a few things. Besides, you're going to need your privacy when you call Kenny, which you will do, right?"

"Yes, Mother Hen, I'll do it."

"Today?"

"Yes, today."

"As soon as I leave?"

"Go home, Carmen."

"I want to hear you dialing Kenny's number before the door slams shut behind me," Carmen said, heading toward the door.

Giving her a light, playful shove, I said, "Go home."

Carmen stopped at the door and spun around. "Why is the phone not in your hand?"

My turn to give the finger.

"You better call," she said.

I nodded. "I will."

"Okay. I'll call you later to find out how the conversation went. Of course if it goes really well, I won't be talking to you until tomorrow because you'll have your ringer off tonight."

"Whatever." I gave her a hug then bent down and planted a kiss on her stomach. "Your mother is stupid," I said to her unborn child.

Carmen covered her belly with both hands. "Don't listen to her."

I laughed and kissed her cheek. "Bye, stupid. Call me if things get rough, okay?"

"I will. Thank you for lifting my spirits a bit."

"Anytime, girl. And thank you for doing the same, Mother Hen."

"I'll be a fly Mother Hen, though, won't I?" Carmen said with a smile.

"Yes, you will. Hey, before you go, have you spoken to Reesa lately?" I hadn't spoken to her since Christmas Eve and wondered if she had confided in anyone other than Shay about her pregnancy.

Carmen shook her head. "I spoke to her on Christmas morning, but not since then. With all that's been going on, I just didn't get around to it."

"Understandable," I said. Obviously Carmen was still keeping the pregnancy under wraps. "Does she know about the baby?"

"No."

"What about Shay?"

"Nope. You're still the only one who knows."

"When are you going to break the news to them?"

"I'll call them both tonight. I just didn't want to say anything until I knew for sure what I was going to do."

"They're gonna be shocked."

"Yeah, I know."

"I'm sure Shay'll be glad you're joining the club."

Carmen smiled. "True. Anyway, let me get going. I'm sure Anthony will start calling me all paranoid soon."

"He's really excited, huh?"

"Extremely. Believe it or not, this baby's really changed him. He's not the same Anthony that used to get on my nerves."

"I'm happy to hear that. I guess what happened between you and Jordan can't necessarily be all that bad."

In a slightly deflated tone, Carmen said, "No, I guess not. I just hate how it all went down."

"I know you do, girl, but that's past now. No more dwelling on coulda, woulda, shouldas, okay?"

Carmen sighed and gave me a single nod. "Okay. Anyway, I'm out of here. Call Kenny."

"Yeah, yeah," I said, not sure if I actually would.

"I'm serious, Erica. Take a chance and call him. You promised."

223

"I know I did, but it's not that easy."

"At least think about it, then."

"I will."

Carmen gave me another hug, told me to call her, then took her pregnant behind home. I watched her head to the elevator just like I had done when Kenny left. I couldn't help but wonder what would have happened had he heard me call out his name and never gotten on that elevator. Instead of spending New Year's apart, would we have rung it in together with resolutions to bring nothing but happiness to each other's lives? To love each other without holding back? To be what we used to be before he tore us apart?

I sighed and closed the door. Take a chance. Call him.

Could I?

I asked myself that as I walked into the kitchen and put the empty mugs in the sink.

Could I?

As I threw away the napkins we'd used and put away the place mats.

Could I?

As I grabbed the phone, went into the living room, sat on the couch, and started dialing his number.

Could I?

I knew I was doing it, but it didn't really register with me until his phone started to ring in my ear. For a split second I thought about disconnecting the call. But in that split second, Kenny answered.

"Erica?"

I didn't speak for a moment. *Could I?* That question popped into my head again. I'd made the call, but could I take the chance?

"Erica, are you there?"

"I'm here," I said after another couple seconds of contemplation.

"You called," Kenny said, his voice filled with surprise.

I closed my eyes and exhaled. "Yeah."

"Why?"

I didn't answer him. Instead I said, "Did you hear me call you before you got on the elevator?"

Kenny cleared his throat. "Yes."

"Why didn't you stop and turn around?"

"You told me to leave, so I was leaving."

"But I called you."

"You also flipped the script on me. I didn't feel like dealing with the instant replay."

"I-I'm sorry. Damn it, no I'm not." I shook my head slowly and massaged my temples. Babbling is a pet peeve of mine. I hate when others do it and I hate when I do it even more. "I'm scared, Kenny." I didn't know I was going to say that. I was thinking about Carmen's advice about putting everything out on the table, and the words just slipped out.

"I know," Kenny said. "I want to tell you that you have nothing to be scared of, but I won't."

"Good. Because I have *everything* to be scared of. I don't know if I could ever completely trust you again."

"I know. But believe me, I'll be working for it."

"I don't want you to work at anything. I just want you to be real with me."

"What are you saying, Erica?"

"I don't have a clue about how I'm going to deal with your son."

"What are you saying, Erica?" he asked again.

"Baby momma drama. Don't want it, and I damn sure don't need it. So keep that in check."

"Erica."

"Yes?"

"What are you saying?"

"Isn't it obvious?"

"Nothing's obvious with you."

"I'm not going to say it."

"Say what?"

"That I miss you."

"Good. I don't want to hear that anyway."

"Good. And I'm not going to tell you that although I'm scared like hell of being hurt, I want to give us another chance."

"I didn't want you to tell me that either."

"I love you. I need you. My world, as turbulent as it's been since you came back into it, hasn't been this balanced in a long time. I'm not saying any of those things either."

"Please don't."

"Kenny."

"Yes, Erica?"

"Come over."

"I'm getting my car keys now."

Reesa

"Another nightmare?"

I took a deep breath, let it out slowly to calm my racing heartbeat, and said, "Yeah. Fourth one in a row."

"Tell me about it."

I sighed. This was the third straight night that I'd disturbed Shay's sleep in the early hours of the morning. I promised myself I wasn't going to disturb her like this again, but this nightmare really had me shook. "My unborn child kept morphing from a boy to a girl and telling me about what he could have been if I would have let him live," I said softly.

"Oh, Reesa . . ."

I blew out an anxiety-filled breath and massaged the hell out of the back of my neck as a tear slid out from the corner of my eye. "Shay, I feel so guilty. What if I prevented the world from getting to know the next Michael Jordan or Serena Williams? The next Martin or Malcolm. The next Oprah or Condoleezza Rice." I stopped talking and inhaled deeply, trying to keep myself from breaking down.

"Come on, girl," Shay said. "We talked about this before. Don't torture yourself by asking what if. You made your decision—the best decision for you. Just go with that. You're only going to drag yourself down into a deep state of depression if you keep asking yourself what-if questions. And you don't want to do that."

"I know. It's just that the dream was so vivid and heart-wrenching. It's hard to not ask what if."

"No what-ifs, Reesa. Leave the past behind you and focus on the future. Focus on your happiness from this point on."

"I want to, Shay. I just wish the nightmares would stop."

"They will when you commit yourself to being happy. When you stop beating yourself up emotionally for making a very tough decision that you had to make."

I sighed. "But what if it was the wrong decision?"

"I told you no what-ifs."

"But—"

"Reesa, did you want to have a baby right now?"

I dropped my chin to my chest and breathed in and out for a few seconds before I answered as honestly as I could. "No."

"Then go to sleep and stop stressing yourself out. You weren't ready to have a baby, and there's absolutely nothing wrong with that."

I nodded slowly, and for the first time saw light at the end of the tunnel I didn't think I was going to go through. "I didn't think having the abortion was going to affect me like this." My voice was solemn as I spoke. "I guess I psyched myself up so much into thinking that because I was ready, it was going to be a piece of cake. I mean, I knew it wasn't going to be completely easy, but still, I really didn't think I'd be stressing too much afterward. It actually didn't hit me until after you and Ahmad dropped me off. That's when the cramping from my uterus contracting really got to me. And I don't mean the pain. I mean it got to me emotionally. I was all alone and it just kind of came down on me that I was feeling what it would have been like to have a real contraction, only there was no baby inside of me. That really messed me up. I cried for I don't know how long. I couldn't do anything. Just lay on my bed and cried. That night I had my first bad dream."

"You never called me that night."

"You'd already given me your shoulder so much and been there for me, I just didn't want to bother you anymore."

"It wouldn't have been a bother, and you know that."

"I know, but I just wanted to try to deal with it myself."

"I was actually expecting you to call me that night. When you didn't, I was surprised. Even more so when I called you the next day to see how you were holding up and you sounded so normal."

"I could have won an award that day," I said, remembering how difficult it had been to mask my sadness.

"I'm just glad you came to your senses and finally called me."

"So am I."

"Reesa, it's going to take time to get over this, but you will get past it."

"I wish I could control time."

"We all do, girl. Listen, I didn't say anything before, but I've been through what you're going through."

"You have?" I was surprised.

"Yes. I was eighteen when I thought I had everything under control and had sex without a condom. I knew better than to let him come inside of me, so I made sure he pulled out before it happened. Unfortunately, no one ever warned me about premature ejaculation. Girl, I was messed up. I was all set to go to school, get my degree, and start living. Then that happened. Just like you, I wrestled with the idea of having an abortion. I mean, how could I abort my child? How could I not want to be a mother?

"I cried so many nights. Cried until my eyes, head, my whole being hurt. Two months before I was set to go to college, I went to the clinic and had the abortion. It was the hardest thing I've ever had to do, but I had to do it because I wasn't ready. I had a life to live. I had a woman to become. Being a mother was an absolute must for me, but it was a must when the time was right, and my time hadn't come yet."

Shay became silent for a few seconds. I was silent, too, not knowing what to say. Silence passed as conversation until she spoke again.

"I was in pain for a long time after that day. I was burdened with so much grief, so much guilt. I didn't know that it was going to be so hard on me emotionally."

"How did you get past it?"

"Time. Time and a letter."

"A letter?"

"I know it may seem a little off the wall, but I wrote a letter to my child and explained why I did what I did. I'd apologized in my prayers so many times, but that letter made my apology tangible."

I sighed and wiped away tears as they fell from my eyes. "I don't know if I could do that, Shay. What could I possibly say to earn my child's forgiveness?"

"You're not looking for forgiveness, Reesa. You're just explaining why you made the decision you made. This letter is really for you. I know it would be hard, but I really think it would help. I'll tell you what, as bad as it seemed then, I have absolutely no regret about my decision, because I know in my heart that I wouldn't be the woman, mother, or wife that I am now had I had that child."

I dropped my chin to my chest and squeezed my eyes shut tightly. A letter to my child. The child that I killed. How could I do that?

"Think about it, Reesa. You don't have to do it, but seeing your words on that paper may really help."

"What would I do with it when I finished it?"

"Keep it. In your closet. In your drawer. In your Bible. Under your pillow. Keep it somewhere safe, and read it when you feel yourself drowning. Read your words and see that you didn't have an abortion out of selfishness, but out of love. Love for yourself. Because, Reesa, if you didn't love yourself first, you wouldn't have been able to give all of your love to that child. Keep the letter until you're ready to move on without it."

I couldn't help it. I let the phone fall to my lap and cried hard tears. I cried for selling myself short and settling with a man like Simon. I cried for allowing myself to fall backward into his arms when I knew that moving on without him was the best thing for me. I cried for the life I prevented. Most importantly, I cried for the decision I made, because I knew it was the right one for me. I cried until I couldn't anymore, then picked up the phone again. "Still there?"

"You know I am."

"I'm going to try and write it," I said, wiping away a stray tear.

"Okay."

"I love and appreciate you, Shay. Although the nightmares haven't stopped, having you to talk to has truly helped. Thanks again for your friendship."

"Stop thanking me, girl. We're supposed to be there for each other. That's what friends do. And don't worry about those nightmares. They'll pass."

"I hope so."

"Just remember what I said, girl. There's nothing wrong with the decision you made because you made it for you. You weren't ready now. But the time will come when you will be, and when that time does come, the experience is going to be something you'll always treasure."

Tears fell as I smiled. "Thank you, Shay. Thank you so much for everything."

"Anytime, Reesa. Just remember to be there for me when Ahmad gets on my nerves."

I laughed. "I will. Speaking of Ahmad, please tell him I'm sorry for disturbing his sleep by calling in the middle of the night like I have been."

Shay sucked her teeth. "Disturbing his sleep? Please. Ahmad doesn't even know you've called me. He's dead to the world when he sleeps."

I laughed out loud, something I hadn't done in a while.

"I'm serious, girl," Shay continued. "I don't know what he dreams about, but whatever it is, it must be damn good. He even talks in his sleep sometimes."

"Get out!"

"For real. I tried to listen to him one night, but I couldn't make out what he was saying. It's probably a good thing I didn't, though, because if I heard the wrong things, there would have been some drama up in this household. And God knows Ahmad and I have had enough of that."

"I hear that," I said, chuckling.

"So anyway, I'm glad to hear you laughing."

"I'm glad to be laughing," I said.

"Keep it up."

"I will. Thanks again, Shay."

"Anytime."

"Go and get some sleep. I've kept you up long enough."

"You going to be all right?"

"Yeah. I think I'll be fine."

"All right. You make sure and get some sleep, too, okay?"

I smiled. "I have a feeling that I will finally do that."

"Good. I'll call and check on you tomorrow."

"Okay. Talk to you then. Bye."

"Bye."

I hung up the phone, lay back on the bed, and stared up at the ceiling.

A letter.

Words on a paper.

Words for my child and more importantly, myself. What would I say? How would I start? Could I really do it? Tears fell slowly from my eyes and ran down onto the pillow.

A letter.

Words on paper.

Shay was so happy now, with such a beautiful life.

She'd had an abortion too.

I sat up, reached into my night table and removed a pen and pad and began writing without thinking. Two hours later, after shedding more tears and nearly giving up several times, I folded a sheet of paper full of words I never really saw as my pen flowed, and slid it into an envelope, sealed it, and placed it inside my night table drawer. I know Shay said to read it whenever I felt the need, but for better or worse, I wouldn't. I said all I had to say and from this point, I would move on.

Someday, I thought, exhaling and placing my hand on my stomach.

I didn't know when, but I knew that, just like Shay, someday I'd have another opportunity to be a mother. If I met the right man and it happened before I hit thirty-five, that would be great. If not, and it happened a little later, that would be fine too. Either way, I'd survive because I knew that day was going to come.

I looked at my alarm clock. It was three o'clock in the morning. I lay back down as what I felt would finally be a good sleep called out to me. Before drifting off, I thanked God for my family, my friends, and for having the right to make my own choice about what to do with my body and my life.

Someday. Whenever that would be.

I looked at the drawer with my letter inside then did something I hadn't in a while—I smiled. Five minutes later, sleep welcomed me with open arms, and I was drooling on my pillow.

One Year Later

Carmen

I left him.

I should have left him a few months ago. Hell, I should have left him before I ever slid his ring on my finger, but I didn't because I was foolish enough to believe that things had actually changed and gotten better. But a leopard's spots never change. I admit, for the first six months of my pregnancy, Anthony did a damn good job of making me think he'd changed. He was attentive, nurturing, and selfless with his time. I was the top priority. Work, his boys, the gym, his videos, even his own mother—they all came second to me. I was in heaven because she absolutely hated that. For six whole months, Anthony made me feel like I was a true queen. So much so that I was eventually able to let go of the regret I had over the way I'd lost Jordan, who'd left the company soon after the New Year started. His departure hurt at first, but with Anthony catering to me the way he was, I got over it faster than I thought I would.

Things between Anthony and me were great. So great that when he suggested a shotgun wedding at the Justice of the Peace, I was all for it. One, because I loved the man I thought he'd become, and two, because I didn't want my baby to be born out of wedlock.

We were married just a little after my sixth month started. My mother was there, although she didn't particularly want to be. She still hadn't warmed up to the idea of Anthony being her son-in-law. Reesa, Shay, and Erica were there too. Three of Anthony's boys were to represent, and so was his cousin. His mother, of course, refused to take part in our union, and that was just fine with me. Anthony and I got married without a hassle and enjoyed a relaxing mini-honeymoon in Florida, where we visited some of my family who didn't get to see me often.

For the first time in a long time, I was truly happy. I was looking forward to being a mother. Anthony was finally the man I wanted. I knew that all of our days together weren't going to be bliss, but I just knew that Anthony and I were finally going to be all right. I knew that leopards didn't change their spots, but I just knew with all my heart that Anthony had, and he and I were never going to have the same type of drama we'd had before.

And then the seventh month arrived.

I don't know what the hell happened to cause Anthony to switch from being Mr. Wonderful to being a son of a bitch, but that's just what happened. All of the catering and attentiveness disappeared almost overnight. The sudden lack of attention really bothered me. I mean, there I was going into the last trimester, and he was reverting to his old self again. Already uncomfortable with the forty pounds I'd gained, instead of making me feel better by talking about how beautiful a pregnant woman I was, he had the nerve to talk about how fast I needed to lose the weight because he didn't want a fat wife.

Asshole.

The further along I went in my third trimester, the more self-conscious I became as Anthony continued to stress me out with his ignorant remarks and his disgusted looks whenever his eyes would rest on me. Not surprisingly, with each day that passed, I began to build up more and more contempt for him. Thankfully, I had my girls to help keep my blood pressure down and keep me sane in the midst of Anthony's madness.

My seventh month passed with the communication between Anthony and me all but disappearing, and my eighth month crept by with him becoming nothing more than a stranger who occasionally slept in his bed at night, opting instead to sleep on the couch in front of the television.

Because it wasn't good for the pregnancy, I tried to not think about the possibility of Anthony seeing another woman, but it was hard not to. I was pregnant, irritable, and not interested in sex, and Anthony was a man with a high libido.

Maybe if he were a different type of man, I would have given him the benefit of the doubt and thought that instead of cheating, he was just abstaining until after the baby was born. But Anthony was Anthony, and I'd given him the benefit of the doubt before.

Thoughts of him cheating disappeared during my final month, not because I didn't think about it, but because I was just too damned anxious to have the baby. That's all I thought about day in and day out. Giving birth. I was ready. No, I was past ready. I was tired of being pregnant. Tired of the huge belly. Tired of the swollen ankles and feet. Tired of the pain in my back. Tired of waddling around everywhere I went. Tired of taking forever to get out of bed or a chair.

Tired.

And then the moment finally came. Eleven o'clock at night—that's when the contractions started, and as was usually the case, Anthony wasn't around. After calling his cell phone about fifty times, calling his mother, and then all of his friends, I gave up and called Erica to have her take me to the hospital. Arriving within twenty minutes, she and Kenny helped me to the car, grabbed the duffle bag I'd packed for my stay in the hospital, and rushed me to the maternity ward. Anthony's name was never mentioned.

Amazingly enough, he managed to show up just before it was time for me to start pushing. I didn't even bother to say anything to him when he walked in and relieved my mother, who was by my side. I just focused and bore down when the doctor told me to push. I did squeeze Anthony's hand extra hard, though.

Giving birth was by far the most exhausting experience I'd ever been through, but when the doctor announced that I'd just delivered a healthy seven-pound, eleven-ounce baby boy, all of the pain and fatigue disappeared and was replaced immediately by sheer joy. Cradling my newborn son, Antonio Jose, against my chest, I looked down at his tiny, bawling face and wondered how I could have ever thought of not having him. He was perfect. I'd heard people say that the love I'd feel for my child would be intense, but I didn't really understand just how powerful those feelings would be until that moment. And then when I pulled my breast out and he latched on and started feeding, forget it—I would do anything to protect my child.

That's why I left Anthony. To protect my son.

Anthony had never laid a hand on me before then. Continuing his nomadic ways, he came and went as he pleased, and did little to help me with Antonio. He didn't change him, didn't bathe him. I was breastfeeding, so he didn't have to feed him. He barely even held him, and when he did, he seemed unsure about what to do with him. As excited as he'd been when he first found out I was pregnant, and as ecstatic as he'd been when the doctor announced that we had a son, the last thing I expected was for him to act like he didn't want to be a father.

Whatever. Saying to hell with him, I went about my business as a wife and working mother, and held things down.

And then I found the condom in Anthony's jeans pocket.

Although I was happy with my son and preoccupied with taking care of him, I never stopped thinking that Anthony was cheating on me. All of the classic signs were there. Coming home late and heading straight for the shower; leaving early in the morning to "work out" before work; taking his cell phone calls outside because all of a sudden he couldn't get a good signal inside. Like I said, the signs were there. I just never had proof. Until that condom.

It was Saturday morning and I was sorting the dirty clothes to wash them. Anthony's jeans weren't in the hamper, but hanging in the closet. I only decided to wash them because they had a faint cigarette odor coming from them. If not for that smell, I would have never touched them.

The condom fell out of the back pocket when I threw the jeans into the darks pile. At first I just stared at it. A condom? Anthony and I didn't use them. I must have been seeing things, right? I stepped closer to get a better look. After all, it was early, I hadn't gotten much sleep, thanks to Antonio. Maybe my eyes were playing tricks on me.

But they weren't.

Ribbed for extra sensation. Trojan brand. I didn't know whether to be mad, glad, or sad, so I didn't do anything. I just went about my day and waited for Anthony, who'd left just before I'd woken up, to come home. He said he was going to take his mother to visit family in New Jersey.

I was fine all day until I pulled the condom from my back pocket to look at it. Why I did that, I don't know. Holding it tightly between my thumb and index finger, I stared at it with unflinching eyes and became pissed. A condom. That ass was fucking another woman. Some might say I deserved it for what went on with Jordan. Some might say I didn't. Either way, the more I looked at the condom, the more enraged I became.

When he came home, I lit into him verbally in two languages. He tried to come up with some bullshit lies about the condom not being his, but I wasn't a fool. I threw it in his face, and with my Puerto Rican rage in overdrive, slapped him for disrespecting me after all the shit I put up with from him. Then I slapped him again for the pain I endured giving birth to his son, who he didn't seem to give a shit about.

That's when he hit me. In my face. One slap. Hard. Unchecked. And then he wrapped his fingers around my neck, pushed me back against the wall, and told me to never lay a fucking hand on him ever again.

I wiped a few tears away as I thought back to that moment. I'd been so stunned by Anthony's uncharacteristic outburst that for a long while, I sat on the couch with an ice pack on my bruised cheek. He hit me. If not for the stinging, I don't think I would have believed it. I sat in stunned silence until Antonio started crying. I went to him, held him tightly, and thanked God that he'd been in his crib sleeping and not in his playpen watching me like he usually was.

I packed a bag for myself and Antonio, left the house before Anthony came back, and went to stay with my mother. Anthony called her house begging and pleading to speak to me. He was sorry, he insisted. He never meant to hurt me. He wanted another chance. I heard all of this as I stood beside my mother, shaking my head no, that I wasn't willing to talk to him. He hit me. That night, I decided I'd had enough of him. Like I said, I should have come to my senses sooner and left, but all things happen when they're supposed to, and had I left earlier, I would have never known that Anthony could lose control like that, and I might have gone back. A slap was always the first thing to happen in an abusive relationship. I wasn't about to find out what the next thing was. And I damn sure wasn't trying to end up like Laci Peterson, the pregnant California woman who was murdered by her husband.

I left him.

For good.

I kissed Antonio on his forehead then shut off the overhead light, leaving only the nightlight on. In a few days I'd be meeting with a lawyer to file for a divorce. I hated that Antonio was going to grow up in a single-parent household, but I'd rather that than a chance at a worse alternative. I kissed my son again then left the room and went to the living room and sat down.

I was drained physically and emotionally, and I was looking forward to getting some sleep, especially now that Antonio was sleeping through the night. But before I could go to bed, there was something I had to do. Something I'd been thinking about doing for a while.

I picked up the phone, took a breath, and dialed Jordan's number. I knew I was taking a bold chance by calling him, considering the fact that I hadn't spoken to him since the night I did him wrong, but for the past couple of months, he'd really been on my mind. Even though he'd said good-bye, I still felt like the door hadn't been completely closed on us yet. Call me crazy, but I just had this feeling that maybe, just maybe, there was still a chance for Jordan and me to rekindle what we had. We truly did have a special connection between us; a connection I believed could get us past my mistake. He'd said good-bye, but that good-bye, I think, was more emotional than it was heartfelt.

"Hello?" It was a woman's voice. Soft. Pleasant. I didn't speak for a second as I wondered if I'd dialed the wrong number. But even with a year gone by, I knew I hadn't. "Hello?" the woman asked again.

I cleared my throat. "Uh, hello. Is Jordan home?"

"No, he's not. But this is his wife. Is there something I can help you with?"

I know it didn't, but I swear to you my heart stopped beating.

His wife?

Stunned and wondering if I'd heard correctly, I didn't speak.

"Hello?" the woman said. "Are you still there?"

I closed my eyes and exhaled softly as they filled with tears. "Yes. I'm . . . here."

"Is there something I can help you with, Ms. . . ."

"Scott," I answered, giving my married name. "Mrs. Carmen Scott."

"Well, Carmen, is there something that I can help you with?"

Tears spilling slowly from my eyes, I said, "No . . . I'm an old coworker of Jordan's. I was just calling to say hello."

"Oh, okay. Well, he won't be home until tomorrow. He's away on a business trip. I can take your number down and have him call you when he gets back."

Wiping tears away, I said, "No. That's . . . that's okay. I'll catch him some other time." *Another lifetime,* I thought.

"Are you sure?"

"Yes."

"Okay. Well, I'll tell him you called."

"Thank you. . . Oh, Mrs. Combs."

"Yes?"

"Just out of curiosity, when did you and Jordan get married? I never even knew he was seeing someone."

"Oh, we actually knew each other back in high school, but lost contact when we left for college."

"Really? How did you manage to get together?"

"Well, as luck would have it, we actually met up with each other again at a new-hire business function a few months back. We've been together ever since, and we exchanged vows just two months ago."

I struggled to keep my emotions in check as tears ran down my cheeks and fell from my chin. I cried hard and silently for a few seconds, unable to respond. A new-hire business function— a function he would have never attended had it not been for me.

"Are you there, Carmen?"

I cleared my throat, clenched my jaw, and did my best to sound normal enough to say "Good-bye, Mrs. Combs" before I hung up the phone and buried my face in my hands. He was married. I guess the door had been closed after all.

Reesa

Happy birthday to me.

I checked myself out in the mirror and smiled. Not bad for a thirty-four-year-old. My breasts were still up for the cause. My stomach was sticking out a bit, but wasn't out of control. My hips weren't small, but they weren't too wide. And my ass was still firm and worth an "Oh, damn!"

Nope. Not bad at all.

If someone asked me a year ago how I saw myself in the future, my description would have been completely different. I had the whole glass-is-half-empty mentality thing going. Everything was on the downward slope, heading straight toward a black pit. That's how I saw things.

But now everything is different. I'm a young thirty-four, loving and enjoying the hell out of my life.

There were two things responsible for the changes in my outlook. Getting rid of Simon had been the first step. Not until I'd done that had I realized what life and living it was all about. He'd been dragging me down and holding me back in a major way financially, emotionally, and spiritually. Blinded by the sex, his negative energy penetrated my mind, body, and soul, and had me thinking that giving up and settling had been the right thing to do. Again, my glass was half empty. I never even realized how stressed out I'd been until he was gone. Like I said, he knew how to maintain in the bedroom.

I was blind, baby. Blind to the facts. . . . Sorry for my Public Enemy, Flava Flav moment. Old school was playing from the radio, and it just seemed appropriate.

Anyway, the next major step was the abortion. Right for some, wrong for others, choosing to forego motherhood had been the best decision for me to make. I never thought I would have gone through an experience like that, but you know the saying: Never say never. Life threw me one hell of a curve, and instead of striking out, I swung with everything I had, hit that ball, and got on base.

Not an easy decision. I regressed every once in a while and had moments where guilt and regret would press heavily down on my shoulders, but as time passed, those moments decreased. Guilt did hit me extremely hard two times, though. The first was when Carmen broke the news about her pregnancy, and the second when she gave birth to her beautiful son. Make no bones about it, I was ecstatic and so, so happy for her, but I'll be honest; hugging her and offering congratulations had been tough because I wanted more than anything to go and lock myself in a closet somewhere and cry my eyes out.

I was being punished. That was the way I looked at it back then. God was throwing Carmen's son in my face as a way to reprimand me for my choice. I felt that way for a long while after she'd broken the news, but that feeling disappeared the day Antonio came into the world. On that day, standing alongside Shay and Erica, I got to see the joy on Carmen's face as she held her son in her arms, and I knew right then that God had not been punishing me, but in fact had been showing me what it was going to be like for me when I was ready. That was my crystal-ball moment. I haven't regretted my decision or felt guilty about it since.

Happy birthday to me.

I looked at myself again and flashed a smile.

Then the doorbell rang. I took a glance at the clock. It was seven o'clock. He was right on time.

I gave myself the once-over again and smoothed the red, ankle-length dress I was wearing the hell out of. Normally I'd wear black, but my new man likes me in red. Oh yes, I did say new man.

Thirty-five. Six-four. Two hundred and twenty pounds of lean, cut muscle. Skin the color of mocha. Eyes the very definition of bedroom.

Mekhi. Not the actor, but an architect from New York. I met him at the MVA a few months ago. I was renewing my driver's license. He was there trading in his New York permit for a Maryland one. Mekhi was a beautiful, sensitive, gentle, romantic man. He was taking me out on the town to celebrate my thirty-fourth. The dress was one of the gifts he'd given me.

Mekhi.

Not sure where we were headed, although the outcome was looking damn good. But I wasn't pressed. Whatever happened between us happened.

I sprayed on some Victoria's Secret Very Sexy For Her perfume—another gift he'd bought me—flashed another smile, thought, *Nope, not bad at all* again, then went to get the door.

And oh, I wasn't blind to the facts like I was with Simon, because I wouldn't allow myself to be that way again with anyone, but Mekhi could damn sure teach Simon a thing or thirty. When he said he was an architect, I didn't know he'd meant he was one in bed too.

Erica

I did it.

I took the step.

The leap.

I gave in to what I'd been fighting. But I also flipped the script on him again. Did it whenever the fear became too much for me. Did it when his baby momma called him. Did it when the piece of wall I'd had up fell and I started to lose myself in his arms completely. It wasn't easy. I wasn't easy. Hell, sometimes I was a straight bitch. But I was entitled.

True to his word, though, Kenny remained strong and played one-sided emotional tennis with me. Taking everything I threw at him, he did whatever he had to do to show me how much he loved me. If it meant giving me the space I needed and sometimes demanded, he did it. If it meant being the man I needed, he was all man.

Never say never.

No way, no how.

No chance in hell.

Never again.

I said it, but now there I was sitting beside Kenny, my hands intertwined with his. Happy and crying as my mother stood to dedicate a toast to us.

It was our engagement party. Yup. Engagement.

Kenny popped the question.

I said yes.

Never say never.

I finally gave in completely and took a second chance at love with Kenny. Said to hell with it, dropped my guard just enough to let Kenny have a piece of my heart. But only just enough.

I may have given in and said yes, but my guard wasn't down completely. Kenny had broken my heart once, and lowering my guard just enough ensured that I wouldn't go through the same emotional wringer I'd gone through when I was naive enough to think he was never going to hurt me. This time, I was prepared. And Kenny knew that because I reminded him every day. Sometimes with words, sometimes I did it with my actions; other times, it was my looks. I would never let him forget that I would never forget what he'd done. That was my way of keeping him in check.

Honestly, a big part of me truly believed that I didn't have anything to worry about. But a small part of me did. Who knows? Maybe one day that small part would disappear. But for now, he would have to continue to be the man of steel.

Almost as though he were listening to my thoughts, he gave my hand a gentle squeeze. I looked at him. He looked at me. We smiled. Didn't speak. Just smiled.

I leaned toward him and gave him a soft kiss on his cheek then looked over to where Reesa, Carmen, and Shay were sitting. Their eyes were focused on my mother, so they didn't notice that I was looking at them. I smiled. The past year had been a true challenge for all of us. Well, all of us except Shay. She and Ahmad continued to enjoy their lives together with little drama. But the rest of us . . .

I looked at Reesa. Her new man, Mekhi, was sitting beside her, his arm draped on the back of her chair. She had an abortion. She never told me, but I know she did. She was a much different person than she had been a year earlier. She smiled more, laughed more; she had a glow about her that never existed. I was glad she woke up and finally got rid of Simon's tired ass. Mekhi was good for her. He complemented her new personality nicely. Not only that, but the brother was fine, educated, and paid. He was definitely a keeper.

Go, girl. I knew she had it in her.

I looked from her to Carmen. Having just signed divorce papers a few hours earlier, she was officially a single woman again. I was glad she had sense enough to leave Anthony's sorry ass before he had a chance to put his hands on her again. Too bad she didn't leave him before she exchanged vows. She could have saved herself the emotional and legal hassle, and instead of sitting there solo, she'd be sitting there with Jordan's arm on the back of her chair.

She told me about finding out he was married. I can't say that I was particularly surprised. Although I never met him, I knew from the way she smiled whenever she mentioned his name that he was a special man. The right man. Someone would have snatched him up eventually. Carmen had her chance. I bet she'd never make that mistake again.

But even though she was by herself, Carmen was all right. Wanting and needing no man, her life revolved completely around her son. She was definitely destined to become a mother. I think that's why she and Anthony were put together— to bring Antonio into the world. Motherhood came so naturally to her that whenever I looked at her now, it was with envy. When my time came, I hoped that I'd be at least half the mother Carmen was. I was proud of the way she stayed afloat when things seemed to be sinking for her. My girl looked good, and she was happy. She was blessed.

Speaking of being blessed . . .

I squeezed Kenny's hand this time. As hard and scary as it was to go give in, I was glad I finally decided to leave the past behind me and move forward with him. Kenny had always been the man for me. I knew it when we were dating, knew it when he broke my heart, and I knew it when I saw him again after not seeing him for more than two years. He was my soul mate. I loved him, and I don't think I would have ever been truly happy until he and I got back together. I was glad he wrote the book.

Speaking of his book, I finally finished it. I have to admit, just like everyone said, the book was intense and deep—so deep that it brought tears to my eyes. He really did strip naked and bare his soul, going so far as to tell the readers at the end that no matter what it took, he was determined to win my heart and trust again. Who knows? Had he brought the book to me right after he finished it, we might have been together much sooner.

But things happen when they're supposed to, and I had a lot of healing to do. I needed those two years to let the anger die down just enough for Kenny's reemergence in my life to be something I could handle.

I squeezed his hand again.

He looked at me.

I looked at him.

We smiled.

We'd made it.

Reading Group Questions

1. Reesa's decision to terminate her pregnancy was a difficult one for her to make. Do you feel it was a selfish decision?

2. Considering how badly Erica had been hurt by Kenny, should she have given him another chance?

3. Why do you think Anthony's mother was so disrespectful to Carmen?

4. Have you ever settled with a man the way Reesa did with Simon? Is, why?

5. Who was the strongest character and who was the weakest?

6. Have you ever look down on a friend because she's settled in her relationship?

7. Do you think Carmen should have left Anthony to be with Jordan? And what do you think Jordan's reaction to her pregnancy would have been?

8. Have you ever wanted a man to fight to be with you the way Kenny did over Erica?

9. Do you think Erica was too hard on Kenny? Or not hard enough?

10. Have you ever had a cut-off age to have a baby? And did you stick to it?

An Excerpt From

Dwayne S. Joseph's

next novel

If Your Girl Only Knew

September 2006

Prologue

Jocelyn.

She was whispering my name as she stood before me naked, swaying her hips rhythmically to music that only she could hear. Her dance was slow, hypnotic and arousing and made bumps rise from my skin. I couldn't help but catch my breath as she traced a finger from inside of her mouth and dragged it down in between her breasts, licked her lips and smiled. Whispering my name seductively again, she came toward me slowly, grabbed hold of my throbbing member, straddled me, and slid me inside of her. I couldn't help but exhale from the warmth and wetness of her. Little by little, my body began to move in tune with hers, until we were both dancing to the same sexual groove. Up and down. Back and forth. In circles. We danced passionately this way for what seemed like hours. As her movements became more intense, I could feel myself nearing the point of explosion. I tried as hard as I could to hold it back, but with her fire, I couldn't, and I released powerfully. Seconds after that I felt her buckle on top of me with her own climax. "Oh David!"

I quickly opened my eyes at the sound of my fiancé, Janelle's voice. She was naked above me and breathing heavily. Her dark-chocolate skin was coated with a light sheen of perspiration. I was naked and covered with sweat too.

"David," she whispered, "that was incredible. Baby, what got into you? I can't remember the last time you were so intense."

I shrugged my shoulders but didn't respond. Thankfully Janelle didn't wait for a response. She kissed me on my neck and lips, then rose from on top of me and walked off into the bathroom. As she closed the door behind her, I sat up and dragged my hands down over my face. "Jocelyn," I whispered. "Damn."

I couldn't believe that just happened. Jocelyn Alvarez. My ex. My first love. The one that I always felt "got away." She'd been on my mind constantly ever since I ran into her a month ago back in Philly when I was there for a book signing. I hadn't seen her since we broke up six years ago. Our breakup hadn't been pretty. Dating since we were sixteen, I turned twenty-one and fucked up by cheating on her with her rival, Theresa Cueves. Jocelyn and Theresa were like oil and water; they just didn't mix. They'd hated each other since before I came into the picture. Apparently back in junior high, Jocelyn had stolen Theresa's boyfriend. I guess Theresa had been looking for revenge ever since then, and like a fool, even though I knew how Jocelyn felt about her, I helped Theresa get it. I got all caught up in Theresa's firm breasts and J.Lo like ass, and had sex with her at a party that Jocelyn, who was supposed to be away for the weekend, ended up coming to. In my defense, I was drunk. But that didn't matter. Jocelyn dumped me on the spot, and no matter how hard I tried, no matter what I said or did, she wouldn't take me back. That was the worst.

Jocelyn was my everything. Ask me who my ideal woman was in both looks and personality, and Jocelyn's name would have been the one coming from my lips. My moment of drunken weakness with Theresa was a major slip-up that I would never forgive myself for. I dated other females after Jocelyn, but none of them ever gave me the feeling that Jocelyn gave me. Not even Janelle, who I'd been with for the past year and a half.

Damn.

That dream was just too intense.

Too real.

I shook my head. I should never have sent Jocelyn that e-mail.

After bumping into her, we spent almost three hours reminiscing and filling each other in on the happenings in each other's lives. After what I'd done, and the way Jocelyn had swore she'd never talk to me again, the last thing I expected was just to be talking as though I'd never been a fool. But there we were, talking, smiling, laughing; staring. We gazed into each other's eyes so many times, even if we wanted to, there was no denying the spark that still existed between us.

Before we parted, we exchanged e-mail addresses, with the intent of keeping in touch with one another occasionally. We were both busy after all—me as an author, and she as an exec in advertising. So once in a while should have been all the time we had. Beside, I was engaged—something that I hadn't told Jocelyn—so my time was definitely limited. Once in a while is how things started initially. I'd e-mail her and say hi. She'd email me and say bye. Nothing wrong with that right?

But a couple of weeks ago, I was at home alone, supposedly to work on my new book, when I did something that I shouldn't have done. Something that would have major repercussions.

Sitting in front of my laptop, I e-mailed Jocelyn and bared my soul.

Even though we were apart for all these years, I'd never truly gotten over her. Like I said, she was my ideal partner. Bumping into her only brought feelings, which I'd tried to bury, back to the surface.

That night, alone with my laptop, everything came to a head, and I started typing. And then I hit send. And now here I was, having incredible sex with my fiancé, only it wasn't my fiancé I was sexing.

Damn.

It's a good thing I didn't call out Jocelyn's name.

When Janelle came out of the bathroom, like a woman in love, she wrapped her arms around me, kissed me, and pulled me down on the mattress to cuddle. Eventually with her head on my shoulder, she fell asleep. As for me, I couldn't sleep. I just lay in bed, staring up at the ceiling.

I sent the e-mail.

She hadn't yet, but how was Jocelyn going to respond?

More importantly, what would she say when I told her about Janelle, which I knew I had to do sooner or later.